▶▶▶ACCEL·WORLD 26
CONQUEROR OF THE SUNDERED HEAVENS

REKI KAWAHARA
ILLUSTRATION BY HIMA
DESIGN BY bee-pee

AIRI SAGISU
Grade nine at Eternal Girls' Academy.
Student council vice president.

NANAKO JUHOLT
Grade seven at Eternal Girls' Academy.
Student council secretary.

TOMOCHIKA KYOBU
Grade nine at Shirakabanomori Academy.
Student council president.

RIOH KOSHIMIZU
Grade nine at Shirakabanomori Academy.
Student council vice president.

TSUBOMI KOSHIKA
Oscillatory Universe executive.
Third of the Seven Dwarves.
Duel avatar: Rose Milady.

PLATINUM CAVALIER
First of the Seven Dwarves.
Also called Bashful, Basher.

IVORY TOWER
Full proxy of the White King, White Cosmos.
Fourth of the Seven Dwarves.

SILVER CROW
Formerly of the new Nega Nebulus, currently a member of Oscillatory Universe. Possesses the sole flight ability in the Accelerated World.

HARUYUKI
Boy in the lowest school caste.
Duel avatar: Silver Crow.

KUROYUKIHIME
Legion Master of the new Nega Nebulus.
Vice president of the Umesato Junior High student council.
Duel avatar: Black Lotus.

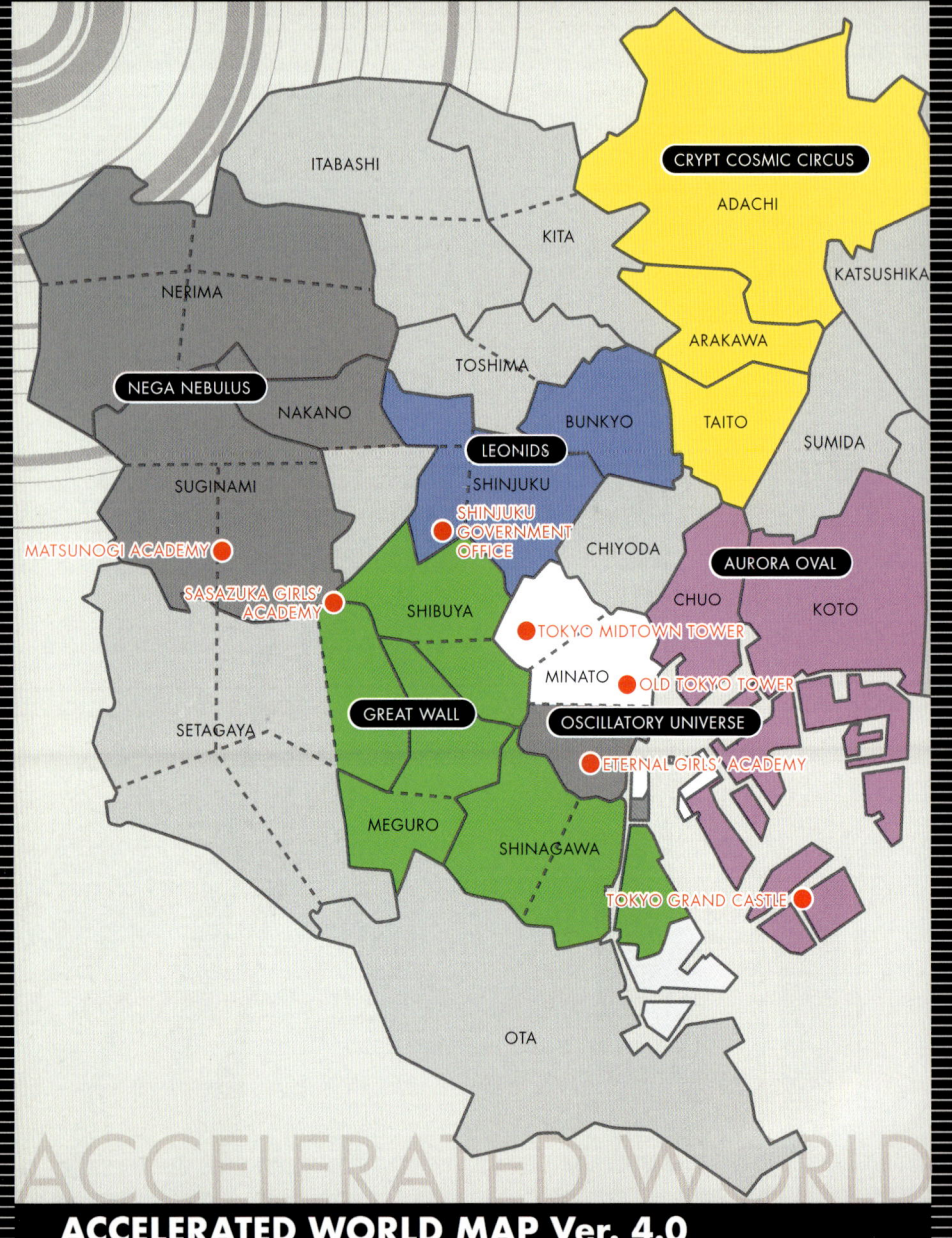

ACCELERATED WORLD MAP Ver. 4.0

Eternal Girls' Academy

Famed K–12 girls' school in Minato Area No. 3 with over 130 years of history, nicknamed EG. It is the headquarters of Oscillatory Universe and is attended by many of the Legion's core members, including Rose Milady (Tsubomi Koshika). It is also the base for the Acceleration Research Society.

Deity of Demise, Tezcatlipoca

Giant Super-class Enemy over 100 meters tall that appeared from inside the Sun God Inti. Its confirmed methods of attack are Toxcatl, gravitational waves released from its right hand; Miccailhuitontli, incandescent flames released from its left; and Level Drain. According to the White King, its power surpasses that of the Four Saints and the Four Gods combined.

▶▶▶ ACCEL · WORLD

CONQUEROR OF THE SUNDERED HEAVENS

Reki Kawahara
Illustrations: HIMA
Design: bee-pee

NEW YORK

■ Kuroyukihime = Umesato Junior High School student council vice president. A "machine child" produced by parents who were researchers at Kamura, she had her brain overwritten with someone's soul. Her duel avatar is the Black King, Black Lotus.

■ Haruyuki = Haruyuki Arita. Grade eight at Umesato Junior High School. After numerous battles with powerful foes under his "parent" Kuroyukihime, he reached the high-ranker level. His duel avatar is Silver Crow.

■ Chiyuri = Chiyuri Kurashima. Haruyuki's childhood friend. As a Burst Linker, she possesses the extremely rare ability to go back in time and is active as the Black Legion's healer. Her duel avatar is Lime Bell.

■ Takumu = Takumu Mayuzumi. A boy Haruyuki and Chiyuri have known since childhood. When he had level seven in his sights, he was sent back to level four because of Tezcatlipoca's Level Drain. His duel avatar is Cyan Pile.

■ Fuko = Fuko Kurasaki. One of the Four Elements. Rules wind. Taught Haruyuki about the Incarnate System. Her duel avatar is Sky Raker.

■ Uiui = Utai Shinomiya. One of the Four Elements. Rules fire. Grade four student in the elementary division of Matsunogi Academy. Uses the advanced curse removal command "Purify." Her duel avatar is Ardor Maiden.

■ Centaurea Sentry = Seri Suzukawa. The Third Chrome Disaster and one of the strongest players in the Accelerated World. Taught Haruyuki Omega style Whole Blade.

■ Rose Milady = Tsubomi Koshika. Ranked third of the Seven Dwarves, the White Legion's executive, but is fighting together with Haruyuki for the time being in order to save Megumi Wakamiya.

■ Ivory Tower = Identity unknown. Ranked fourth of the Seven Dwarves, full proxy of the White King. Also the true identity of Black Vise, vice president of the Acceleration Research Society.

■ Graphite Edge = Identity unknown. Burst Linker who belonged to the old Nega Nebulus. One of the Four Elements. His identity is still shrouded in mystery.

■ White Cosmos = Identity unknown. Master of the White Legion Oscillatory Universe. Also known as Transient Eternity. Kuroyukihime's older sister and "parent."

■ Neurolinker = A portable Internet terminal that connects with the brain via a wireless quantum connection and enhances all five senses with images, sounds, and other stimuli.

■ Brain Burst 2039 = Trial No. 2. Neurolinker application sent to Haruyuki by Kuroyukihime. Viewed as mainly a fighting game with Enemy hunting.

■ Accel Assault 2038 = Trial No. 1. High-speed shooting, one-on-one. A separate Accelerated World from Brain Burst, which declined because it was filled with excessive fighting.

■ Cosmos Corrupt 2040 = Trial No. 3. Hack-and-slash, mainly fighting Enemies. A separate Accelerated World from Brain Burst, which declined because it was filled with excessive harmony.

■ Duel avatar = Player's virtual self operated when fighting in Brain Burst.

■ Legion = Groups composed of many duel avatars with the objective of expanding occupied areas and securing rights. There are seven main Legions, each led by one of the Seven Kings of Pure Color.

■ Normal Duel Field = The field where normal Brain Burst battles (one-on-one) are carried out. Although the specs do possess elements of reality, the system is essentially on the level of an old-school fighting game.

■ Unlimited Neutral Field = Field for high-level players where only duel avatars at level four and up are allowed. The game system is of a wholly different order than that of the Normal Duel Field, and the level of freedom in this field beats out even the next-generation VRMMO.

■ Movement Control System = System in charge of avatar control. Normally, this system handles all avatar movement.

■ Image Control System = System in which the player creates a strong image in their mind to operate the avatar. The mechanism is very different from the normal movement control system, and very few players can use it. Key component of the Incarnate System.

■ Incarnate System = Technique allowing players to interfere with the Brain Burst program's Image Control System to bring about a reality outside the game's framework. Also referred to as "overwriting" game phenomena.

■ ISS kit = Abbreviation for "IS mode study kit." ("IS mode" is "Incarnate System mode.") The kit allows any duel avatar who uses it to make use of the Incarnate System. While using it, a red "eye" is attached to some part of the avatar, and a black aura overlay—the staple of Incarnate attacks—is emitted from the eye.

■ Seven Arcs = The seven strongest Enhanced Armaments in the Accelerated World. They are the greatsword Impulse, the staff Tempest, the large shield Strife, the crown/scepter Luminary, the straight sword Infinity, the full-body armor Destiny, and the Fluctuating Light (form unknown).

■ Mental-Scar Shell = The emotional scars that are the foundation of a duel avatar (mental scars created from trauma in early childhood)—this is the shell enveloping them. Children with exceptionally hard and thick "shells" are said to produce metal-color duel avatars.

■ Artificial metal color = Refers to a metal-color avatar that is not generated naturally from the subject's mental scars, but rather produced artificially by a third party through the thickening of the Mental-Scar Shell.

■ Unlimited EK = Abbreviation for Unlimited Enemy Kill. The subject avatar is killed by a powerful Enemy in the Unlimited Neutral Field, and after they regenerate once more after a fixed period of time, they are killed again by that Enemy, falling into an infinite hell.

▶▶▶ ACCEL · WORLD

Duel Avatar and Enemy List

Black Legion: Nega Nebulus

Provisional Master: Black Lotus (Kuroyukihime)

Provisional Submaster: Scarlet Rain (Yuniko Kozuki)

Four Elements	Wind: Sky Raker (Fuko Kurasaki)
	Fire: Ardor Maiden (Utai Shinomiya)
	Water: Aqua Current (Akira Himi)

Lime Bell (Chiyuri Kurashima)

Cyan Pile (Takumu Mayuzumi)

Silver Crow (Haruyuki Arita)

Chocolat Puppeter (Shihoko Nago)

Mint Mitten (Satomi Mito)

Plum Flipper (Yume Yuruki)

Magenta Scissor (Rui Odagiri)

Trilead Tetroxide

Centaurea Sentry (Seri Suzukawa)

Triplex	No. 1: Blood Leopard (Mihaya Kakeya)
	No. 2: Cassis Moose
	No. 3: Thistle Porcupine

Blaze Heart

Peach Parasol

Ochre Prison

Mustard Salticid

Lavender Downer

Iodine Sterilizer

Ash Roller (Rin Kusakabe)

Bush Utan | Temporarily transferred from Great Wall

Olive Grab

Blue Legion: Leonids

Master: Blue Knight

| Dualis | Cobalt Blade (Koto Takanouchi) |
| | Manganese Blade (Yuki Takanouchi) |

Frost Horn

Tourmaline Shell

Cerulean Runner

Green Legion: Great Wall

Master: Green Grandé

Six Armors	First seat: Graphite Edge
	Second seat: Viridian Decurion
	Third seat: Iron Pound
	Fourth seat: Lignum Vitae
	Fifth seat: Suntan Chafer
	Sixth seat: ???

Jade Jailer

Yellow Legion: Crypt Cosmic Circus

Master: Yellow Radio

Lemon Pierrette

Sax Loader

Purple Legion: Aurora Oval

Master: Purple Thorn

Aster Vine

White Legion: Oscillatory Universe

Master: White Cosmos

Seven Dwarves	No. 1: Platinum Cavalier
	No. 2: Snow Fairy
	No. 3: Rose Milady (Tsubomi Koshika)
	No. 4: Ivory Tower
	No. 5: ???
	No. 6: Cypress Reaper
	No. 7: Glacier Behemoth

Shadow Cloaker

Orchid Oracle (Megumi Wakamiya)

Acceleration Research Society

Black Vise

Argon Array

Dusk Taker (Seiji Nomi)

Rust Jigsaw

Sulfur Pot

Wolfram Cerberus (Armor of Catastrophe, Mark II)

Computation and Martial Arts Research Club

Aluminum Valkyrie (Chiaki Chigira)

Orange Raptor (Yuko Hori)

Violet Dancer (Kurumi Kuruma)

Iris Alice (Lilya Usachova)

Affiliation unknown

Avocado Avoider

Nickel Doll

Sand Duct

Crimson Kingbolt

Lagoon Dolphin (Ruka Asato)

Coral Merrow (Mana Itosu)

Tin Writer

Enemies

Four Saints

Archangel Metatron (Shiba Park Underground Labyrinth)

Amaterasu (Tokyo Station Underground Labyrinth)

Goddess of the Dawn Ushas

Queen Mother of the West Xiwangmu

Four Gods of the Four Gates

East gate: Seiryu

West gate: Byakko

South gate: Suzaku

North gate: Genbu

Eight Divines of the Shrine of the Eight Divines

???

Highest-ranking Beings

Goddess Nyx (Yoyogi Park Underground Labyrinth)

Abandoned Princess Bari

Storm King Rudra

God-class Enemies

Sun God Inti (Deity of Demise Tezcatlipoca)

1

Here comes a new challenger!

Haruyuki glanced dispassionately at the burning letters. He did feel the usual pre-duel thrill, but the core of his being was cool as ice. He kept his emotions in check and his mind sharp as he waited to be sent to the duel stage.

The flames faded away, and a sinking sensation came over him. He fell through an infinite darkness until eventually, his feet touched hard ground, and his field of view took on brightness and color once more.

He had been walking down Oume Highway on his way to Umesato Junior High when he was challenged. The scene that manifested before his eyes now was roughly that terrain as it had been. But cruel cracks cut across the sidewalk, and the multiuse buildings and apartments to either side of the road were charred as though they had been exposed to intense heat. The sky that had been a clear, cloudless blue in the real world was now blanketed by a roiling yellow sandstorm.

A lower nature-type—the flame-affiliated Scorched Earth stage—Haruyuki realized right away. He turned his gaze toward the guide cursor displayed in the overlay in the center of his field of view. The light-blue triangle pointed southwest and trembled slightly. His opponent was apparently closing the distance between them in a straight line, but judging from the pale color of the cursor, it would be a little longer before they made contact.

Haruyuki looked up and to the right. The enemy avatar name displayed below a health gauge there read "Zelkova Verger." He had learned neither of these words so far in junior high, but he knew what they meant nonetheless. "Zelkova" was some kind of tree, and a "verger" was a guard. So tree guard. But this didn't mean someone who guarded the tree; his opponent's affiliation was the tree part.

It was no mere chance that he knew this much about his opponent, despite the fact that this was his first duel against them. This knowledge was the result of a lot of hard work day and night for the last few days to memorize the details of Burst Linkers active in the Tokyo area.

Naturally, he had made similar efforts in the past, but his focus had mainly been limited to the members of the seven—well, excluding Nega Nebulus, the six Great Legions. But now he had expanded that focus to Burst Linkers from small and mid-size Legions, as well as to those without any Legion affiliation. Given that there were around a thousand Burst Linkers in total, remembering every little thing about all of them wasn't as simple as memorizing mathematical formulas or historical eras, but he was currently in no position to complain.

At any rate, it was a good omen that Zelkova Verger was among the just under five hundred people whose names, Legion affiliations, and characteristics he'd memorized thus far. Zelkova was a member of the small Legion Gallant Hawks based out of Mitaka, which neighbored Suginami to the west. The fact that he had appeared from the southwest likely meant he'd taken the Keio Inogashira Line to come on an expedition to Suginami Area No. 3, although one could not call that a particularly far expedition.

The reason Haruyuki had never had the chance to fight Zelkova before, despite being neighbors, was simply because he had never gone to Mitaka with the objective of dueling, plus the fact that he was protected by the right to refuse challenges in the Suginami area, given that it was Nega Nebulus territory. However, that privilege had been stripped away three days earlier, on July 24.

He yanked back his thoughts as they threatened to slip away into reminiscence. He had to concentrate on the duel before him. Zelkova Verger was an M-type, level six. Haruyuki's Silver Crow was also level six, so in light of the principle of "same level, same potential," there was no significant difference in the abilities of their duel avatars. The contest would be decided by the knowledge and experience, insight and judgment, and inspiration of the Burst Linkers themselves.

The enemy was still approaching in a straight line. He was able to do that, despite the dense clusters of buildings and houses that filled Suginami Area No. 3, because the majority of structures in the Scorched Earth stage were essentially skeletons, nothing more than floors and pillars. The burnt-out walls were much more brittle than they looked, and most would crumble to dust if stormed by a heavyweight avatar. So a player could charge up their special attack gauge while they smashed through the shells of the structures.

But Silver Crow was a metal color and lightweight, so he couldn't break through the thick walls just by running at them. To charge his special attack gauge, his only option was to break whichever walls looked like they would crumble from his punches and kicks.

Haruyuki turned his gaze upward. He could see seven or eight Gallery members encamped on the roofs of buildings with frames laid bare. Some among them probably intended to challenge him once his duel with Zelkova was finished. Silver Crow's specs had long been public knowledge, but he was under no obligation to reveal his pre-fight routines.

He returned his gaze to the guide cursor and saw that the blue had gotten quite saturated. Estimating that the distance between him and Zelkova was down to five hundred meters, he started running west on Oume Highway.

Before too long, a large intersection came into view up ahead. If he proceeded straight, he would reach the gates of Umesato Junior High, but there was no point in going to school in a duel stage. Although luring an enemy to familiar terrain was an effective strategy, it also came with the risk of being cracked in the real world.

He turned left at the intersection, started down Itsukaichi Highway, and picked up speed. After a minute or so, he turned left onto a random road and went around to the rear of his charging opponent, smashing the buildings to his left as he did so. But naturally, Zelkova would realize that Haruyuki was trying to get behind him and adjust his own course accordingly.

The guide cursor bobbing in his field of view turned just a little bit faster; Zelkova had shifted to the left. Haruyuki also turned left at the same time and plunged into a narrow residential alley. This movement would have been communicated to Zelkova through the cursor, but he still had plenty of time to set a trap.

Although the buildings in the Scorched Earth stage were burnt-out husks, walls and fences in this dense residential area still more or less remained, so visibility was poor. Duelers had nothing to rely on but the subtle movements of the guide cursor to estimate their enemy's location and direction of movement. But too great a focus on the cursor in an attempt to gain the upper hand would lead you to forget a single fundamental rule: The guide cursor only spun around three hundred and sixty degrees horizontally. It did not take into account vertical movement.

"Hup!" Haruyuki kicked off the ground with a soft cry after he'd gone some ways down the alley.

He found footholds on a half-destroyed wall and a charred tree, and leapt up to the roof of a two-story house. If he stopped there for even a moment, Zelkova might notice something was up, so he jumped from rooftop to rooftop at the same speed as he had been running.

In other stages where the buildings were more solid, running across rooftops was a standard technique, but it became dramatically more difficult in the Scorched Earth stage. Reinforced concrete buildings and apartments were one thing, since even burnt-out, their roofs would not break so easily as that. But the roofs of residential houses were about as tough as thick cardboard, so the most lightweight of avatars could easily step through them by accident.

The reason he was nonetheless able to advance without falling through one of these cardboard roofs was thanks to the super-high-level task given to him by his new master—or rather, teacher. And that task was to first step onto the surface of a body of water with his right foot, and then take a step forward with his left foot before his right sank. Repeat this process to take ten steps in a row on top of that body of water. He very much wanted to insist that she had assigned him an impossible task, but she had apparently mastered it in the distant past. Now she had the Surface Walk ability, which allowed her to walk across water without sinking.

So these last few days, before Haruyuki went to bed, he had been diving into the Unlimited Neutral Field to train his water-walking on whatever random water surface was around if it was a Water stage, or on the temple pond or school pool if it wasn't. He'd been doing this for nearly two months of inside time, but all he had to show for his efforts was a mere five steps in a row. To be perfectly honest, he was starting to feel pretty jaded about the whole thing, but he also couldn't quite bring himself to abandon the endeavor after getting this far.

It would probably take him another year or two to make it to the ten steps he'd been assigned, but it turned out that he'd already gained something from all his training: His ability to minimize his weight had seriously improved. Compared with water, into which even a grain of sand would quickly sink, the charred roofs of the Scorched Earth stage were as sturdy as steel.

After thirty seconds of racing along the densely packed rooftops with a light bouncing motion that felt weird even to him, he heard the dry roar of destruction up ahead and saw yellowish smoke drift into the air from the left. Zelkova had smashed the wall of a building.

The destruction of this object filled Zelkova's special attack gauge. Now he would no doubt attempt to blindside Haruyuki with a large attack, and thereby gain initiative. Even though the other Burst Linker was still thirty meters away, Haruyuki could feel this energy crackling in the air around him.

Naturally, Zelkova would have been well prepared for Silver Crow's flight ability. And he would know its limitations—top speed, altitude. And the fact that he couldn't fly unless his special attack gauge was charged.

He had probably kept an eye on the sky at the start of the duel for a surprise attack from above, but then let down his guard when Haruyuki dared to approach without charging his gauge. He was now likely relying on the exclusively horizontal gauge to determine Silver Crow's whereabouts.

Haruyuki kicked gently at an especially fragile roof and leapt upward. The cursor disappeared from his view. Close range.

"Cubic Squelcher!"

A powerful cry came from the other side of the wall of the house to his immediate left, and half of Zelkova's special attack gauge vanished. A heartbeat later, the concrete wall exploded into millions of tiny pieces.

Shooting up out of the cloud of dust with a thunderous roar was a semi-transparent fist, three-dimensional and fifty centimeters across. The massive mitt shot below Haruyuki, cut across the small yard, and smashed through the wall of the neighboring house as well.

The precision of Zelkova's attack was truly magnificent, given that he had only the guide cursor to go on and was aiming into a room invisible from the outside. If Haruyuki had been moving along on the ground, that special attack would have slammed squarely into his chest, and half of his health gauge would have been shaved away. The only advance information he had to go on was the technique name, Cubic Squelcher. But it was one thing to picture it and entirely another to actually see it.

But the duel was no simple show of technique and strength; it was a contest of insight and deception.

Haruyuki leapt into the massive hole in the wall, an even greater calm ruling the core of his being. The cloud-of-dust effect hadn't yet disappeared completely, but he could clearly see the large silhouette standing inside of it.

Zelkova was frozen with one fist thrust out in front of him, unable to move for a fraction of a second as the immediate after-effect of his attack. Haruyuki had no sooner landed in front of his enemy than he was grabbing that defenseless fist and flipping the other avatar with everything he had in a one-armed shoulder throw.

His opponent went flying right through what was left of the wall he'd put a hole into with his special attack, and groaned loudly when he landed flat on his back in the yard.

"Nnngh."

The majority of terrain objects were weak and brittle in the Scorched Earth stage, but the ground itself was one of the few exceptions. As a general rule, it was indestructible, so in a certain sense, it was heavier and harder than any weapon. Thus, for an armor-specialized avatar like Zelkova Verger, a throwing technique was often more effective than any half-baked striking attack.

That said, however, Haruyuki couldn't actually do enough damage with a one-armed shoulder throw to decide the match. Zelkova bounced to his feet right away and snapped into a fighting posture, seeming to pay no mind to the fifteen percent eaten away from his health gauge.

"An impressive performance indeed, Silver Crow!" he cried in a clear, low voice. "I could not fathom that you would come from above when your gauge is quite empty!"

His tone was polite, but not because he was trying to show Haruyuki respect. He was simply creating a character similar to that of the Yellow King, Yellow Radio.

It wasn't that you couldn't *fathom it, you didn't* let *yourself fathom it,* Haruyuki thought, though he kept this to himself.

Instead, as he stepped outside through the hole, he replied, "I must say to you as well, your sighting's pretty accurate, even through the wall."

"..."

Perhaps his response was unexpected. Zelkova Verger fell silent as if taken aback, and Haruyuki took the opportunity to study him.

Just as in the advance information Haruyuki had memorized, Zelkova was a fairly large duel avatar, but there was no sense of sluggishness to him. His shoulders, chest, and limbs were covered with heavy, square armor, but the naked body of the avatar beneath looked even more slender than Cyan Pile.

The wooden armor, Zelkova Verger's most prominent feature, was a reddish-brown, more matte than glossy. It had a high resistance to all kinds of piercing attacks, including slicing, striking, and physical bullets, but given that it was wooden, it was obviously weak to fire. Haruyuki, however, had no flame-affiliated weapons or techniques, and there were no sources of fire in the stage, either.

Other effective attacks were throwing and submission techniques. But after that one-armed throw, Zelkova would now be on guard against such strategies. And Haruyuki faced the same issue with any submission technique, as with a throwing technique: He first had to grab on to his enemy. But it had long been the case in fighting games that a throwing technique was not easy to pull off when your opponent was expecting it.

Thus, he didn't move to close the distance between them himself or even drop into a fighting position.

The moment he saw the name of his challenger, he had expected it to more-or-less go down like this. Which was why he'd gone after the first strike a bit forcefully. As long as the amount left in his gauge was greater, Zelkova would have no choice but to come and attack him, knowing full well the risk he faced of Haruyuki grabbing hold of him.

After about ten seconds of this stalemate, an impatient voice called down from above somewhere, "Heeeeey! How long are you gonna stare at each other?!"

"If you don't want to fight, then just resign already!"

Jeers came from the Gallery, which had been automatically transported to the surrounding tall buildings as the scene of the battle shifted.

Neither the timbre nor the tone of the voices was familiar. The crowd was made up of Burst Linkers from small or mid-size Legions who, like Zelkova, had traveled to be there in the hopes of raising their standing by defeating "Speed Star," aka "Betrayer," aka Silver Crow.

Zelkova, below him in a fighting stance, shifted his center of gravity ever so slightly. The rude cries from the Gallery were upsetting his concentration. He was the same level six as Haruyuki, but his primary means of earning Burst Points might have been hunting Enemies, so that he didn't have as much experience in duels.

As Haruyuki gleaned this, he was already stepping forward. The movement was neither running nor walking, but rather sliding along the ground. He was still far, far from the absurdly smooth interval between motion and stillness of his teacher, Centaurea Sentry. But thanks to the lessons drilled into him in his water-walking training, he felt like he had sheared away a great deal of unnecessary motion.

"Yaah!" Zelkova cried, as he tried to launch a right straight, but Haruyuki had already closed the distance between them.

Given that he had much more left in his health gauge, Haruyuki could have patiently waited for his opponent to attack. But recent events had put him into a mode where his body reacted automatically whenever there was an opening. Actively considering and discarding strategies was only an option until contact with the enemy. Once contact was made, all he could do was leave himself to the flow of things.

He thrust a hand at Zelkova's chest, and the other Burst Linker's massive bulk staggered backward. One hand clutched at the air in front of Haruyuki in an attempt to regain balance.

Haruyuki immediately grabbed on to that arm with both hands and whirled around. He twisted the joints in the limb to their limits, and then used up the special attack gauge he'd charged in the previous shoulder throw to vibrate the wings on his back at full power for a single second. The finely tuned thrust of his flight ability hit the joint of Zelkova's left shoulder.

Crack!

However sturdy the armor, it couldn't defend against submission attacks on the naked body of the avatar itself. And physical stature was practically irrelevant when it came to the durability of the avatar body.

Using this combination of a joint lock and his striking technique, Aerial Combo, Haruyuki ripped Zelkova Verger's sturdy arm off at the base.

"Ngah!" Zelkova staggered backward, groaning.

Although the sensation of pain in the normal duel stage was half that felt in the Unlimited Neutral Field, it was still genuinely hard to ignore the agony of losing a limb. However, if you got lost in the sensation, you were basically begging your opponent to come at you with follow-up attacks.

Haruyuki tossed away the arm he'd twisted off and jumped toward Zelkova again.

The other Burst Linker tried to open up a space between them with a leap backward. But he was a heavyweight avatar and needed a moment's preparation to jump.

Haruyuki shot out with a low kick, legs neatly aligned side by side. The damage from the kick was minute, but because Zelkova was destabilized from the loss of his arm, he flipped over so force-fully, he nearly spun around again. He slammed into the ground on his back, and another chunk of his health gauge vanished.

It was plenty possible for Haruyuki to push forward with another attack, but he decided instead to step back.

Silver Crow's health gauge was still full. Zelkova Verger's, on the other hand, was already down by half.

In the battle so far, it was fair to say that Haruyuki had over-whelmed his opponent. Zelkova had to have understood now that the reason for this was the difference in duel experience.

Of course, it had only been a little over nine months since Haruyuki himself had become a Burst Linker. He was just barely a mid-ranker, having graduated from the ranks of new-bie at long last. But he'd spent so much of his time in this world in an increasingly harsh battle against the Acceleration Research Society and the White Legion, with his many duels featuring the fiercest of fierce warriors, names known throughout the Acceler-ated World, that his avatar had gleaned tremendous experience for the amount of XP his avatar had collected.

"Plunderer" Dusk Taker.

"Quad Eyes Analyst" Argon Array.

"Restrainer" Black Vise.

"Sneezy" Glacier Behemoth.

"Grumpy" Rose Milady.

"Sleepy" Snow Fairy.

"Bashful" Platinum Cavalier.

And the White King, "Transient Eternity," White Cosmos.

All of these fights had been literal life-or-death struggles. He could have easily lost all of his Burst Points in any one of them. And the only one he could say he had clearly won was against Dusk Taker; all the others had been losses or at best draws. The White King, in fact, had defeated him without even fighting him directly. But having somehow survived any number of extreme situations, he no longer got particularly nervous in a normal duel against an opponent of the same level.

He could tell at first glance that he was calm, and Zelkova Verger was too worked up. It was fine and normal to want to keep from losing, but Zelkova's desire to win was too strong. It bled into his actions and allowed his opponent to predict his next move.

The high rankers who fought me probably thought the same thing, Haruyuki thought, and he reined in his feelings. The line between confidence and arrogance was razor thin, and he was still too much of a baby in terms of inside time to consider himself among the strongest warriors of this world.

He retreated to the opposite side of the garden, and Zelkova, perhaps convinced now that Haruyuki was not coming in for a follow-up attack, finally got to his feet, the red of the damage effect spilling from his empty shoulder socket. The gaze from behind his rough face mask was full of rage.

"It almost seems as though you're suggesting I resign," he said, his voice tense.

Haruyuki shrugged. "Well, it'd really help me out if you did."

"What is this attitude of yours?!" Zelkova punched a stone pillar with his remaining hand. The pillar crumbled without resistance, chunks of it flying out into the small yard. About ten percent of the stones hit Zelkova himself, but he seemed to pay this no mind as he roared in anger.

"It's not like you don't know what Tezcatlipoca has done to the Unlimited Neutral Field! Many Legions are in real crisis now that they can no longer hunt Enemies. And the culprit behind it all is Oscillatory Universe. And yet you, traitor that you are, went over to their side. And now you act as though you're above it all. You disgust me!"

This was fairly mean, but the blade of words did not pierce the shell surrounding Haruyuki's heart. He'd heard all this and worse over the course of the last few days.

"I'm not trying to be above it all," he replied evenly. "I'm just saying if I can get an easy win, I'll take it."

The wrath radiating from Zelkova grew even more intense.

Haruyuki instinctively realized that Zelkova was going to come at him with something, but he still didn't drop into a fighting stance. Zelkova's special attack gauge was fully charged once again, thanks to the serious damage he'd taken. If he had some way of turning the tables on this almost-certain defeat, Haruyuki wanted to see it.

Zelkova seemed to understand this desire. He threw his remaining fist high into the air, as if to say, *You want to see? Then I'll show you.* The eight or so meters between them couldn't be bridged with any regular attack, but there were no binding-type abilities in the details Haruyuki had memorized. And if Zelkova turned to special attacks, he wouldn't use Cubic Squelcher again, not when Haruyuki had already grasped its potential.

Offensive special attacks in Brain Burst were not so easy to get a hit with, whether long- or short-range. The standard practice was to use them in a surprise attack or to combine them with a normal attack to somehow chip away at the enemy's ability to evade.

Zelkova was also level six, so he would have been well aware of all this. Which meant that he had some kind of plan that would allow him to attack and make that attack hit Haruyuki as they faced off here.

I hope it's some kind of trick, Haruyuki thought, as he waited for the activation of the technique.

Zelkova Verger stretched out the fingers of the hand brandished above him and plunged them down into the ground.

"Conic Smiter!!"

This name was not in Haruyuki's advance information. Had he kept this card hidden up his sleeve all this time? Or had he recently learned the technique?

Zelkova's hand shone a bright red. But his special attack gauge did not decrease.

It can't be an Incarnate technique? Haruyuki tensed up. And then he felt a faint vibration in the soles of his feet and reflexively leapt away.

Zelkova's special attack gauge finally dropped. At the same time, something sharp and pointy shot up from the ground at lightning speed.

The cone-shaped spike was a meter and a half long and thirty centimeters across. It was the same color as Zelkova's armor and looked pretty hard. Haruyuki got the gut feeling that Silver Crow would have been skewered from bottom to top if he hadn't jumped.

He would never have been able to dodge this long-distance attack and its entirely invisible trajectory on his first encounter with it if he hadn't noticed the faint shaking in the ground. But now that he had dodged it, it would definitely be a slight and a sign of contempt if he didn't counterattack.

He'd seen what he needed to see; it was time to end this. Haruyuki crouched and was about to make a dash toward Zelkova until he saw that the other Burst Linker's special attack gauge had dropped a mere ten percent.

He'd already started to move, so he didn't feel any vibrations. He relied on his gut this time and jumped in the opposite direction from before.

Two spikes ripped through the ground thunderously to pierce the space where he had been only an instant before.

Zelkova's fingers were plunged all the way into the ground, and he still had eighty percent of his gauge left. Which meant…

Haruyuki had no sooner landed than he was throwing himself backward in a somersault. The third spike popped up a millimeter in front of him. Another somersault, another spike shooting past his nose. On his next somersault, the fifth spike grazed Silver Crow's back.

Zelkova's aim was steadily getting more accurate, and with the walls of houses closing in behind him, Haruyuki didn't have enough space to do another flip. Rather than relying on Zelkova to send it one way or another with his gaze or some other signal, this Conic Smiter special attack was likely able to automatically follow its target. An ideal high-performance technique for localized defense, befitting someone with the name "Verger."

Judging from the speed at which Zelkova's special attack gauge was decreasing, there were likely ten spikes. It would be impossible to evade all of the remaining five in this small yard.

Making this split-second judgment, Haruyuki narrowed his options down to three and assessed each of them in an instant.

The first thing he thought of was to flee into the air, but that risked him being hit in the hint of an opening between when he deployed his wings and generated thrust.

The second thing he thought of was to counter the spike with a striking palm. If he cut through the minimal, single point that was the sharp tip, he was certain he could destroy it. But if his aim was off by even a millimeter, his hand would be shattered.

And the third option was one he hesitated to use, but it had the greatest chance of success. It was also the option that would settle this match the quickest.

In his hyper-accelerated awareness, with time slowed to a crawl, Haruyuki somersaulted through the air three times, and just as he was about to land, he said to himself, *Gou.*

Waves rippled through his field of view. His mind expanded and melted into the air.

Bam!

The sixth spike jutted up out of the ground. But it was in the middle of the yard, three meters away from where Haruyuki had landed.

"Huh?!" Zelkova cried out, stunned. And this was no wonder. The automatic targeting couldn't be knocked off target, and yet it had been seriously knocked off target.

The "Gou" technique that Haruyuki used was one of the Omega style secrets he had learned from Centaurea Sentry. By completely interrupting the signals output by his own consciousness, he caused an error in the predictive abilities of the BB system (also known as the Main Visualizer) and erased his presence not only from this duel opponent, but also from the detection of the system itself. Automatic tracing-type special attacks were no longer able to follow, and Zelkova Verger himself would have lost sight of Haruyuki for an instant.

Gou was not an Incarnate technique, but the proviso "strictly speaking" did apply. His teacher Centaurea said that Incarnate techniques, which overwrote phenomena using powerful images, and Gou, which disconnected every kind of image, were based on entirely opposing logic. But both were the same in that they used the BB Image Control System, so Haruyuki couldn't help feeling that there was a bit of Incarnate to Gou.

But when he really thought about it, image power was indispensable to all Burst Linkers. A clear image was required in both the instantaneous choice of how to move your avatar and the long-term vision of how you wanted to grow. When he really drilled down to it, even the water-walking he worked at was actually practice, with the image of making his weight zero.

The boundary between normal and Incarnate techniques was in point of fact fuzzy, and if there was a line to be drawn between them, then he would have to follow the definition of the Red King, Scarlet Rain: Incarnate techniques shone.

The so-called overlay of Incarnate techniques was the result of the excess signal when the user's imagination passed through the BB Image Control System, thereby being processed as a system light effect. Gou, reducing image output to zero as it did, naturally did not shine. Thus, it was not an Incarnate technique. This was the line that Sentry insisted on.

Having shaken Conic Smiter, Haruyuki landed and immediately kicked off the ground again with all his might. He accelerated full-power using the wings on his back and closed in on his baffled opponent.

Zelkova quickly shook off his shock, but he made no move to pull his hand out of the ground. He probably couldn't pull it out until a spike hit or his gauge was entirely depleted. Given the power of the technique, Haruyuki wasn't surprised that it had that kind of constraint to it.

He'd been planning to rip Zelkova's right arm off like he had the left, but that was impossible if it was affixed to the ground. All the better, then.

Quickly changing his plan on the fly, he kept charging and jumped up when he was practically on top of Zelkova.

As he floated up into the air, the Conic Smiter spike automatically retargeted him and jutted up from the ground. But the sharp tip just skimmed the air a centimeter below the soles of his feet.

Missing its intended target, the spike shot through Zelkova, who was crouched directly below Haruyuki, from the thin armor over his stomach all the way up to the nape of his neck.

The forty percent remaining in his health gauge vanished in an instant, and the massive reddish-brown body shrank into itself before shattering into a million pieces.

2

Haruyuki easily beat back the three middle rankers who challenged him after Zelkova Verger and then waited for a new challenger for a minute or two. When none came, he determined that he was done for the morning and cut the global connection on his Neurolinker.

If he stayed disconnected twenty-four-seven like Kuroyukihime had, he wouldn't be chased by this group of self-styled bounty hunters. But he left his connection on as a general rule, except for when he was at home or at school. In fact, he even made sure that the times when there was the greatest possibility of his name appearing on the matching list were widely known.

Thanks to that, he had a minimum of ten daily duels, and on busy days he fought in as many as twenty. He was always completely wiped out by the time he got home in the evening. But even if it meant collapsing on the side of the road in the real world, he had no intention of refusing any challenger. He figured that was the least he could do now.

He let out a short sigh and looked up at the sky. Even though it was only ten in the morning, the sun was practically setting fire to the city. He had no sooner had the thought that today was going to be another scorcher than sweat was beading on his forehead. He wiped it away with a terry-cloth handkerchief and started toward school once more.

He tried to stay in the shade as much as possible as he traveled the remaining three hundred meters, and then slipped through the school gates that appeared on the left side of the sidewalk. He immediately connected to the Umesato local network and sighed with relief. The local network was significantly limited compared with the global net, but even so, the connection did a lot to ease his sense of helplessness.

He went around to the right instead of going to the building entrance facing the front courtyard. He walked down the path that was always gloomy, even in the middle of summer, until the small hut set up in the space between the second school building and the concrete wall came into view.

It was a solidly built structure that made lavish use of precious natural wood, but its inhabitant was not human. The front of the hut was a stainless steel lattice, and Haruyuki peered through this to the inside as he offered a quiet greeting.

"'Sup, Hoo. Pretty hot again today, huh?"

A gray bird raised his eyelids from where he sat on a perch in the middle of the hutch. This was the northern white-faced owl, Hoo, the lone animal that the Umesato Animal Care Club, of which Haruyuki was president, was caring for at present.

It had only been just over a month since Haruyuki had started taking care of him, but lately when he said hello, the owl would reply with a little chirp. If he was in a good mood, he would fly up from his perch and do a couple turns around the hutch. He normally did, anyway, but that day, Hoo only glanced at Haruyuki with his orange eyes and quickly lowered his lids once more.

He was supposed to be a more heat-resilient species of owl, but Haruyuki guessed that days of this intense summer sultriness had worn him out. There was an overhang at the top of the wire mesh, so the hut got no direct sunlight, and there was a birdbath for Hoo to play in. But there was basically no breeze, so the heat was just sitting in the air there.

"Hang on a sec, okay? I'll give you a mist shower," Haruyuki said, and turned toward the toolshed. He got out the hose with the multi-spray nozzle and connected it to the tap on one side of the hutch. While cleaning the hut, he had accidentally discovered that Hoo liked to be sprayed with the mist setting, to the point where just seeing the hose would make him demand a shower.

He was twisting the dial at the end of the nozzle to set it to the mist mark and pulling the lever to test it, to confirm that misty water did in fact come out, when a chat window opened up in the bottom of his virtual desktop. Text scrolled in a cherry-pink font.

UI> HELLO, ARITA.

Haruyuki automatically started to turn around before muttering "whoops" and letting go of the trigger. He'd almost sprayed her once before in a similar situation, and he couldn't go around repeating the same mistake.

He turned around for real this time and greeted the sender of the chat message. "Hello, Shinomiya."

Standing there was the "super president" of the Umesato Animal Care Club, Utai Shinomiya. She was very much the picture of an elementary school student on summer vacation in her printed T-shirt and shorts, but in the Accelerated World, she was a true high ranker, inspiring fear with the nickname Testarossa.

When she held her longbow Flame Caller, she had strength on par with that of a fearsome god, and yet she was always giving Haruyuki the gentlest of guidance. She was a priceless friend and senior to him in the Legion. Or at least she had been, but their bond as members of the same Legion had been severed three days earlier.

A sharp pain shot through his heart as he had this thought. But he kept that off his face and tried to keep going with a smile. "I was just about to give Hoo a mist shower. Why don't you—?"

But he couldn't finish. Because Utai dropped the bag she was carrying and charged into him. Even though he was over twice her size, the tackle very nearly knocked him over. He managed to stay on his feet somehow, and with a shrill voice, he asked, "Wh-wh-what's wrong, Shinomiya?!"

Clutching Haruyuki's pudgy, round body with her right hand, Utai tapped at her holo keyboard with her left.

UI> Arita, please stop the reckless duels.

"Huh?" He was stunned at this comment out of nowhere.

She looked up at him with tears in her large eyes and kept typing at lightning speed.

UI> I took the liberty of watching your earlier duel. You fought wonderfully, but if you keep winning in that fashion, you will only see an increase in the number of people who harbor ill will toward you.

"Um." After thinking for a second about how to respond to this, he asked quietly, "You were watching? I didn't notice you at all."

UI> Because I used a dummy avatar.

"O-oh, you did...?"

A dummy avatar was for viewing alone, an avatar with a different appearance from your duel avatar, set for those times when you wanted to hide your true identity and enter the Gallery. And indeed if Ardor Maiden, one of Nega Nebulus's Four Elements, had been seen there, the other members of the Gallery would no doubt have started bothering her in one way or another. But why would she go to such lengths to watch his duel?

Guessing at his confusion, Utai answered before he could ask any questions.

UI> People are talking about it. They're saying that you fight dozens of duels a day, and yet you haven't lost once. I won't criticize you for the pursuit of victory. But there's something more important. And that's to—

"—have fun with the duel," he muttered, before she could finish typing the sentence out. This was the philosophy Haruyuki himself had long held in his heart. He'd even said it to other people on multiple occasions.

Utai pulled herself away from him the tiniest bit and nodded firmly.

UI> THAT'S EXACTLY RIGHT. BUT YOU DID NOT LOOK LIKE YOU WERE HAVING THE LEAST BIT OF FUN TODAY, ARITA. YOU CLAIMED OVERWHELMING VICTORY IN ALL FOUR DUELS, BUT TO MY EYES, IT LOOKED ALMOST AS THOUGH YOU WERE FIGHTING IN ORDER TO FOCUS HATRED ON YOURSELF.

He met Utai's deeply anxious eyes for only a moment before averting his gaze.

"I guess so," he said. "That's why I'm accepting these duels."

Utai raised her left hand just a little, but then dropped it lifelessly without typing a single character. The right hand holding on to his shirt also slowly let go.

Ashamed of putting an unprecedentedly sad expression on the face of the Shinomiya he so deeply loved and respected, Haruyuki went on to explain.

"You know that the Deity of Demise, Tezcatlipoca, is wreaking havoc on the Accelerated World. In just three days, it's had a huge impact on the small and midsize Legions that used Enemies as their point supply. Right now, they're focusing their anger on Oscillatory Universe, the group behind all of these disasters. But at some point, I think they'll also turn on the six Legions that released Tezcatlipoca."

UI> WE'RE NOT LEAVING THEM TO THEIR OWN DEVICES BECAUSE WE WANT TO, Utai interjected, typing at the speed of light with both hands.

Haruyuki swallowed hard and looked up into the sky toward the city center. "Yeah. I know you did whatever you could on that front a long time ago. And I get that mustering the strength of the six Great Legions won't do anything now, so you can't attack or whatever."

He brought his gaze back to Utai and continued. "But the Burst Linkers from the small and midsize Legions assume that the six Great Legions will naturally solve the problems of the Accelerated

World. Just like that time with Chrome Disaster, and with the ISS kits, too. If they keep not being able to hunt Enemies, there's gonna be people in those Legions asking why the kings aren't doing anything. And when that happens, there'll obviously be a backlash from the members of the six Great Legions."

Utai seemed to grasp the danger contained in the map of the future that Haruyuki was drawing. A new anxiety, different from her earlier concern, rose on her childish face.

UI> IF IT'S AT THE LEVEL OF SIMPLY ARGUING ON THE NET, IT'S FINE. BUT WE DON'T KNOW HOW IT WILL ESCALATE ONCE THE SKIRMISHES START, CHALLENGING AND BEING CHALLENGED.

"That's exactly what I think. I know they're the 'Great Legions,' but even the biggest of them, Great Wall, only has a hundred or so people. There are definitely way more people in the small and midsize Legions, and Burst Linkers who are unaffiliated with any Legion. If serious fighting breaks out, the Great Legions won't make it out unscathed. I mean, there are tons of really powerful fighters in the smaller Legions."

Utai nodded. She had said earlier that he hadn't lost once, even while dueling a dozen or more times each day. That was a fact, but he'd had several close calls. In the Zelkova Verger duel, for example, he might have lost if he hadn't played his secret Gou card. If that level of user kept coming at him, they could make up the gap with the mainstay members of the six Great Legions. And if these small and midsize Legions put together a select team and entered the Territories, areas under the control of the six Great Legions might actually fall.

After that, it would be all-out war, blood spilled on top of blood. Who knew how many Burst Linkers would be driven to total point loss before the warring ended?

Likely thinking the same thing, Utai lowered her eyes briefly, but then eventually raised both of her hands and tapped resolutely at the air.

UI> EVEN SO, THAT'S NO REASON FOR YOU ALONE TO BE THE RECEPTACLE OF THE DISPLEASURE OF THE SMALL AND MIDSIZE

LEGIONS, ARITA. THE ONES RESPONSIBLE FOR ALL OF THIS ARE THE WHITE KING AND OSCILLATORY UNIVERSE. NO ONE WOULD HAVE A WORD TO SAY AGAINST YOU IF YOU CUT YOUR GLOBAL CONNECTION AND TOLD THEM TO GO TO MINATO AREA NO. 3 AND NOT TO SUGINAMI IF THEY HAVE A PROBLEM WITH THAT! This was an entirely correct assertion.

It was true that in the Territories exactly a week earlier, on July 20, Minato Area No. 3—which housed Eternal Girls' Academy, the White Legion's headquarters—had fallen under the control of Nega Nebulus, and the members of Oscillatory Universe, estimated to be around thirty in total, were stripped of the right to refuse challenges.

That said, however, they seemed to have cut their global connections, unlike Haruyuki, so even if a player were to march into Minato Area No. 3, they wouldn't be able to challenge them. But there was one exception: the Legion Master and White King, White Cosmos herself.

Ever since she lost in the Territories, the White King had left her name on the matching list. Sky Raker/Fuko Kurasaki hypothesized that the reason for this was a challenge to the Six Kings—and to the Black King, Black Lotus in particular. The truth was unknown, but at any rate, if they wanted to, currently any and all Burst Linkers could freely duel the White King, of whom they had previously not even been able to catch a glimpse.

In fact, there were apparently more than a few Burst Linkers who challenged her out of curiosity or in pursuit of a tale to tell. But they had all been attacked by a massive, monstrous avatar and killed instantly before facing White Cosmos herself. There weren't supposed to be Enemies in the normal duel stage, and it wasn't as though she'd have a Legion member as a bodyguard in duels that weren't tag team matches. Most people assumed that it was likely the ability to automatically produce a puppet, something along the lines of Chocolat Puppeter's special ability Puppet Make or Viridian Decurion's Viridian Legionary, but no one knew for sure.

There were also rumors of the names of the Legion's executives, the Seven Dwarves, appearing on the list from time to time, but these were fierce and powerful warriors. Unless you were a skilled high ranker, they would kick you to the curb without giving you the chance to protest.

Because of this, it was next to impossible for Burst Linkers like Zelkova Verger to register their complaints directly with the members of Oscillatory Universe, even if they did make the trip to Minato Area No. 3. Still, Haruyuki didn't shy away from Utai's gaze as he said, "Thanks, Mei."

He called her by the nickname derived from her avatar name rather than her real name and placed a gentle hand on her small shoulder.

"I'm really happy you're still keeping an eye out for me like this, even though we're not in the same Legion anymore. But I was the one who cut open the Sun God Inti and revived Tezcatlipoca sealed away inside of it. And I was the one the White King kidnapped, the cause of everything that's led to where we are now. The members of the small and midsize Legions have a right to complain to me. If that releases even a little of the pressure building up, then I can't exactly go refusing challenges—"

UI> Of course I'm worried about you!!

Utai typed with such force that he felt like he could hear the keys clacking, even though it was a holo keyboard, and then she leapt at Haruyuki once more. Tears pooled in her wide eyes, and her lips trembled like she was going to try to produce words, before her ten fingers flashed once more.

UI> Even if we're not Legion members in the system anymore, that doesn't mean that our bond has disappeared! After all, you left Nega Nebulus to help Lo. And to go back further in time, you cut Inti open to save the five Kings. And yet you alone are being treated like a traitor, and you constantly get challenged every day, I just—

Perhaps she couldn't continue any further. She grabbed on to his shirt with both hands and pressed her forehead firmly against his chest.

The instant he felt her silent sobbing, Haruyuki's own eyes grew hot. But he couldn't go crying now. He had chosen all of this of his own free will.

Instead of holding the shuddering slender back, Haruyuki gently patted it.

"I'm sorry to make you worry, Mei. But I really am not pushing myself. It's maybe true that I don't have the mental energy to enjoy the duels, but…compared with training with Master Raker or my teacher Sentry, twenty or thirty duels a day is nothing. I'm only on standby on my way to school and back home, and most of the time, it's the first time I'm going up against that avatar. So I actually am learning all kinds of things fighting them.

"And we're Burst Linkers, so there's only the duel, right?" he finished in a joking tone.

Utai still took a while to lift her face away from his chest, but eventually, she took a step back, pulled a handkerchief out of her pocket, and wiped her eyes. Head still hanging, she took a few deep breaths before finally looking at him. She blinked red-rimmed eyes a couple times, and a faint smile spread across her face as she nimbly made the fingers of her left hand dance.

UI> THE WAY YOU SAY THAT, IT SOUNDS AS THOUGH YOU THINK YOU COULD BEAT ME ALREADY IN A DUEL.

"Wh-what?!" Stunned, Haruyuki threw his hands up around either side of his face and began waving them frantically as he protested desperately. "I—I—I don't think that even a bit! If you saw the duels today, then you know I'm totally nowhere near that level, Mei!"

Utai giggled before exhaling once more. Recomposing her expression, she typed a tiny bit more slowly.

UI> I UNDERSTAND YOUR THINKING, ARITA. IF YOU WILL PROMISE ME THAT YOU WON'T BE RECKLESS, THEN I WILL NOT TELL YOU TO STOP THE DUELS ANYMORE. BUT I DO HAVE ONE REQUEST.

She paused for an instant and looked directly at him.

UI> WOULD YOU PLEASE MEET WITH LO?

Haruyuki couldn't answer her right away.

The person that Utai called Lo was of course the leader of Nega Nebulus, the Black King, Black Lotus—Kuroyukihime.

After the mission to rescue Silver Crow had ended in disastrous failure that evening three days earlier, Haruyuki explained what had happened to his comrades in a dive chat. Naturally, Kuroyukihime had also been there. But from the time the meeting had ended after midnight on July 25 until the present moment, Haruyuki hadn't been in touch with her, and she'd made no attempt to contact him.

He did feel like he needed to sit down and actually talk with her. But what to say and how to say it? Kuroyukihime was the very person who had rescued him from Hell, the parent who had given him Brain Burst, and the swordmaster to whom he'd sworn his eternal loyalty. He owed her so much, and yet he had betrayed her, leaving Nega Nebulus to transfer to Oscillatory Universe.

If he hadn't done that, though, Cyan Pile, Trilead Tetroxide, Lavender Downer, Graphite Edge, Centaurea Sentry, and the Archangel Metatron, the six who had volunteered for the dangerous mission of rescuing him, would have all been slaughtered by Tezcatlipoca under the thrall of the Arc Luminary.

If it had simply been death they faced or losing however many points, then it would have been possible for them to come back from that. But Tezcatlipoca had the same Level Drain ability as Seiryu, one of the Four Gods, and had in fact forced Cyan Pile down from level six to level four.

On top of that, unlike the Burst Linkers, Metatron couldn't regenerate as long as she had points left. Strictly speaking, once the Change came over the Unlimited Neutral Field, Metatron would be revived as an Enemy in the deepest part of the Shiba Park Dungeon, but this would be an entirely different individual, one whose memories and thinking had been reset.

Thus, in the moment, Haruyuki could only surrender himself

to the White King and beg her mercy. He had no other option but to bow his head to her, the only one with the potential to stop Tezcatlipoca, and pledge his loyalty in exchange for those six lives. Kuroyukihime also had to understand this, but whether or not she accepted it and agreed with him was another question.

To be honest, he didn't know how she would take his decision. But the fact was that even now after three days—to be more precise, sixty hours—had passed, he still hadn't heard from her. He was forced to assume that Kuroyukihime was still in no mind to talk to him. He wasn't sure how to explain all this to Utai.

But before he could open his mouth, his ears picked up new sounds: the crunching of feet against the gravel of the rear courtyard and a cheerful whistling.

Hurriedly taking a step back from Utai, he lifted his hanging head. Approaching them was a girl wearing the school-mandated gym clothes. Fortunately, because she was looking at her virtual desktop as she walked, she hadn't noticed this moment of closeness between Haruyuki and Utai.

After glancing over to make sure that Utai's face was dry now, Haruyuki called out to the girl, "Izeki! Distracted walking's dangerous."

The girl, Reina Izeki, lifted her face from her desktop and grinned. "It's totes fine. I'm a pro."

"A pro at what, though?" Haruyuki retorted, and she let this slide with a smile.

"Hey there, Utaicchi," she said. "That's a cute shirt."

UI> THANK YOU. I BOUGHT IT WHEN I WENT SHOPPING WITH GRANNY.

Utai shrugged bashfully and grabbed the hem of her T-shirt to pull it smooth. It was printed with three rows of silhouettes of small birds.

Reina had a little sister the same age as Utai, and a fond smile crossed her face before she at last shifted her gaze to Haruyuki.

Instantly, her smile faded, like she could sense something amiss with him. But her usual playful expression quickly returned, and she yanked on the collar of her gym uniform, to flap it open and shut.

"And like, Prez, this heat is seriously deadly," she complained. "Make it so we can come in our street clothes for summer break at least."

"Huh?!" Haruyuki shook his head, vigorously. "N-no way, we can't!"

"How come only Super Prez gets to be different?!" she argued, somewhat overbearing, and Haruyuki cleared his throat.

"Um," he started. "Shinomiya's entry permission uses the shared study program of Umesato and Matsunogi Academy, but the program rules don't specify the clothes to wear when visiting the other school. But for us, there's a rule that says anything other than our uniforms, gym clothes, or team uniforms is no good, even during summer break, so..."

"So striiiict." Reina pursed her lips before she snapped the fingers of her right hand. "I know! So we make our own uniforms then!"

"Whaaat?!" Haruyuki yelped.

"Our gym clothes are so thick and stuffy," she said, matter-of-factly. "We could do some SC design with fabric that breathes better and stays drier."

"E-ess-see?!" Haruyuki repeated the letters that most likely were a contraction for "super cute" and turned his gaze to the left, seeking help. But super president Utai merely grinned and made no move to tap at her keyboard.

"O-oh. Clubs don't usually have uniforms, though," Haruyuki replied, even as he thought that this was a very uninteresting response.

Reina raised an eyebrow at him. "I think it'd be good, though," was all she said as she looked down at her feet. The tote bag Utai had dropped earlier was standing there. She picked it up and turned her face toward the hutch.

"We'd better get cleaning before it gets too late," she said. "And Hoo's gotta be hungry."

"Yeah, I guess we should get to it." Haruyuki nodded, and Utai also voiced her agreement.

UI> YES, LET'S DO THAT!

If they had followed the agreement to each take their turn watching over Hoo, Reina would have been on duty that day. But Haruyuki ended up coming to school every day, and Reina also came every two out of three days, so they'd stopped mentioning it when the other showed up on their off-duty days.

The group quickly finished cleaning the hutch and changing the water in the birdbath to arrive at the long-awaited feeding time. Utai was left to purchase and prepare Hoo's food—either quail or mouse meat cut up into small pieces, or live crickets and mealworms. But despite the fact that Hoo would only eat from Utai's hand when he first came to Umesato, he had recently started eating the food that Haruyuki and Reina gave him, albeit only when he was in a good humor.

It seemed like he was in a bit of a listless mood that day, so Haruyuki thought maybe there was no chance he would take food from anyone other than Utai. But after he swooped down to perch on Utai's arm, he quickly gulped down the quail meat Reina offered him with tweezers. After she'd fed him five pieces, they traded, and Haruyuki brought a piece of meat toward Hoo's beak in the same way.

"Skree!" Hoo opened his beak wide and made a threatening sound, so Haruyuki jumped and dropped the tweezers.

But Utai didn't panic; she simply covered Hoo's face with her free hand. His field of view blocked, Hoo flapped his wings several times, but soon quieted right down.

As Haruyuki reeled from the shock of Hoo's reaction, especially since he thought the owl had grown comfortable with him, he remembered his earlier greeting to Hoo through the wire mesh of the hutch. Hoo had quickly closed his eyes without a cry, instead of flying up from his perch, not because the heat had drained him of energy, but maybe because he had been on guard against Haruyuki.

"Did I do something to Hoo?" he murmured, processing the shock of it bit by bit.

"Oh," Reina said, unexpectedly. "Actually, I kinda get how he feels."

"Huh?!" Haruyuki cried.

"Nah, I don't mean like you did anything to me, Prez. But like, lately, you're, I dunno..." She trailed off, and the hesitant expression she'd had when she first saw Haruyuki that day returned to her face.

If she'd sensed a change or some anomaly in him, then he could think of only one reason for that: the fact that he'd been forced to leave Nega Nebulus and transfer to the enemy Legion Oscillatory Universe. He'd thought he had a handle on his mental state, but given that he'd caused both Utai and Reina worry and had even put Hoo on guard meant that he didn't have the shock he'd received three days earlier or his anxiety about the future completely under control.

"I'm sorry, Izeki," he apologized. "I had a kind of shock recently, and...if I'm different from usual, it's probably because of that."

"Like, what kind of shock?" Her brow furrowed in concern.

"Um." He was sure she was actually worried about him, so he wanted to tell her the truth without any lies or evasions. But he couldn't exactly go talking about Brain Burst stuff when she wasn't a Burst Linker.

After thinking earnestly about it for a second, he said, "I betrayed someone I really care about. Someone really important to me. I guess you could even say I owe her my life."

"So then you just gotta say you're sorry and you're good to go."

Reina's response was so straightforward and to the point that he was briefly at a loss for words.

If I could do that, I wouldn't be having such a hard time, he said to himself.

Reina peered into his eyes as if she could read his thoughts.

It was true that the only thing for him to do was apologize. Utai had said the same thing. And he did want to see Kuroyukihime and tell her how sorry he was. Otherwise, these feelings casting a shadow over his heart would never go away. He understood this painfully well, and yet...

When he fell silent, Reina patted his shoulder lightly. "This sort of thing, the longer you let it go, the harder it gets, y'know? Instead of getting all in your head about whatever, the best thing is just to go. Do the thing. Not like I'm one to talk, though. I'm not so great with people that I can get up on my high horse or anything."

She grinned as she crouched to pick up the tweezers and meat Haruyuki had dropped.

"Ah, sorry. Thanks," he said hurriedly, coming out of his reverie, but he didn't reach out to take them from her. Most likely, the way he was now, Hoo wouldn't eat from his hand no matter how many times he tried.

Taking the dirt-covered bit of meat, he told the girls, "I'm going to clean up outside," and left the hutch.

He tossed the piece of meat in the garbage and washed his hands, and then stared at his wet hands. They were chubby hands that appeared to have never touched anything other than a virtual desktop and a holo keyboard. But even so, he felt like the skin on them had gotten a bit thicker from gripping a broom or a mop every day, cleaning up after Hoo.

He thought his insides had changed as well, just like these hands. He had been changed in overcoming the many life-or-death struggles, the intense battles as a Burst Linker. He'd gotten so that he could hold his head a little higher. But had he only thought he was stronger now? Was he dressed up in paper armor? He acted tough now, but if that hardened shell was peeled away, would there still be the same old him inside, clutching his knees to his chest?

He lowered his wet hands and headed for the toolshed. On his way, he had a sudden thought and changed course for the concrete wall on the west side of the animal hutch.

At the base of the wall were flower beds about eighty centimeters wide. They were beautiful, made with natural rock in neat piles, but they contained not even a blade of grass at the moment, much less a flower.

He crouched in front of them and stared hard at the black earth. If a weed had popped its head up there, he would have to yank it up, although he would be sad to do so. He checked the bed from the left end, and by about the time he'd gotten to the middle, he noticed a single tiny green leaf about the size of his pinky fingernail poking its face up.

Wondering if the wind had blown a seed there or if it had been mixed into the soil from the start, he was about to pluck the leaf out when he stayed his hand.

"Ah!" he cried out unconsciously, and brought his face in closer. The slightly shiny, simple elliptical leaf looked to be neither grass nor tree. He stared very hard at it for five seconds, and then leapt to his feet.

Forgetting for a moment the weight on his heart, he ran back to the animal hutch. He peered through the mesh to find that Utai and Reina had just finished feeding Hoo. He waited for them to come outside before calling, "Sh-Shinomiya! The seed is maybe growing!"

Utai's jaw dropped. She blinked several times and then raced over to the flower bed. Haruyuki and Reina chased after her.

She bent forward, hands on her knees, to scrutinize the little leaf before looking back and tapping at her holo keyboard.

UI> THERE'S NO MISTAKE. THIS IS THE SAME SHAPE AS THE PICTURE THAT WAS ONLINE!

"R-right?!" Haruyuki bobbed his head up and down, while beside him, Reina cocked her head to one side.

"What's growing?" she asked.

He belatedly realized that Reina hadn't been with them when they were doing the planting and explained rapid-fire, "Um. I guess it was about four days ago? Me and Shinomiya planted some cherry seeds in these flower beds. To be honest, I thought they wouldn't germinate, but they are!"

"Whoa! Look at you kids! You gotta let me in on the fun, too!" Reina whapped him on the back.

Flustered, Haruyuki wasn't sure how to respond, and Utai replied on his behalf.

UI> I'M SORRY, IZEKI. WE WEREN'T TRYING TO KEEP IT A SECRET. IF YOU'D LIKE, WHY DON'T YOU HELP US TAKE CARE OF IT?

"Yeah, totally!" Reina cried, and reached out both hands to pat Utai's cheeks.

Haruyuki watched them happily fooling around and looked at the new bud shining like an emerald in the sunlight. He felt a tiny bit of the ice choking his heart melt away.

By the time they had watered the little cherry plant and finished carefully cleaning the animal hutch, it was 11:50 AM. Normally, this would have been the end of their club duties, but they had one other big event scheduled for that day.

Haruyuki left Utai and Reina in the rear courtyard and returned to the front of the school. As he approached the gates, the designated meeting spot, he felt like his stomach was curling up into itself. He tightened the muscles of his lower abdomen to try and rid himself of this anxiety and then stepped behind one of the gate pillars, about to launch his messaging app. But there was no need.

"Yo, Haruyuki! We're here!"

He yanked his face up at the sound of this voice and saw a flash of vivid color.

Oversized T-shirt, canvas sneakers, hair tied up in pigtails—all of it a flaming red. The shorts with drawstring hems and the messenger bag draped across the chest were black, maybe to express the merged status of their Legions. Or maybe not.

"H-hey, Niko. Sorry for getting you to come all the way here when it's so hot out. But I've got some good news—," he started to say, but then he noticed someone walking up behind Niko, aka Yuniko Kozuki, and his jaw dropped.

His age or maybe younger—the girl looked to be in seventh or maybe even eighth grade. Ever since he'd become a Burst Linker, he'd had significantly more opportunities to interact with girls this age, but this was a type he hadn't encountered before.

Hair that fanned out into slight spikes with fine silver highlights, black tank top with a flashy pink splash pattern. Her black miniskirt had a ridiculous number of zippers, and even in this heat, she wore black leather gloves on her hands and thick-soled black boots on her feet. If he was forced to say one way or the other, her look resembled Rin Kusakabe's regular avatar, but it had a different feel when seen in the real world.

Heavy boots thudding against the sidewalk as she approached, the girl came to a stop directly in front of Haruyuki and blinked eyes rimmed in black eyeliner.

"'Sup," she said, her voice surprisingly sweet, with a hint of an edge to it.

"'S-Sup," he managed to reply, while wondering who exactly this was. He was only supposed to meet Niko here this morning, and she hadn't said anything about someone coming with her. He figured the girl was most likely a member of Prominence, but he had absolutely no idea who her duel avatar was just from looking at her. He glanced at Niko for help, but she merely grinned at him, as if to say "take a guess."

Happily for him, Niko's attitude hadn't changed in the least. It had been three days since he'd seen her in person, but she seemed to not care at all about his Legion transfer. Or maybe she was just acting like she didn't.

In which case, he couldn't exactly be the one moping around with a long face. *Just act normal!* he told himself, before turning his gaze back on the punk girl. But her avatar name still eluded him, and she would probably get angry at him if he kept staring at her forever.

"Um," he hedged. "This is the first time we've met in the real. Right?"

The punk girl's sparkly purple lipsticked lips curled upward, and she glanced at Niko standing next to her. "Yah. I win, man."

"Whoa, hey, Haruyukiiiii!" Niko stretched out that last syllable and marched over to him to impose successive karate chops to his side.

"Hngh!" He doubled over. "What do you mean, win…?"

"Obviously, we had a bet, okay?" Niko snapped. "About whether or not you'd guess who she is."

"H-huh?!" He gaped at her. "But there's no way I could! How am I supposed to know the name of someone I've never met in the real?"

"You have, though," the punk girl interjected, grin still plastered across her face.

"I—I have? Where?" he asked, baffled.

The girl tapped at her virtual desktop without a word and snapped out her index finger.

Haruyuki's jaw dropped even farther as he watched the silver highlights coloring the girl's hair vanish. It was probably that new high-tech discoloring powder—a micromachine dye that controlled how light was reflected and refracted by manipulating the microscopic surface structure. It had only just gone on sale to the general public and was astoundingly expensive.

"W-wow," he gasped. "So the other colors…"

He swallowed the rest of his question about whether she could manipulate the rest of her look the same way. Now that her hair had changed—transformed into a uniform black short cut—he felt a belated sense of déjà vu as he looked at her face. The Goth makeup made it hard to picture her unadorned face, but if he subtracted the thickness of the soles of her boots from her height and turned the punk look into a sailor-style uniform…

"Oh!" he cried, in realization. "A-are you maybe Pokki?"

Pokki was the nickname of Thistle Porcupine, a member of Prominence's Triplex. Haruyuki had indeed come face-to-face with her on this side last Saturday at the time of the expedition to Minato Area No. 3, the location of the headquarters of

Oscillatory Universe. But Thistle then had been wearing her school uniform, and of course, she hadn't been wearing makeup, nor had she had the dye in her hair. Haruyuki had also been nervous before the big fight, so the only real impression he'd taken away of her was "lively and clever."

Had she gone so far as to use discoloring powder to disguise herself in order to win the bet with Niko? Or was that how she usually looked? Haruyuki couldn't help but wonder this as he hurriedly extended his right hand.

"I-I'm sorry. I'm Haruyuki Arita. Welcome to Umesato."

The smile disappeared from Thistle's face, and she looked at his hand, seemingly troubled.

And small wonder when he thought about it. Even if she was a veteran high ranker serving as an executive of a Great Legion in the Accelerated World, she was still a junior high school girl in the real world. It was only natural that a boy suddenly demanding to shake her hand would be an issue.

"Oh! S-sorry." He hurriedly withdrew the offending hand, but Thistle didn't move to lift her face. He was stuck for what to do when Niko slid over to him.

"Sorry, my dude," she murmured. "It's a whole thing. No handshaking, please and thanks."

"S-sure thing. Um. So should we go, then?" He tapped at his virtual desktop and sent the two girls the school visit permits he'd applied for using his authority as the Animal Care Club president. Unlike the permit issued to Utai, there was a limit built into these for the maximum time they were allowed to stay. And although visitors were generally required to wear the uniforms of the school they went to or clothing in line with that school's regulations, it was summer vacation, so they had a little leeway with that.

Once Niko and Thistle set up the permits in their Neurolinkers, he led them to the animal hutch in the rear courtyard. Utai appeared to know who Thistle was at first glance, and Reina and Niko had met at the school festival at the end of the previous month. But this was the first time Reina and Thistle were meeting, so he would have to introduce them.

"Um. This is Reina Izeki. She's a member of the Animal Care Club. And this is…" He'd gotten that far when he realized he didn't know Thistle's real name, much less what school she went to. *Yikes!* He started to panic, but fortunately, the girl in question gave her name for him.

"Kao Fukaya. Nice to meet you, Izeki."

"Same. And call me Reina."

"Then call me Kao."

The two girls grinned at the same time. Reina was the beach-blond, miniskirt type, and Thistle/Kao was on the punk side of things, so they belonged to pretty different subcultures, but something clearly clicked between them nevertheless.

Smile fading, Kao turned her gaze toward the animal hutch and said admiringly, "That's some animal hutch. Looks big enough for you to have an eagle or a falcon or something in there, too. But it'd be pretty hot for them in the middle of summer."

"Right?" Reina agreed. "I mean, dang, it's only July, and I'm already dying."

"Can I go say hi to Hoo?" Kao asked, and Reina glanced at Utai. Utai was quick to nod, so Kao approached the hutch on quiet feet to peer in through the wire mesh. Haruyuki and the others also moved to a position where they could see inside.

"'Sup, Hoo?" Kao called softly.

Having just eaten his fill, Hoo was drowsing on his perch, but he raised an eyelid at the sound of her voice. He apparently wasn't actually in a bad mood or feeling poorly; he spread his wings out wide in greeting and then returned to his afternoon nap.

"Whoa, what a beautiful white-faced owl," Kao said in quiet awe, and then looked back over her shoulder. "So it's totally okay with my fam. We can definitely take him over the summer. But the big thing is whether Hoo'll be comfortable with us. Anyway, how about we just have him overnight first and see how it goes?"

UI> THAT WOULD BE GREAT, Utai replied instantly, and continued to tap at her holo keyboard. UI> WE UNDERSTAND ONLY TOO WELL THAT WE'RE ASKING A TREMENDOUS FAVOR OF YOU. EVEN IF IT DOESN'T WORK OUT, PLEASE DON'T FEEL AS THOUGH YOU'RE PUTTING US OUT IN ANY WAY.

"Uiui, way too together. As usual." Kao grinned wryly, and then looked at Haruyuki and Reina. "Uiui said that she'd bring Hoo. But you two are welcome to join if you want."

"Huh? Um," Haruyuki stammered, and Reina answered first.

"Thanks for asking us, Kaocchi. But I gotta go pick my kid sister up in a bit."

"She in nursery school?" Kao asked.

"Mm-nn." Reina shook her head. "Kindergarten day care. It's Saturday, so I gotta pick her up earlier than usual."

"Yeah? I guess you can't come with your little sis, huh?"

"Ha-ha-ha! No way!"

Listening to the two girls talking, Haruyuki had a slightly guilty thought.

If Reina couldn't come, then everyone going to Kao's house would be Burst Linkers. Once Hoo's move was finished, there was a good chance that talk would turn to his Legion transfer. He couldn't avoid it forever, but he wasn't sure he could talk about it calmly yet.

"So then, Cr—I mean, Haru. What're you doing?" Kao turned to him, and Haruyuki lowered his eyes.

"Um," he said, "I actually have a thing after this, too. And like, Hoo won't really settle down today with me around for some reason."

"What? You're not coming?" Niko pouted.

He hadn't been in touch with her for the last three days, either, so he really did need to sit down and talk with her for real at some point. But all he could do now was bring an awkward smile to his lips.

Fortunately, the clouds on Niko's face cleared quickly, and she clapped her hands together. "Well, if ya got something going on, ya gotta go. At least help us get ready to go, though?"

"O-of course." Haruyuki bobbed his head up and down and ran to the toolshed to get Hoo's carrier.

While Utai and Kao were putting on Hoo's jesses and leash, Haruyuki led Niko to the flower beds.

Seeing the new cherry sapling shining a bright green, Niko threw a fist into the air so forcefully it nearly pulled the rest of her up with it, and she gave Haruyuki three high fives in a row. And then she suddenly shifted into worrywart mode, muttering about how the sprout might wither and die, or be eaten by insects or birds. So Haruyuki promised to put a net up over the flower bed to keep the bugs out and set up a solar-powered camera to watch their future cherry tree, and managed to soothe her anxiety.

When they returned to the hutch, the girls had just finished tucking Hoo away in his carrier. Haruyuki and Reina went with Niko, Kao, and Utai to the school gates to see them off.

He had assumed that Kao lived in Nerima Ward, but she was actually in Nakano. When he thought about it, the north side of Nakano—Nakano Area No. 1—had long been the territory of Prominence, so it made sense that she lived there.

"And there they go," Reina muttered, as the girls disappeared into the crowd on Oume Highway.

"Yeah." Haruyuki nodded. "I just hope Hoo likes Fukaya's house."

"He'll be fine?" Reina raised an eyebrow at him. "I mean, Kao-cchi, she's all right."

"I guess. Yeah." He could agree with that wholeheartedly.

When Kao—Thistle Porcupine—first learned of the plan to merge Prominence and Nega Nebulus, she had been opposed to it becoming a reality. But once she saw how firmly determined Niko was, she had apparently done everything she could to win over the other Legion members.

Which was exactly why her feelings about Haruyuki's transfer were almost certainly not peaceful, probably more akin to betrayal than anything else. And yet none of that had shown in her voice or her face as she took on the serious role of caring for Hoo.

Maybe I should message them and say I'll come after all. Explain what happened in my own words. And apologize?

Haruyuki pushed back this impulse. He could talk all he wanted, but talk wouldn't begin to make up for what he'd done. He had to keep on fighting every comer until there was no one left to challenge him before he even deserved the chance to apologize to everyone.

"Prez, you're making that scary face again," Reina said abruptly, and Haruyuki blinked a few times before turning to his side.

Reina's face was tense with the same concern as when she had first seen him that day. She glanced around quickly before lowering her voice and continuing.

"I basically get that you've got something I don't know about with Utaicchi, and Nikocchi, and Kaocchi. And those two who visited before, Shihoko and Rin. That stuff you were saying before about betraying someone important to you, that's connected to them, too, right?"

"Huh?!" Haruyuki's jaw dropped, and he was stumped for a second about how he should answer this.

He'd had plenty of guests from other schools visit the animal hutch, so it was natural that she would figure they had some kind of connection with each other. She maybe couldn't guess that it was a full-dive fighting game, but from her tone, she seemed to have at least realized that it wasn't something the general public was especially aware of. If he kept on dancing around the subject, he might end up causing some groundless misunderstanding.

What if I just invited Izeki to Brain Burst?

The thought popped up in his head, but he quickly pushed it back down to the bottom of his brain.

He didn't know if Reina even met the very first condition for becoming a Burst Linker—having worn a Neurolinker since immediately after her birth—and there was no guarantee that she liked video games. Plus, even assuming she made it past these two hurdles, he would have been hard-pressed to say that the Accelerated World as it was now was a place where beginners could have fun with duels.

What came out of his mouth instead was something he'd been thinking about for a while, although it was a bit out of the blue in the current conversation.

"So, um, Izeki?" he asked.

"Hmm?" She angled her head to one side curiously.

"You wanna run in the student council elections with me?"

"Huh?!" she cried, stunned, and waved both her hands in front of her, frantic. "Wh-where'd that come from, Prez?! Way to sucker punch a girl! And I'm totally, obviously not council material."

"I mean, if you're not, then neither am I," he responded. "Um, do you know Mayu Ikuzawa, the Class C rep?"

Reina blinked a few times before nodding. "I mean, I know her to see her. But I've basically never hung out with her."

"Yeah? So like, a little while ago, she came to me and Taku—Takumu Mayuzumi—and asked us to run with her," he explained. "But you have to have a team of four for the election, so we're short one."

She shook her head, exasperated. "That is definitely not enough of a reason to ask me. There's gotta be someone better for the job, like Kurashima or someone."

"Ohh."

It wasn't that he hadn't entertained the idea of asking Chiyuri to be the fourth member of their team. However.

"She's totally not interested," he told her. "And Ikuzawa said we should pick someone we think would be good on student council instead of just someone we're friends with."

"So then I'm even less—" Reina was interrupted by the sound of a bell.

If this had been in the middle of a school term, the sound would have signaled the end of fourth period and the start of lunch. But now, on summer vacation, it was nothing more than a synthetic noise to inform them that it was twelve thirty.

Once the bell had finished ringing in their aural receptors via their Neurolinkers, Reina groaned. "Sorry. I gotta go change and pick up my sister pretty quick here. Prez, can we talk about this tomorrow?"

"Sure, that's fine. But..." Haruyuki turned his eyes to the rear courtyard, and Reina seemed to remember that Hoo had moved. "Right." She nodded thoughtfully. "No job for us here tomorrow. Um, so then I'll call you tomorrow night. I'm out!" Reina waved at him and ran off toward the entrance to the school.

"O-okay. See you!" Haruyuki wondered if this would be a voice call or a dive call or...

Left alone at the gates, he exhaled at length and then slipped through the stone archway. He could faintly hear students on various sports teams yelling from the courtyard on the other side of the main school building. Track team member Chiyuri was probably at practice there, and Takumu was likely working hard in the dojo, given that he and the kendo team had the Kanto Tournament in the middle of August. That said, however, they would still have lunch breaks, so if he messaged them right now, he could probably see them for a bit.

But he kept standing there, rooted to the spot, arms dangling by his sides. He hadn't talked to either Takumu or Chiyuri since the meeting after the Tezcatlipoca mission. He'd gotten a mail from each of them, but he'd simply replied, "I'll message you later" and left it at that. It was true that he didn't know how to face them exactly, but there was also one other rather large issue.

Today was Saturday—the day the Territories took place in the Accelerated World. Minato Area No. 3, location of Oscillatory Universe headquarters, was currently the domain of Nega Nebulus. Naturally, Oscillatory would attack with a lineup of its best members in order to recapture it. Haruyuki hadn't been told whether Nega Nebulus would defend this territory or decide there was no need for that and abandon it. And there was no reason for anyone to tell him. Because he was now a member of Oscillatory Universe, and if the White King or her executive were to seek information related to Nega Nebulus from him, he couldn't exactly *not* answer them.

On this point, the movement of Oscillatory Universe was in fact a little unsettling. He'd given them his mail address and contact info, but he hadn't heard so much as a peep from them these last three days. There were only three and a half hours from the time when the bell had rung earlier to mark twelve thirty until the start of the Territories at four o'clock. Haruyuki had thought that the White King intended to use him as a spy, but even if she did get some good information from him at this late stage, she wouldn't be able to reflect it in their strategy for the Territories, would she?

And then, as if the universe was reading his mind, his mail icon blinked.

He swallowed hard as he stared at the name of the sender to the right of the icon. "Sleepy" in roman letters. Oscillatory Universe's Snow Fairy.

How had he gotten a message from the outside when he was only connected to the local in-school net? He felt a shiver run up his spine as he raised a tense hand to tap the icon. The window that popped up contained a single line of text.

YOUR RIDE WILL PICK YOU UP AT 12:40.

Behind the overly simple message was a taxi reservation link. When he tapped it, a map of the area opened, and the movement of the car was displayed in a glowing blue line, along with a scheduled arrival location in a marker of the same color. The vehicle was currently heading east on Oume Highway.

"Gah! It's practically here!" he gasped, and whirled his head around, looking for help. But none of his comrades were there. And given that he was no longer a member of Nega Nebulus anyway, he would have to decide on his own how to handle Fairy's instruction.

After looking toward the school one more time, Haruyuki whirled around and ran out the gates.

3

He crossed Oume Highway at the intersection a little to the east of the school gates and hurried to the specified coordinates on the opposite side of the street. As he ran, he connected his Neurolinker to the global net. The moment he left the Umesato grounds, he was cut off from the in-school local net, so the only way he would be able to get into the taxi was to connect globally. There was the chance of someone challenging him, but he would deal with that then.

A holotag that only he could see was floating in the taxi area along the sidewalk. The displayed timer had twenty seconds left on it. If the reserved passenger wasn't in the pickup location, automatic taxis on main roads would quickly drive off again, so he was really cutting it close.

"At least give me five minutes," he grumbled, but the moment he saw the car that pulled up in front of him, his jaw dropped in amazement.

It was definitely an automatic taxi, but instead of the compact two-seater often seen on the roads, this was a large black SUV. He looked to both sides of himself, thinking this car had to have been reserved for someone else. But he was alone in the taxi area, and he could see the holotag rotating quite obviously on the roof of the car.

The SUV stopped in front of him with exquisite precision, and the passenger side door opened. He felt a cool breeze from the air conditioner as he peered inside, but naturally, the driver's seat was empty, and the steering wheel and instrument panel were tucked away.

Taking a deep breath, he slid into the vehicle, sat down on the cushy passenger seat, and fastened his seat belt. The door closed with a luxurious click, and the planned route and anticipated arrival time were displayed on the windshield. The destination was a spot in Shirokane Yonchome, Minato Ward.

The map was a simple thing, so there were no names attached to the buildings on it. But he knew what lay at this particular destination without having to look it up. The time had finally come for him to step inside Oscillatory Universe headquarters in the real world.

He heard the flicking of the turn signal and the low hum of the powerful engine as the SUV smoothly pulled out into traffic. It quickly slid over to the right-hand lane, merged with the flow, and began to drive.

Since he was here anyway, he was determined to enjoy the drive. He basically never got to ride in a luxury vehicle like this. He leaned back in his seat and inhaled deeply, filling his lungs with the sweetly scented air. As he exhaled slowly, he wondered at the fact that he hadn't yet heard any of the usual announcements from the vehicle.

"Hello, Crow."

"Hyaah?!" He shrieked at the greeting that came out of the blue from behind him. He froze for a minute before ever so timidly looking over his shoulder to peer into the back seat.

Sitting there were two girls who looked to be about his age. There had been no announcement because there were already passengers in the vehicle.

The adjustable tinted windows in the back seat had been set to the darkest level, and his eyes, used to the strong light of day, couldn't immediately make out the girls' faces. He blinked several times as he squinted until he finally realized who they were.

The small girl sitting directly behind him in the light-blue dress-type uniform was Tsubomi Koshika. Third of Oscillatory Universe's Seven Dwarves, Grumpy, aka Rose Milady. She was the one who had greeted him.

The girl sitting beside her had short, kind of fluffy hair.

"Whaah?! Wa-Wakamiya?!" he cried out, even more surprised.

Megumi Wakamiya gave him a hard stare. "Why are you 'whaah'-ing, Arita? You really that unhappy to see me?"

"N-no, that's totally not it. Honestly." He shook his head from side to side before asking tentatively, "And, like, how are you feeling?"

A faint smile rose on her pursed lips. "Mmm, I'm totally fine now."

"You are?" He let out a sigh of relief. He'd only learned that Umesato Junior High student council secretary, Megumi Wakamiya, was also a Burst Linker by the name of Orchid Oracle a mere week earlier, in the middle of the territory battle against the White King that had taken place the previous Saturday.

With Paradigm Breakdown, an Incarnate technique Blood Leopard/Mihaya Kakei praised as the pinnacle of techniques in the Accelerated World, Oracle had cut an area four kilometers across out of the Territories stage and shifted it to the Unlimited Neutral Field. The White Cosmos had forced her to do this, and the reason Oracle had followed her orders was because Cosmos had told her that she would bring back to life the parent of Oracle and Milady, Saffron Blossom.

But once Oracle had learned from Haruyuki that it had been the White King herself who had pushed Saffron to total point loss, she had restored the battleground to the Territories stage with her opposing Incarnate technique, Paradigm Restoration. Thanks to this, Nega Nebulus was able to defeat Oscillatory Universe, albeit with difficulty. But Oracle had paid a high price for this.

He still wasn't clear on exactly what had happened, but Oracle's mind ended up connected to a light cube that wasn't hers, and the real-world Megumi had fallen into a coma.

Haruyuki and Tsubomi had gone and found Oracle in the Unlimited Neutral Field and rescued her this past Monday. It had only been five days since Megumi woke up in the large hospital in Setagaya, but she had apparently recovered enough to be out and about. Haruyuki was overjoyed, but…

"Um, Koshika, Wakamiya? Do you know that this taxi is heading for Eter—I mean, EG?" he asked, twisting his body around as far as possible in the passenger seat.

The girls nodded at the same time.

"Why would we not know?" Megumi replied calmly.

"It's right there on the windshield," Tsubomi noted, with similar equanimity.

"Well, if you know, then I guess that's fin—," he started to say, but was quick to reject that idea before he'd even finished saying it. There was no way any of this was fine. "No, no, but then why did you get in?! You both left Oscillatory and transferred to some midsize Legion somewhere, right?! If you go to EG now, they'll hang you. Or worse, they'll beat you senseless in duel after duel."

"We'll take them down in a flash!" Tsubomi snapped a finger out at him before resuming her serious expression. "Well, we both know we're not going to get off with just a chat. And it's not like me and Orkki have formally stated we're leaving the Legion. Even Cosmos wouldn't judge us based on nothing."

"Mmmmm." Haruyuki simply could not accept this. He craned his neck as far as it would go to try to meet her eyes. "But you're up against *the* White Cosmos. I seriously doubt she can actually be reasoned with. And, Wakamiya, you got stuck in the Unlimited Neutral Field like that as punishment for disobeying her and turning the stage back in the Territories last week. Can you really say she wouldn't try the same thing on you again?"

"Oh right. I haven't properly thanked you yet," Megumi said, as she sat up straighter and bowed. "Arita, thanks for rescuing me."

"U-uh, Koshika did most of the work, so…" Haruyuki shrugged.

"I'm not saying anything here," Tsubomi interjected. "I don't like this whole humble hat-in-hand routine."

"Th-that's okay. You don't have to say anything," he stammered. "Anyway, to go back to what I was saying, I feel like if you go to EG like this, Wakamiya…you'll be forcibly possessed by Cerberus again."

The moment he spoke the name of Wolfram Cerberus, something throbbed deep in his heart, but he managed to push this pain aside and waited for the two girls to answer.

Megumi glanced at Tsubomi, a serious look on her face, before replying slowly, "I don't entirely understand the logic myself. But Cosmos's ability to revive the dead can rewrite Main Visualizer access privileges."

"R-right," he said, hesitant.

Now that she mentioned it, that was exactly it. White Cosmos could interfere with the light cube of each Burst Linker that existed in the Brain Burst central server—also known as the Main Visualizer—and through this power had brought about many miraculous, or perhaps demonic, phenomena: reviving the first Red King, Master Gunsmith, Red Rider, and putting him to work producing a huge number of ISS kits; forcing Twilight Marauder, Dusk Taker to possess the right shoulder armor of Cerberus and create the Armor of Catastrophe, Mark II; and even locking Orchid Oracle up inside of Cerberus and making her activate Paradigm Breakdown. Haruyuki agreed with Megumi that these deeds were likely caused by direct manipulation of the Main Visualizer.

To put it in terms of other video games, this was akin to hacking the server and directly overwriting internal data. The BB system had thus far crushed without exception any player's cheating behavior, such as with the backdoor program Takumu once used. So why was it overlooking the White King's hacking? Or did this actually mean that her power to revive the dead was a legitimate ability given to her by the system?

Perhaps sensing Haruyuki's indignant questions, Megumi warned, "As a rule, Cosmos can only exert power over the light cubes of Burst Linkers who have already lost all their points and been banished from the Accelerated World. She can't manipulate the circuits of active Linkers. If she could, she'd have killed the kings a long time ago and reached level ten, wouldn't she?"

"Oh. I—I guess so." Haruyuki started to nod his head in agreement, and then suddenly shook it from side to side. "B-but! When you were forced to possess Cerberus, Wakamiya, the system was treating you as an active Linker, right? So then how?"

"'As a rule' means that there are exceptions," Tsubomi cut in. "Especially when it comes to Brain Burst."

Haruyuki looked toward the smaller girl, and she pushed away the hair hiding her right eye.

"There's a command," she said abruptly.

"A command?" He had not expected this. "Do you mean a voice command? Like Burst Out or Physical Bu— Yikes!" He clamped his mouth shut, to very narrowly escape wasting five points.

"Hey!" Megumi snapped. "Are you stupid or something?!"

"Whoa! No one could be *that* stupid!" Tsubomi yelled, and then sighed.

Megumi glared at him. "The PB that you almost carelessly activated just now, Arita, is a public command that's on the Instruct menu. But there are also secret commands like PFB—the full burst—and one of those is a command to remove the lock from your own light cube. And I am not telling you what it is, so you can forget it."

"I—I don't even want to know." Haruyuki shook his head vigorously before asking hoarsely, "B-but why would there be a command like that?"

"I don't know that," Megumi said simply. "But Cosmos…I guess it would be more accurate to say that Doc forced me to say it and stole the access privileges to my light cube."

"Doc?" He raised his eyebrows at the unfamiliar name, but then realized that it must have been one of the seven dwarves who appear in *Snow White*, like Grumpy and Sleepy. He was pretty sure it was translated as "doctor" in Japanese. And if he were to pick the Burst Linker in the Seven Dwarves who most suited this nickname...

"By 'Doc,' do you maybe mean Ivory Tower?" he asked.

"Correct," Megumi assented and leaned back in her seat, her dislike of the White Legion executive member on full display.

He belatedly noticed that she was wearing her Umesato uniform. Her perfectly white shirt was neatly ironed out to the edges of the collar, and he supposed he should have expected nothing less from a current student council member. The moment this thought struck him, he wanted to asked her a bunch of things about last year's election, but he held his tongue; now was not the time for that.

"Um, so then, Wakamiya," he started to say. "Your quantum circuit, your light cube, is still under the control of the White King? In that case, I really do think it's too dangerous for you to go to EG—"

"There's a thirty-minute time limit for the lock removal command," Megumi interrupted.

Haruyuki started to heave a sigh of relief, but a new fear quickly rose in him. "Who told you there's a time limit? If it was Ivory Tower..."

"Relax." She rolled her eyes, slightly. "It wasn't Doc or Cosmos. When I spoke the command in the Unlimited Neutral Field, there was a system message that the effect would expire in thirty minutes."

"O-ohh." Now at last he was convinced, and the tension drained from his shoulders.

But then another possibility popped up in his mind, and he once again leaned in to the back seat area. "Um, Wakamiya!"

She jumped visibly. "Wh-what?"

"So when you were forced to possess Cerberus, he was there, too? Right?"

"Of course he was."

"Then do you know who he is? Like his real name or where he lives or something," he said urgently, and Megumi shook her head.

"Mm-nn. That was the first time I'd ever met Wolfram Cerberus. And it goes without saying we've never met in the real, either. He didn't say a single word the whole time."

"He didn't? What about you, Koshika?" He looked at Tsubomi, clinging to a thread of hope, but her answer was the same.

"I only know his avatar name," she said. "There's basically no mixing between the members of Acceleration Research Society and Oscillatory."

"Oh, really? Thanks anyway." He bowed his head and felt a pain in his neck from spending most of this car ride twisted around toward the back seat. He turned to face forward again for the time being, leaned into the artificial suede seat back, and let out a sigh.

Right before Kuroyukihime and the team had set out on the mission to attack the God Genbu, Haruyuki had called to Cerberus from the Highest Level and promised to save him, to purify the Armor of Catastrophe, Mark II, and end the scheming of the Acceleration Research Society. And then they would duel again.

He was definitely going to fulfill this promise. But right now, he needed to focus on the situation at hand. He took a few deep breaths to calm himself and set his thoughts to the future.

At any rate, there seemed to be no danger of Megumi's mind being held captive once more, and as long as Haruyuki and Tsubomi didn't say the lock removal command—whatever it was—they couldn't end up in that position, either. But in that case, why would Snow Fairy go so far as to pay the fare for an expensive taxi to bring the three of them to Eternal Girls' Academy? And why would Tsubomi and Megumi not make up a reason to refuse to answer the summons?

Wait. I could ask myself the same thing, he muttered to himself, as he pulled a thermos out of the grocery bag twisted around in front of him and took a gulp of the nicely chilled sports drink inside.

He'd been at school when he got the mail from Fairy, so he could've said he was in the middle of club work and escaped that way if he'd wanted to. But in the end, he'd followed her instructions, basically because he was a member of Oscillatory Universe. He had no attachment to the Legion or any sense of loyalty or camaraderie, but he couldn't lie to avoid a summons, and he didn't want to. That was what being a Legion member meant. It was probably the same for Tsubomi and Megumi, even after the King had treated her so cruelly.

Lifting his face to look out the windshield, he saw that the taxi had at some point left Suginami and entered Nakano. If he'd been alone, he would have wanted to get into the driver's seat and pretend he was driving. But he couldn't do something so childish with Tsubomi and Megumi in the car. He decided to settle for enjoying the view from up on high in the tall SUV.

"Right. I should say this while we're here."

He heard Megumi's voice abruptly from the back seat, and he looked back once more. "Wh-what is it?"

"Arita." She looked at him solemnly. "When we get back to Suginami, you have to actually talk to Kuroyuki."

"Huh?" Haruyuki froze, and the next attack came raining down from Tsubomi.

"Honestly! Call her right away when you get home. That's an order."

"That's...I don't think you're in a position to give me orders, though, Koshika," he grumbled.

Tsubomi arched an eyebrow at him. "Who was it again who gave you the points to enhance your sword?"

"Hngh!" He couldn't argue with that.

He'd needed to enhance his beloved Lucid Blade to nullify fire damage in order to slice into the Sun God Inti. But the price at the blacksmith NPC's had been astronomical, and when he panicked about not having nearly enough points on hand, Tsubomi had paid the entire sum for him.

Naturally, he intended to pay her back one of these days, but he definitely couldn't cover this debt with a month or two of Enemy hunting. And more importantly, just as Zelkova Verger had said during their duel, hunting in the Unlimited Neutral Field right now was simply too risky. Before he could pay Tsubomi back in full, he needed to do something about Tezcatlipoca. As he had this thought, he gasped in realization.

He'd completely forgotten because he'd been on challenge standby these last few days and hadn't looked at his Instruct screen. But he should've had a serious influx of points when he destroyed the Sun God Inti, and he remembered there had been a drop of three or four items. If even one of them was a super-special rare item, he might be able to sell it for enough to pay the debt in full. He'd been planning to distribute any Inti drops to everyone on the mission, but no one would complain if he used them to pay Tsubomi back.

He wanted to check his item storage right that second, but the only thing he could check without accelerating was his duel avatar status. And it was a waste to use up a point and accelerate just to look at his storage.

As he stared, undecided, at the BB icon on his virtual desktop, he heard Tsubomi's voice once more.

"I'll tell you right now, you don't have to return those points. Instead, you can actually obey that order. Got it?!"

"I understand." Haruyuki sank deep into his seat, forced to acquiesce.

Their tones were harsh, but the fact that Megumi and Tsubomi were worried came through loud and clear. The same went for Utai, Niko, and all the rest of his friends. The more Haruyuki put off apologizing to Kuroyukihime, the more they would all worry. He knew that. Painfully well.

The right turn signal flickered, and the SUV turned onto Yamate-dori Street from Oume Highway. Although it was a Saturday afternoon, the road was relatively deserted, and the navigation system said that they would arrive in another twenty minutes.

Wanting simultaneously to arrive as soon as humanly possible, and to be delayed as long as possible in a sudden traffic jam, Haruyuki continued to stare at the tail of the car in front of them. He'd had to skip lunch, but he was so nervous that he didn't feel hungry at all.

It was unclear exactly who would be awaiting them at their destination. At the very least, however, he felt certain that the person who had invited him, Snow Fairy, would be there.

"The whims of the King are so troublesome, hmm? Even though we're approaching the last page of the story," Fairy had said when he'd encountered her on the Highest Level.

The last page. Did that mean their current situation, with the Deity of Demise, Tezcatlipoca, freed from the shell that was the Sun God Inti? Or were there still pages left to turn?

The taxi passed the Hatsudai-minami interchange and slipped onto the Central Circular Route running below Yamate-dori Street. The midsummer sun receded behind them to be replaced by orange artificial light.

"I hate tunnels," Megumi said simply, from behind him.

In the end, they did not get trapped in a single traffic jam, and the taxi reached their destination at exactly the predicted time. Since Fairy had paid the fare in advance, they merely got out of the car when it stopped.

Instantly, the heat of the sun threatened to melt Haruyuki into a puddle on the sidewalk. But he stood rooted to the spot, not even noticing the intense sun shining down on him.

The chalky white gate rising up on the other side of the sidewalk formed a majestic arch. ETERNAL GIRLS' ACADEMY was etched into a nameplate in Japanese on the left pillar, while the right-hand pillar displayed the school's name in English. A lush tree-lined path stretched out onto the grounds beyond the gate.

He had learned that the campus was much larger than that of Umesato when he'd visited the school in the Accelerated World long ago. But he'd had his hands full then with rescuing Niko after she had been abducted by Black Vise, and he hadn't had time for a leisurely look around. Viewing EG for the first time with his actual eyes, it looked to be less school and more historic ruins.

"Okay, here we go," someone said, grabbing his arm, and he jumped before looking to his side.

Tsubomi stood there in a white capelin hat, while Megumi held a pale peach parasol over herself. Both looked disgusted with the heat, but neither seemed the least bit nervous. He could understand that Tsubomi might not be tense, given that she was a student at EG, but Megumi's total calm was a testament to her fearsome courage.

"Um," he stammered, "can we really just walk through the gates? Don't we need, like, a permit or something?"

"Fairy'll handle it," Tsubomi said simply, and all he could do was believe what he was told.

He chased after the girls as they walked away briskly and slipped under the stone arch. He waited for an alarm to begin to wail, and a security drone to come flying over, but there was none of that. He had no doubt that a school this famous and wealthy would have top-notch security, but they had probably taken a number of measures to keep that security discreetly out of sight. With that in mind, he did a scan of the area and realized that the social cameras were cleverly blended into the landscape with the trees and lampposts, rather than having the blatantly obvious placement seen at most schools.

When he stepped onto the tree-lined path, completely covered in a canopy of leaves, the heat felt a little less intense. He walked along the twisting cobblestone path, listening to the chorus of cicadas, so loud and numerous it was hard to believe they were still in the city. After the group had gone about two hundred meters, the trees finally opened up in front of them.

This was likely an inner courtyard, but it was larger than the entire Umesato campus. The ground was covered in a gray brick reminiscent of a European plaza, and snowy-white school buildings rose to the right, left, and dead ahead of them. Although old, the buildings were not unfashionable, and the overall impression was more of a museum rather than of a school. There was no sign of any students, perhaps because it was summer break.

Tsubomi came to a stop at the entrance to the courtyard and pointed at the buildings in turn as she spoke. "The one on the left's the main building, the right's the central building, which is where the junior high and high school are, and way in the back's the elementary division and the chapel."

"Th-the chapel?" he repeated.

"I'm pretty sure it was built in 1928," Tsubomi added.

"So then…it's almost a hundred and twenty years old?!" Haruyuki was stunned.

Megumi giggled. "If we have time afterward, you should take a look inside. So…where's the meeting, Rosie?"

"The usual place, probs," Tsubomi replied, and started walking toward the central building on the right.

This four-story building looked more like a school than the main building and the elementary school division, but the face of the central wing jutting outward featured an enormous stained-glass window, which made the building look like a palace somehow.

He put on the visitors' slippers in the entryway and at last stepped inside the school. The natural wood floors, unusual in this day and age, were polished to a shine, and a faint, sweet floral scent wafted through the air. Regrettably, the air conditioners weren't on, but given that there was absolutely no one around, this was only natural.

"This way." Tsubomi beckoned Haruyuki with a hand and headed toward the stairway hall adjacent to the entryway. The stairs they climbed intently were illuminated by the light of the sun through the stained glass. Just when he was running out of breath, they finally reached the top floor.

The party advanced north down the silent hallway. From the windows on the left, he could see the large inner courtyard.

A mere month earlier, Haruyuki had in this very spot in the Unlimited Neutral Field fought against Argon Array, Black Vise, and the Armor of Catastrophe, Mark II, with Wolfram Cerberus inside. Naturally, he could find no sign in the real-world courtyard of that violent battle, but if he listened carefully, he felt like he could almost hear the echoes of that thunder.

In the middle of the fight, Haruyuki had linked with one of the Four Saints, the Archangel Metatron, and become a "contractor," to borrow Centaurea Sentry's word. Metatron had previously joined him in a number of battles, and she even transferred to Oscillatory Universe with him in the end. But these last three days, he hadn't gotten a single link request from her, not even during times when he was accelerated.

He knew that she was currently recovering from the damage she'd sustained in the Tezcatlipoca fight at Sky Raker's player home, Fufuan, but she had said that there was no need for her to go into complete withdrawal mode like she had before. As he followed Tsubomi and Megumi, he wondered if he should try reaching out to her if he returned alive from EG.

The long hallway finally ended, and a single door appeared at the end. This one was not the sliding type like all the others they'd passed, but rather a heavy double door. The brass plate posted on the upper half of it read, JUNIOR HIGH STUDENT COUNCIL OFFICE.

So far, Tsubomi Koshika had advanced unhesitatingly from the gates to this place, but now she stopped abruptly a meter in front of this door.

Megumi Wakamiya placed a gentle hand on her shoulder. Megumi was tall for a ninth-grade girl, and despite being in the same grade, Tsubomi had such a slight build that she could have been mistaken for an elementary school student. So there was a noticeable difference in their heights, but even from behind, he could sense very clearly that these two girls were linked by a powerful bond.

"Let's go," Megumi murmured.

"Yeah." Tsubomi nodded, and the two of them started toward the door. Megumi gripped the left handle, Tsubomi the right, and they pulled at the same time.

Inside the student council office was…actually, he couldn't see all the way in. Because there was a stained-glass partition on the other side of the doorway.

Stepping into the room, Tsubomi and Megumi split to the left and right to go around the partition, and Haruyuki wasn't immediately sure which one of them he should follow. After a moment of confusion, he went around to the right, after Tsubomi.

"Aaah, you're finally heeere!" came a drawled exclamation.

Now that he could see it, the student council office was even larger than he'd imagined. It was maybe five meters wide and eight deep. The wall to his right was covered in bookshelves, while the walls to his left and directly ahead of him were taken up with windows with old diagonal lattices. An enormous elliptical meeting table ruled the center of the room, surrounded by high-back mesh chairs.

There were nine chairs in total, but five were empty. Meaning there were four members of Oscillatory Universe waiting for Haruyuki, Megumi, and Tsubomi.

One of them, a girl with her hair in braids, sitting in the chair to Haruyuki's immediate right, bounced against the seat back as she said, "Honestlyyyy, you took so long, Bomi. I was getting sick of waaaaiting!"

"You're the one who sent the car for us. So don't whine at me about it. And quit calling me that," Tsubomi snapped, apparently known to the EG student council as "Bomi."

But the girl ignored Tsubomi's foul temper and giggled, long braids swinging. "Ooh, you're so cuuuute! Rio-Rio, you think so, too, riiiight?" she asked the boy occupying the chair on the opposite side of the table, stretching out the end of the question at length.

Even seated, it was obvious at a glance that he was fairly tall. His body, clad in a simple white shirt and black slacks, was sturdy, like he did martial arts of some kind. Both sides of his head were shaved in a clean sporty cut, and he wore glasses with thick black frames.

Why is there a boy at a girls' school? Haruyuki blinked rapidly in surprise.

"No, no," the boy said in a husky, low voice. "Please don't come looking to me for support. I also don't recall agreeing to that nickname."

The courteous tone and the mismatch with his muscular appearance tugged at Haruyuki's memory, but he couldn't place where he'd heard it before. Furrowing his brow, he glanced at the boy in glasses as he continued speaking.

"At any rate, we mustn't ignore our guests to have this conversation now. Weren't you on tea duty today, Sagisu?"

"Whaaat? Was I?" The girl with the braids—Sagisu, apparently—replied vacuously, as she stood up and walked to the back of the room, the same light-blue dress as Tsubomi wore swinging around her. There was a sofa set and a simple kitchen on the other side of the meeting table, and this part of things resembled the student council office at Umesato a little.

But Haruyuki's gaze was sucked in by the two other members sitting on the far end of the table.

A slender boy was leaning back in his mesh chair reading a paper book. His hair was cut in the fashionable two-block style, with the sides shaved up and left longer on the top, and the face Haruyuki could see in profile beneath that hair was likely almost shockingly handsome. But perhaps due to allergies, his face from the nose down was hidden by a surgical mask, even though it was summer, and the hand holding the book was covered by a thin glove.

The other person was a small girl like Tsubomi. The thing that first drew his eyes was the wavy blond hair reaching down to nearly her waist. He could only assume that the natural-looking and magnificent mane was not dyed but rather blond from birth. And with her almost translucent pale skin, she was almost like a doll. No, a fairy.

A fairy.

The avatar names of the girl with braids, the boy in glasses, and the two-block boy were unclear, but he was sure he knew who the blond girl was. He forced his stiff legs to move and stepped past Tsubomi out front.

"Um. Are you...Snow Fairy?" he asked the blond girl, who was apparently typing something on her holo keyboard.

"Hang on a sec," she responded in a slightly muddied, sweet voice, and let her fingers dance in the air for another three seconds before slamming a finger against the return key. She whirled herself and her chair around, and looked up at Haruyuki with sapphire-blue eyes lined with blond eyelashes. "Yep. I'm Snow Fairy. Real name Nanako Juholt. My dad's Swedish, hence the name."

He raised his eyebrows. "So you're half-Japanese?"

"Uh-uh." She shook her head. "Eighth. My mom's a quarter, three-quarters Danish, one Japanese, so one-eighth of me is Japanese."

"Eighth." He'd never heard this way of putting it before, but he supposed that she wouldn't have these very obviously blue eyes and blond hair if her northern blood hadn't been so strong. Given how strongly she physically resembled her duel avatar, she was a perfect match in a sense that was different from the usual abilities and attributes.

Haruyuki was lost in staring at her for a moment before he came back to himself with a gasp. However cute she might have been, this girl had tried to slaughter the members of Nega Nebulus with her powerful Incarnate technique Brinicle and even attempted to sever the link between Haruyuki and Metatron. Although they were currently in the same Legion, she was definitely not someone to let his guard down in front of.

Warning himself to stay vigilant, Haruyuki introduced himself. "Um, I'm Haruyuki Arita. I'm in eighth grade at Umesato Junior High, and I belong to the Animal Care Club."

He felt like he'd accidentally blurted out something entirely irrelevant to the proceedings, but Fairy, aka Nanako, nodded slightly and moved her pale-cherry-pink lips.

"I'm in seventh grade—I mean, I'm first year in the junior high division. I'm the student council secretary." She turned her blue eyes on the boys occupying the opposite side of the table and instructed them in an authoritative voice that sounded like she was used to giving orders. "Introduce yourselves."

"Right, right," the boy in glasses responded right away. He politely stood up from his mesh chair, faced Haruyuki, and cleared his throat. "My name is Rioh Koshimizu. I am in ninth grade in the junior high division of Shirakabanomori Academy, and the vice president of the student council. It is a pleasure to make your acquaintance."

He placed his right hand on his chest and bowed, and the moment Haruyuki saw this theatrical gesture, he finally realized who this boy was. He was curious about the school, too, the name of which he'd never heard before, but confirming the avatar name came first.

"A-are you maybe Behemoth?" he asked hesitantly.

"Well, well! You only came to that conclusion now?" Rioh chuckled good-naturedly. "I am indeed Sneezy, also known as Habakkuk, Glacier Behemoth."

"I-I'm sorry. I recognized your voice, but…" Haruyuki shrank into himself, and Megumi broke her silence to interject.

"Well, it's no wonder, Koshimizu. I mean, you lost hard to Arita in the Territories last week. Demanding that he remember you is pretty nervy."

"No, no, this is truly inexcusable, Wakamiya. While it is true that he did break off one of my horns, the contest itself is still on hold. Isn't that right, Arita?"

Haruyuki did indeed recall Behemoth saying something along the lines of "I will save the deciding battle with you for the next opportunity" after he'd destroyed the horn of the massive avatar with his Lucid Blade. He panicked, wondering if the other boy was actually going to make *this* the place of that battle, but fortunately, Behemoth continued without waiting for his reply.

"I was quite looking forward to going up against you again, but right now, we are facing an important battle. The rest of our match will take place at some point in the future. And so next—"

"It's Airi's tuuuurn!" the girl with braids said as she returned from the simple kitchen, so Haruyuki took two steps back to open up a space and let her pass.

She slowly set the tray in her hands down on the table, and then whirled around to look at Haruyuki. "So you're Silver Crowwww? We finally meeeet! Do you know who Airi is?"

The third-person "Airi" of the girl smiling brightly at him was likely the first half of her real name. Although he knew that much at least, he had absolutely no clue as to what her avatar name might have been.

Since two of the four gathered there were Snow Fairy and Glacier Behemoth, there was a good chance that she was also one of Oscillatory Universe's Seven Dwarves. He was pretty sure that Fairy was the second, Behemoth was the seventh, and Rose Milady/Tsubomi Koshika was the third. That left four seats to choose from. She had a totally different vibe from the first seat, Platinum Cavalier, and if this fluffy, cutesy girl was inside of the fourth seat, Ivory Tower/Black Vise, his socks would be knocked off his feet and into outer space.

So then she was either fifth or sixth. But since he couldn't pull the avatar name of the fifth out of the air pockets of his memory, he decided to gamble on sixth, sink or swim. "Cy—Cypress Reaper!"

"Ding, ding, ding!" she cried, delighted. "Your prize is the biggest slice of caaaake!"

He automatically looked at the tray on the table. Occupying a flat wooden plate was a circular cheesecake cut into pieces. And although there were indeed seven slices, no matter how generous he tried to be, there was a significant difference between the smallest and largest pieces.

"Airi, could you not get a little better at this?" Tsubomi said, exasperated.

Airi Sagisu/Cypress Reaper puffed out her cheeks and sulked. "But there are seven piiiieces. I mean, six or eight is one thiiiing, but even *you* couldn't do seven, Nanaaaaa!"

"I could, too," Snow Fairy replied without hesitation, and all present stared intently at her.

"Whaaat? Hoooow?" Airi wailed.

"If you fold a rectangular piece of paper three times, you get lines dividing it into eight, right?" Fairy replied, briskly. "If you spread the paper out and overlap each of the panels from the outside, you can make a regular heptagon. Press those pieces onto the center of the cake and mark it up."

"Huuuuh? Does that actually make a regular heptagonnn?" Airi asked dubiously.

Haruyuki folded and spread out an imaginary piece of paper in his mind. The moment he understood that the result was exactly as Nanako said, he cried out, "Oh!"

Tsubomi, Megumi, and Rioh all seemed to get it at the same time, too, and began applauding, so Haruyuki joined in.

A few seconds later, Airi finally cried out, "Ohhh! I get iiiiit!"

"You don't have to do all that annoying work," a new voice said. "You could just use an AR app..."

Haruyuki stopped clapping immediately.

The voice was lazy and beautiful, trailing off with each sentence it spoke. Goose bumps popped up on both of his arms, and an icy chill ran up his spine.

He *knew* this voice. He would never forget the cruel words

it uttered to him at the base in Tokyo Grand Castle, the large amusement park on Reiwa Island in the Unlimited Neutral Field: "*Then...should I cut off those wings now?*" First of the Seven Dwarves, with the nicknames Bashful and Basher, the platinum knight riding a snowy white Pegasus.

"Platinum Cavalier." Haruyuki half groaned the name, and the boy with the two-block hair sitting on the opposite side of the table slammed the book he was reading shut.

He rotated his chair slightly and turned his face toward Haruyuki. He was obviously handsome, even with the mask on his face. Haruyuki's own best friend Takumu was a relatively handsome boy, but the two-block boy's regal nose and dazzling eyes with irises that threatened to suck a person in went beyond the realm of the average person. This boy could have been a real model or actor, but unfortunately, Haruyuki had essentially zero knowledge of that world.

Momentarily forgetting to keep his guard up, Haruyuki stood rooted to the spot, and the weary voice came his way once again.

"Shirakabanomori Academy, ninth grade... Tomochika Kyobu... I'm the student council president."

The school name was the same one given by Glacier Behemoth/ Rioh Koshimizu, sitting at the left end of the table. If Behemoth was the vice president and Cavalier was the president, then they had to have been pretty tight. Haruyuki found it a little curious that they were sitting so far apart for some reason, but he didn't actually have the nerve to ask about that, so he gave voice to a different question.

"Um. What's this Shirakabanomori Academy?"

"It's right next doooor!" Airi Sagisu said. She indicated the windows on the north side with the cake server she was using to dish out the cheesecake. "Look! You can see just a hint of it past the elementary division, riiiight?"

"Uh. Uh-huh." When Haruyuki stood up tall and looked out the window, he was indeed able to catch a glimpse of a building that appeared to be a different school on the other side of the elementary division building. The walls were the same white as EG's, but the minimal design of the curved body gave a more modern impression.

"It looks super new, huh?" he said, as he brought his heels back down to the floor.

"Although it looks new, it in fact opened its doors in 2015. Which makes it thirty-two years old," Rioh told him. "Naturally, its history isn't quite as extended as that of EG, but our Shirakaba Junior High student council has long been in communication with the student council of EG's junior high. The King herself used this connection to set up a base for the Legion at both schools."

"So then," Haruyuki started to say, "is everyone on the Shirakaba student council also a member of Oscillatory?"

"No, no." Rioh waved a leisurely hand. "It's only myself and Kyobu from the student council. We do, however, have several regular students in the Legion."

"Several?" Haruyuki repeated, and a sudden hypothesis popped into being in his head and immediately turned to certainty. He was about to ask about it, but quickly stopped himself. If he interrogated Rioh now, there was a strong possibility that the other boy would evade the question.

"Is Shirakaba a boys' school?" he asked instead.

Rioh shook his head as he stood up from his chair. "If it were, our situation here would seem comparable to something out of a fairy tale. But no, it is in fact coed. I will help you, Sagisu," he said, making his way around the table.

"Oh! I can help, too!" Haruyuki hurried to add himself to that list, but he was stopped by a large hand.

"No, no," Rioh said. "You are our guest. Please, sit. We will also extend the same hospitality to Koshika and Wakamiya today."

"That's kinda creepy." Tsubomi wrinkled up her face in a scowl, even as she settled into an empty chair on the bookcase side of the table.

Haruyuki followed suit and also sat down, leaving a chair

between them where Megumi sat down, leaned back, and crossed her legs.

This movement was very reminiscent of Kuroyukihime, and Haruyuki wondered if Megumi didn't have stronger nerves than he'd thought at first glance. But then he noticed that the slender hands in front of her stomach were clasped together so tightly her metacarpals were popping up. So she was nervous, too, probably more so than Haruyuki or Tsubomi.

Whatever new developments awaited them, he couldn't let any harm come to Megumi and Tsubomi. They were both serious veteran Linkers, far above himself, so he absolutely couldn't say to them that he would keep them safe, but he was free to think it.

After resolving to make sure the two of them made it home safely, he gasped in realization. Megumi's house was in Suginami's Shimotakaido area, but Tsubomi lived in Minato Ward's Minami-Aoyama, not too far from EG. In which case, why had she already been in the taxi when it arrived at Umesato?

He was about to whisper this question to Megumi, but Airi's voice rang out a heartbeat sooner.

"Okaaay! Here we aaaare!"

Glasses with iced tea and plates with cheesecake were set out before Haruyuki and the two girls. Just as she'd announced, the slice of cake Haruyuki was served was about 1.2 times larger than the ones before Megumi and Tsubomi.

"Why...would the smallest piece come to me?" Tomochika Kyobu/Platinum Cavalier said from his seat across from Haruyuki, the faintest hint of sadness creeping into his ennui-laden voice.

Haruyuki looked over to see that the cake on the plate in front of Tomochika was indeed rather meager.

"Whaat? Okay, how about all of us rock-paper-scissors, except for Aritaaa?" Airi asked, and Tomochika let out a slight sigh beneath his mask.

"No...This is fine..."

"You're so niiiice, Chikarin!" Airi said before taking her seat next to Rioh, and Haruyuki wasn't sure how much of that was sincerely flaky and how much was actually calculated.

Now they were all seated around the meeting table, with Nanako, Tsubomi, Megumi, and Haruyuki on the bookshelf side, and Tomochika, Airi, and Rioh on the window side. There were two more mesh-backed chairs, but given that the cake had been cut into seven pieces, the executive members not present— Ivory Tower, the fifth position he couldn't remember, and Legion Master White Cosmos—were likely not going to take part in the meeting.

When Tsubomi had previously visited the Arita home, Haruyuki asked her what kind of relationship the EG Oscillatory members had. She replied that it was something like the evil queen and her group of minions out of so many manga and video games. He had been able to imagine this fairly easily at the time, but now that he was actually here in the EG student council office, about the only thing that matched his mental picture was the massive meeting table. The room was bright, and the mood was peaceful.

If the reason for that was the absence of White Cosmos and Ivory Tower, then he wanted them to continue to stay away. Nonetheless, he was disappointed he wouldn't get to meet Ivory Tower or the White King in the real. Naturally, that wasn't coming from any kind of fanboy feeling, but rather from a desire to see with his own eyes the kind of people they were in the real world, these Burst Linkers who could bring about such destruction and chaos in the Accelerated World. He wanted to check if they were even actual human beings who ate and drank and breathed.

"Please, dig iiiiin!" Airi urged.

When he lifted his face, he saw that the eyes of the other six people present had at some point come to rest on him. Apparently, they were waiting for the guest of honor to take the first bite.

"Oh! Th-thanks!" He hurriedly picked up his fork and cut into the end of the golden-brown baked cheesecake. The cake was nicely dense and yet somehow smooth as silk, and it melted into nothing on his tongue. A cheesy sweetness coated his mouth, and the richness of it almost made his cheeks hurt.

"Th-this is great. Really great." When Haruyuki gave his opinion, Airi grinned from her seat on the opposite side of the table.

"I'm glad you like iiiit! Nana bought this cheesecake for uuuus!"

"What? Really?" He leaned forward a little and looked to his right.

Nanako replied curtly from the other side of Megumi and Tsubomi. "I didn't buy it for you. I got it because I wanted it." She took a large bite and focused on chewing before speaking once more. "You should savor it while you can, Crow. You won't have the luxury soon enough."

"Wh-what does that...?" he said, baffled.

"Now, now, let us leave the complicated conversations for later," Rioh insisted with a smile. "Delicious food must be enjoyed."

Haruyuki had no other choice but to sit back in his chair. It did indeed feel like heresy to eat a cake this good with a distracted mind. Maybe it was also because he'd missed out on lunch, but to be honest, it was hard for him to say which was better, this or the rare cheese tart from Patisserie la Plage that Niko and Pard had brought to the send-off party for the Inti mission.

He thought about asking Nanako the name of the store and the price of the cake later. If he had the time and money, he imagined he could maybe buy one as a present for everyone in Nega Nebulus before he realized that even if he did buy the cake, he would have no chance to give it to them.

Pain stabbed at his heart again, and Haruyuki drank it down with his iced tea before taking another bite of cheesecake.

Next to him, Megumi and Tsubomi were also moving their forks silently. Tomochika Kyobu was showing off his cake-eating technique, pulling his mask up with his left hand only at the moment of putting the cake into his mouth with his right, while next to him, Airi had a happy smile on her face. Rioh, directly across from Haruyuki, had such a serious look on his face that there was a crease in his brow.

The Seven Dwarves had made Haruyuki shake in his boots any number of times in the Accelerated World, but they were also boys and girls who could become totally absorbed in a piece of cake in the real world. When he had this thought, a different kind of pain throbbed powerfully in his chest.

All Burst Linkers were supposedly gamers playing the same game. And yet ever since the launch eight years ago, they had been hating each other, deceiving each other, fighting each other, killing each other.

If he were to say that this was the design principle behind Brain Burst, well, yes, that was true. The point and territory systems were created to encourage players to struggle against each other. But if they went along with this design and fought each other mindlessly, weren't the Burst Linkers merely dolls dancing in the palm of the developer's hand?

"This is really good," Haruyuki said once more, wanting to push back against that nebulous something.

"Riiiight?!" Airi agreed with a smile.

What if, despite all the fierce battles they'd fought against each other, he and the members of Oscillatory Universe could come to understand each other over a piece of cheesecake? Maybe they could even someday find a way to transform the culture of struggle that dominated the Accelerated World.

As he let his thoughts wander in this direction, Haruyuki slowly brought the last bite of cheesecake to his mouth.

But a mere ten minutes later, he was made painfully aware of just how naïve he truly was.

4

"We have…two reasons for calling you here today," Tomochika Kyobu said, once everyone was more or less finished with their cheesecake. Having at some point put on a new mask, he clasped his gloved hands together in front of his chest and looked quietly at Haruyuki. "The first is…about how to deal with you, Arita. Given that our King approved your transfer to Oscillatory Universe herself, I have no intention of arguing the pros and cons… But opinion on you is split among us."

Haruyuki wasn't sure how to respond to this. "O-okay?"

"You mean whether or not Arita should be put into the training course?" Tsubomi interjected.

"Well…Quite frankly, yes." Tomochika nodded. "That's it exactly."

Haruyuki frowned, wondering what exactly this training course was. And then he remembered Tsubomi had said something about how Cypress Reaper and Glacier Behemoth were in charge of guiding the younger members of Oscillatory Universe.

He glanced directly across from him at Airi and Rioh before turning toward Tomochika. "Um. If that's the problem, I'm happy to take the training course?"

If he was remembering right, Tsubomi had told him that the training with Reaper and Behemoth was nothing compared with

Sky Raker's special lessons. In which case, at the very least, he wouldn't die. Repeatedly.

"I'll tell you now..." Tomochika narrowed his eyes the slightest bit, as if reading Haruyuki's thoughts. "The training takes at minimum a month in the Unlimited Neutral Field, and can even go on for six months... There have been more than a few who were unable to withstand the severity and asked to leave the Legion."

"Whaaat? It's not thaaaat hard!" Airi cut in unhappily, while Rioh nodded deeply next to her.

"Exactly, yes. The instruction that Sagisu and I offer is the very picture of moderate. We even provide a sufficient amount of points in advance in order to prevent players from accidentally losing all of their points should they die even ten times."

Haruyuki seriously questioned whether dying ten times could be called moderate as Rioh continued, equitably.

"However, the issue at hand now is not whether Arita would be able to endure the training, but rather whether the training is in fact necessary at all? You may not have fought Arita personally, Kyobu, but you have certainly witnessed him fighting, and thus have a measure of his prowess, do you not?"

From the way he was speaking, it seemed like Rioh had a high opinion of Haruyuki's abilities.

But it was hard to read any emotion in the eyes Tomochika kept trained squarely on Haruyuki.

"Arita...," he murmured. "Silver Crow's fights take too much of a mental toll on him."

"That's the same for everyone, though," Tsubomi countered coolly. "Times when you're in the flow, you could beat even a serious veteran. And when you're not, you get your feet kicked out from under you by some newb. That's just how it's going to be so long as BB's a contest of imagination. I mean, you don't have a perfect win rate, either."

Even at this merciless note, the look on Tomochika's face did not change in the slightest.

"It's fine to win and lose in normal duels," he remarked. "But those who can't control their mental state at the critical juncture don't deserve to stand alongside us…"

Even after Tsubomi had stepped forward to back him up, Haruyuki was still unable to say anything in response himself. He could only hang his head.

He'd been painfully aware that he was unable to hold his own ever since he was a little kid. He felt like that had changed a little since he'd become a Burst Linker, but here he was, avoiding Kuroyukihime for three days now, so maybe deep down, he was still the same old "Stupidyuki" in the end.

Well, fine. If they're gonna say I'm not strong enough, then they can just beat it into me for six months or a year or however long on this training course or whatever, he said to himself.

"Bashful. If you're going to go on about 'deserving,' Crow is a level-two contractor, and on top of that, he's also a level-three accessor," Nanako—Snow Fairy—said abruptly, and Haruyuki furrowed his brow.

He knew that "contractor" meant a Burst Linker who had linked with a Being, but he'd never heard "accessor" before. And he also wasn't clear on the meaning of the flags "level two" and "level three."

He waited with bated breath for someone to say something, but the tense silence lasted for more than ten seconds. Eventually, Tomochika unclasped his hands and spread them out gently.

"Sleepy…I thought you also insisted that Crow needs training."

"I am, but for a different reason from you," Nanako replied.

"Specifically…?"

"Not telling," she refused flatly, and began to type at her holo keyboard once again.

Tomochika shrugged and returned his gaze to Haruyuki, while touching the fingers of his right hand to his snowy-white Neurolinker as if checking something.

"Whether Arita is a contractor or an accessor or what have you, my assessment remains unchanged," he said finally. "Because the sole reason for Oscillatory Universe's existence is to guard the

King and execute the King's will...If you want to be a real member of this Legion, then you need to undergo the same training as any other hopeful and show your resolve."

Haruyuki felt that those gray eyes, ringed with long eyelashes, shone with a deep, sharp light. Tomochika Kyobu/Platinum Cavalier clearly didn't trust him at all. And why would he? Haruyuki was utterly and completely sincere when he vowed his loyalty to the White King, but he had no way of proving he wasn't a spy or an assassin sent by Nega Nebulus.

He forced his clenched jaw open. "I understand. I'll do the training or whatever's necessary."

"Whaaaat?"

It was the very person in charge of this training who let out this displeased cry: Airi Sagisu.

"If you really are a contractor and an accessor, Arita, then there's nothing for us to teach," she told him. "We could give you the final task out of the blue, and you could probably finish it in one goooo?"

"Wh-what's the final task?" he asked with trepidation.

"Solo subjugation of a Beast claaaass."

Nuh-uh! No way! Not a chance!!

Haruyuki just barely managed to suppress this scream. A Beast-class Enemy was right in the middle of the five Enemy classes, but since the chance of encountering a Legend- or Super-class Enemy was essentially zero so long as you didn't deliberately go and challenge one, for all practical purposes, this class of foes could be said to be the strongest in the Accelerated World. When he had gone with Tsubomi to rescue Megumi Wakamiya at Tokyo Midtown Tower, they'd fought and defeated the Legend-class Enemy, Einherjar. But it had been weaker than the usual Einherjar because it was tamed by the White King. Even so, Haruyuki had only gotten a bit of a cut in; Tsubomi had been the one to strike the killing blow.

"Um. So do all the members of Oscillatory Universe finish that final task?" he asked, very timidly, and Rioh gave him a wry smile.

"No, no. If that were the case, we wouldn't have such trouble here and there. Outside of us Seven Dwarves, there are only two—no, is it three now?—who have accomplished this."

"Th-that's plenty, though…" Haruyuki wondered if Oscillatory couldn't have beaten Nega Nebulus with just a show of force instead of using all those little tricks, before he banished the thought. No matter what the situation, Kuroyukihime and the rest of the team would have definitely won out in the end.

Right. And they would continue to. Even if Haruyuki went over to the enemy.

He clenched his fists tightly on his lap and said, "I understand. Please let me do this final task."

"Arita," Megumi said in a low voice.

"Goodness." Rioh shook his head, ever so slightly.

But Haruyuki couldn't take back his words now.

When Tomochika heard this declaration, the pristine surgical mask moved the tiniest bit. Maybe he was going to say something and then decided against it. Or maybe he was smiling.

"If you're killed by a Beast-class opponent," came his quiet voice, "there is the risk of unlimited EK…What do you intend to do in that case?"

Haruyuki took a deep breath, held it for a moment, and then replied, "If that happens, please leave me there."

5

Haruyuki had basically always gone through a safety device that automatically cut his connection after a set period of time when he dived into the Unlimited Neutral Field. That way, even if he ended up in an unlimited EK, he wouldn't lose all his points, even if he did die a few times.

But today, after basically standing up and saying "bring it on" to an unlimited EK, he couldn't very well request a safety. What surprised him was that Tomochika Kyobu and the others didn't make any move to use a safety, either. Maybe they had an exceeding amount of confidence in themselves, or maybe they had some other safety plan besides an automatic disconnection device.

As these thoughts were wandering through his mind, Haruyuki connected his Neurolinker to the EG local net with the ID that Fairy had sent him. Normally, a global connection was necessary to dive into the Unlimited Neutral Field, but Oscillatory had apparently found a way around that limitation.

Once everyone was ready, Airi Sagisu began the slightly extended countdown.

"Here we goooo! Threeeee, twooooo, oooone."

""""Unlimited Burst!""""

His senses were taken over by the sound of acceleration, the darkening of his field of view, the sense of falling. And then the feeling of landing.

When he opened his eyes, the look of the student council office had changed completely. The floor and walls and all their decadent natural wood had been turned into grimy metal, rippling in organic curves. In every corner of the once-tidy room, disturbing myriapods wriggled and writhed. The sky he could see through the distorted window glass was an unsettling yellowish-green.

"So it is a Purgatory stage then…," said a voice to his left.

Haruyuki turned to find a large M-type avatar in heavy armor that was a pale, watery blue standing there with his arms crossed. He had two long horns growing from his forehead, and his face mask was also relatively fierce, giving the overall impression of some kind of demon.

He did a quick rummage through his memories, but there was no mistake; he'd never seen this avatar before.

"Um. A-and who might you be?" he asked nervously, and the blue demon avatar raised both hands in surprise.

"Now, now! It's me, Sneezy."

"Huh? Behemoth? But when we fought before, you were super huge, almost like a dragon," Haruyuki said, spreading out his arms as far as he could. The Glacier Behemoth he'd encountered in the Territories a week earlier had been nearly six meters long from head to tail, on par with a Beast-level Enemy.

"It would seriously suck if he were that massive thing all the time. That's this guy's Beast mode," a rose-pink F-type avatar said as she walked toward them. Countless sharp spikes glittered on her worrisomely slender limbs and torso. The face mask framed with gorgeous ringlets was sweetly dazzling.

Grumpy, aka Rose Milady, came to a stop, the needle-like pin heels on her feet clacking, and said with a sigh, "Crow, can you really beat a Beast class solo?"

"I—I don't know," he replied honestly.

Milady shook her head in exasperation and let out a lengthy sigh.

"Now listen." An F-type clad in pale-peach dress-type armor approached from the other side of Milady. "Aaah, this is why I told you not to do this."

"D-did you?" he asked, frowning.

"I did. Telepathically," said the Prophet, aka Orchid Oracle, rather outrageously. The silver hair hanging down her back swung from side to side as she stopped in front of Behemoth. "Sneezy, are we really going to abandon him if Crow ends up in unlimited EK?"

"Oh, well..." The blue demon avatar was at a loss for words when a black shadow suddenly rose up behind him, and Haruyuki shrank back with a gasp.

It was probably a duel avatar. But he couldn't even tell what shape it was, much less its armor color. Its entire body was covered in a dark-gray cloaked hood with absolutely no luster to it. The cloak's ragged hem was about ten centimeters from the floor, but there were no feet to see there. The figure was almost like a ghost. Or the god of death.

The death avatar, which apparently possessed the same hovering ability as the Black King, Black Lotus, wavered from side to side as it spoke in a voice with a faint hint of an echo, "Ohhh, Orkkiiii! You're so sweeeeet!"

Haruyuki had to brace himself to keep from being completely knocked off his feet. Inside the extremely inauspicious ragged cloak was Cypress Reaper, aka Airi Sagisu. He'd forgotten until that very second, but Kuroyukihime had once told him that "cypress" was a kind of tree, and "reaper" meant a taker of souls.

The girl with the braids who gave Haruyuki the biggest slice of cheesecake was a distinct mismatch for this duel avatar that was the very figure of death. But Burst Linkers whose real self and avatar diverged were not uncommon, and it was the height of rudeness to pry into the mental scars that were the mold for the avatar.

As Haruyuki recovered from his shock, Orchid Oracle said, in a slightly thorny voice, "I'm not being 'sweet' or whatever. When you and Sneezy took on the final task, we had a proper rescue team on standby, didn't we? Crow's a member of Oscillatory now, too, so isn't it only natural for us to do the same for him?"

"I agree with youuuu," Cypress said. "But wasn't Crow himself the one who said there was no need for rescuuuue?"

"That's because Crow leaps before thinking," Oracle objected, sticking up for him. Or maybe not.

"Oracle, what you're saying is...an insult to a warrior tackling a trial," a quiet and cold voice said from the opposite side of the room.

Clank, clank.

Walking over to them, metallic footsteps echoing, was a knight-type avatar clad in armor of an elegant and masculine design. The armor was a silver that was almost white. If Silver Crow was a metallic silver, then the knight could perhaps have been called a clear silver.

Because the visor on the helmet with the long decorative horns was pulled down, Haruyuki couldn't see the face mask. But from the large kite shield resting on the knight's back and the long-sword with a cross hilt hanging from his left hip, Haruyuki knew that this knight was the first of the Seven Dwarves, Bashful—Platinum Cavalier.

He stared intently at Cavalier, a user of the Femto style of swordsmanship, according to Centaurea Sentry. He'd had the chance to see him up close on the balcony at Heimwert Castle at Tokyo Grand Castle, but he'd been desperately trying to calm himself down then. He very much had not had the brain space to observe Cavalier coolly.

He'd fought any number of sword-bearing Burst Linkers since his first days in the Accelerated World as a level one, but he'd only experienced the profoundness of the sword arts after he acquired the sword-shaped Enhanced Armament Lucid Blade as his level-six bonus.

Currently, there were three Burst Linkers whom Haruyuki deemed the most powerful sword users in the Accelerated

World. One was of course the Black King, swords fused with her four limbs, able to slice through all things in creation—World End, Black Lotus. The second was the Ain style user, wielding double blades of fused hyper-diamond and graphene that unified defense and offense, Anomaly Graphite Edge. And the third was his own teacher, Omega style user, Ruthless, Asura, Omega Weapon, aka Centaurea Sentry.

Naturally, there were plenty of others proficient with a sword. The Red Legion's Lavender Downer, for example—nicknamed Tranquil, who had joined them on the Tezcatlipoca mission—was a user of a stage-three Incarnate technique; and Graphite Edge's child and sole student, Trilead Tetroxide, was also a swordmaster of the orthodox school, freely wielding the Infinity, one of the Seven Arcs. The Blue Legion's Dualis, aka Cobalt Blade, and Manganese Blade were masterful fencers and powerful warriors, and there was no questioning the strength of their master, the Blue King, "Vanquish" Blue Knight.

The reason Haruyuki didn't count among his top swordmasters the Blue King, who held the Arc Impulse and who had in fact subjugated Centaurea Sentry after she had become the third Chrome Disaster, was simply because he had not experienced that strength firsthand. But there was no doubt that the Blue King was a top-class sword user, widely recognized for having established his own unique sword school, Infinite style. By a similar logic, Platinum Cavalier with his so-called Femto style would have been a swordmaster on par with Sentry, Graph, and Knight.

However.

Now that Haruyuki was getting a good look at him up close for the first time, Cavalier had an almost shockingly soft air to him. Haruyuki didn't have the ability to expand his visual field the way Scarlet Rain did, but even still, he could, to a certain degree, pick up what she called information pressure—Cavalier's aura. But the other Burst Linker was not radiating the pressure that Haruyuki could clearly sense from the Seven Kings of Pure

Color, of course, or even from the members of the executive of each Legion. This, despite the fact that both Behemoth and Milady standing nearby exuded a powerful aura, as did Reaper and Oracle, while none of them appeared to be in direct battle mode.

When he thought about it, the only time he had personally witnessed Cavalier's strength was when the knight had enlarged his kite shield to protect the White King from the explosion of Tezcatlipoca's Miccailhuitontli. Maybe Cavalier's main weapon wasn't the longsword on his waist but the shield on his back. Maybe he was actually a defensive-type avatar like the Green King. Haruyuki's imagination ran wild for an instant.

Standing smack in the middle of the party, Cavalier glanced at Haruyuki. "By cutting off any path of retreat himself," he said, "Crow showed his pride and determination as a warrior...In which case, we, too...should respect his will."

No, no, that was simple desperation, is all!

Unable to actually say this, Haruyuki froze in place, and then heard a voice that was either offering him a life raft or striking a follow-up blow, he didn't know which.

"None of that matters. There's no problem as long as Crow wins."

Clink, clink.

Stepping forward with a distinctive footfall was a woman—no, a girl—avatar clad in dress-style armor with a snow crystal motif. Her limbs and torso were even more slender than those of Rose Milady, and she was nearly twenty centimeters shorter. Her armor was an almost transparent pale blue.

Although adorable as a doll of ice, she was a high ranker with unfathomable power who had annihilated fourteen elite members of Nega Nebulus in the Territories with a single Incarnate attack and frozen Haruyuki so completely that he couldn't even breathe on the Highest Level. Even if she had paid their taxi fare and treated them to cheesecake, she was someone he definitely needed to be on guard against.

"I've got plans after this, so let's get to it already," she said. These words were directed at Cavalier.

Even though he was higher up in the executive order than she was, Cavalier nodded without any sign of irritation at being bossed around, and looked at Haruyuki. "Come along, Crow... We'll move to the trial location for the final task."

They passed through hallways and went down stairs with the somehow living gills and other features characteristic of a Purgatory stage to reach the first floor and step out of the school through the back door on the opposite side, rather than through the main entrance that faced the courtyard.

The woods that had been lush and green in the real world had transformed into a clump of dead trees made of metal. The party wove through this grove toward the south and cut across a large space that was likely the EG sports ground.

As he followed Cavalier, Haruyuki quietly asked Tsubomi about the sudden concern that popped into his head. "Um, Koshi—I mean, Milady—doesn't Tezcatlipoca come and attack if you fight Enemies on the Mean Level?"

"Apparently, yes," she said. "But you would know more about that than me."

"No, I don't hunt Enemies at all," he replied, glancing up at the sky in the direction of the city center.

Three days earlier, in the middle of the night on July 24, the White King had accepted his petition and stopped the Deity of Demise, Tezcatlipoca, which had been about to massacre Takumu and the rest of his friends. But he hadn't had even an inkling of how she planned to do this.

Immediately after returning from the Highest Level to the Mean Level of the Unlimited Neutral Field, the White King had taken the diadem, which was one of the two Luminary parts, extended countless spikes from it, and plunged those deep into her own brain—assuming there was a brain in the head of the avatar body. Then she had held the scepter—the controller—in a backhanded grip and stabbed this into her own heart.

Being injured in a duel avatar's most critical points should have caused her health gauge drop to near-death. And Haruyuki couldn't understand why the act of self-harm was even necessary to begin with, but at any rate, this act stopped the movement of the giant Tezcatlipoca.

Haruyuki's wings had already been completely destroyed in Tezcatlipoca's Blast Wave, so he couldn't go to his friends' rescue. But Graphite Edge and Cyan Pile were still just barely able to move, and they fled the battlefield carrying the grievously injured Centaurea Sentry, Trilead Tetroxide, Lavender Downer, and the Archangel Metatron.

Meanwhile, he took the injured White King in his arms, raced down the stairs of Heimwert Castle, and leapt into the portal in the great hall on the first floor to burst out. In doing so, he achieved his initial objective of escaping from Tokyo Grand Castle, but with the Luminary crowns destroyed, Tezcatlipoca was released from the White King's control and returned to its true form as the god of the end.

That massive deity had been transformed into the worst catastrophe in the history of the Accelerated World, and now prowled the twenty-three wards of Tokyo in the Unlimited Neutral Field, mercilessly killing any Burst Linkers who happened into range of its sensors.

The giant's basic detection range was a circle about two kilometers across, and as long as you stayed outside that range, the possibility of an attack was low. The issue, however, was that when a Burst Linker attacked an Enemy, Tezcatlipoca could detect this even from far away and would immediately make a beeline for the site of the attack.

According to one rumor, a party that went Enemy hunting in Kinuta Park in Setagaya Ward on the far west side of the twenty-three wards, after confirming that Tezcatlipoca was in Minamikoiwa in Edo Ward on the very eastern side of the city, was attacked from the sky a mere ten minutes later and wiped out by the Blast Wave. If that were true, it meant that Tezcatlipoca's flight speed could reach up to 150 kilometers an hour.

Naturally, the size of the party was also a factor, but even a Wild-class Enemy couldn't be defeated in a mere ten minutes, much less a Beast-class. The Green Legion had devoted themselves to experimenting with this and discovered that the god wouldn't notice an attack on an Enemy over a hundred kilometers away. But it wasn't practical to head out to Gunma or Yamanashi for every hunt.

In short, all of this meant that for the majority of Tokyo Burst Linkers, Enemy hunting was for all intents and purposes off-limits. It was, in the end, only natural that the anger and frustration of midsize Legion members like Zelkova Verger be turned toward Silver Crow, who had released Tezcatlipoca from Inti and then immediately transferred to the White Legion.

"Well, I guess Cavalier's planning to take care of that somehow," Tsubomi said, and Haruyuki's eye lenses pulled back from the yellow sky to focus on the duel avatar walking alongside him.

"Somehow?" he asked. "What is he going to do?"

"I have no idea," she replied. "But if he says he forgot about Tezca after we get to the test site, you go ahead and punch him."

"I could never," Haruyuki groaned, feeling pressed, before turning his eyes toward the back of the knight walking at the head of the line.

He felt like he'd managed to make friends with Rose Milady/ Tsubomi Koshika, and he might be able to do the same with Cypress Reaper/Airi Sagisu and Glacier Behemoth/Rioh Koshimizu if given the chance. He might even be able to make it happen with Snow Fairy/Nanako Juholt one of these days. He could almost picture this possible future.

But when it came to Platinum Cavalier/Tomochika Kyobu, he felt like he was completely at sea. He hadn't come across someone from whom he felt this kind of remove, even after meeting in the real, since Dusk Taker/Seiji Nomi.

That said, however, he couldn't exactly go building walls. To keep the vow he'd sworn to the White King from being a lie, he had to accept that he was a member of the White Legion. This was the sole path open to him now to continue doing what he had to do as a Burst Linker.

Right, Metatron? Haruyuki murmured inwardly as he looked over his shoulder at the sky once more.

He couldn't see it, since the buildings of the Purgatory stage were in the way, but the old Tokyo Tower stood a mere two and a half kilometers from where he was now. He sent the gentle thought "get well soon" to the Archangel Metatron, where she was recovering at Fufuan at the top of that tower.

Cavalier cut across the grounds to the southeast, nimbly leapt over the tall wall topped with sharp thorns without any run-up, and exited the EG campus.

Fairy, Reaper, and then even the massive Behemoth also jumped easily over the wall. It was, at first glance, an unremarkable act, but precisely because of that, the fact that these were true masters came through loud and clear.

Milady and Oracle also showed off jumps that made it seem like they were weightless, and left alone on the inside of the wall, Haruyuki considered for a moment faking it with his wings. But his special attack gauge wasn't charged, and there would be no point in putting on airs here. He did a proper run-up and then jumped with the intention of going higher than usual so that he didn't catch his toes on the thorns.

He made it over the two-meter-high wall and landed in an area with small-scale buildings packed together. He assumed this was an upscale residential area in the real world, but the organically twisted town of the Purgatory stage was like being inside a nightmare.

Cavalier looked back for only a moment to check that everyone was with him before choosing a road stretching out to the south and starting down it. As Haruyuki trotted after him, the road butted up against another wall in a mere five or six meters, and he could glimpse a building beyond it as large as the EG school buildings.

They jumped once more at the end of the road to clear the wall, and the building that appeared before them was somewhat palatial. Carving out the shape of a C toward the west, the palace had four floors in the annex and six in the main wing. From where the Burst Linkers stood, they couldn't see through to the courtyard.

Cavalier strode determinedly toward the annex and went inside through an opening that appeared to be the back door. Haruyuki chased after him to find a hall there, and the entire party climbed the spiral staircase.

Alongside Milady, Haruyuki asked in the quietest voice he could manage, "What is this building in the real world? It doesn't feel like it's a school."

"Minato City Local History Museum," she told him. "It was built about a hundred and ten years ago, I guess."

"Whoa. But it's still newer than the EG chapel, huh?" He was impressed for a moment, before realizing the question he should have asked. "So…why *this* building?"

"You'll find out soon enough," Tsubomi replied, and he heard a loud creaking from above.

When he looked up, he saw a yellow-green light pouring in through the door Cavalier had pushed open. He followed the party through the door to what turned out to be the roof.

Cavalier walked over to the railing facing the courtyard and said, without looking back, "Silver Crow…*That* is your opponent."

Haruyuki rushed over to the railing and peered down.

There was a rectangular pond in the courtyard enclosed by the C-shaped building. The water shone like it was actually mercury, and Haruyuki couldn't see beyond the surface. Or so he thought.

But then the silver water surged up, and a massive creature appeared from below.

If he were to describe it, he'd maybe say a whale with four legs. The streamlined body was six meters long, with two of those meters being the head. The legs were solid and sturdy, and there were fins at the tip of the tail. If the head had been a little narrower and the tail more pointed, it would have looked not like a whale but rather an alligator.

As Cavalier stared down at the whale with legs swimming tranquilly around the twenty-meter-long pond, he said, "That is…the Beast-class Enemy, Crococetus. Since it is affiliated with nearly every stage and always appears in this pond, it is the subjugation target for our final task…"

"Crococetus," Haruyuki parroted. He had never heard the name before, and he'd definitely never seen this Enemy. So, first encounter, then.

Fortunately, Crococetus was an animal-type Enemy. The possibility of it coming at him with some annoying special attack was low compared with human- or monster-type Enemies. And it was very obviously not a flying type, so if push came to shove, he could flee to the sky. Naturally, he wasn't taking this Beast-class Enemy lightly, but if two or three Legion members outside of the Seven Dwarves had defeated it solo, then it wasn't outside the realm of possibility for him to do the same.

"So if I can defeat that," he said, "you'll also accept my Legion membership, right, Cavalier?"

"A knight…does not go back on his word," Platinum Cavalier recited emotionlessly, and Haruyuki glanced at him.

"Understood." He nodded. "Okay, then—"

"Hang on a sec!" Snow Fairy interrupted. "Bashful, what are you going to do about Tezcatlipoca? If Crow attacks that Enemy, it'll come flying straight for us in a couple minutes, yeah?"

"No need for concern," Cavalier replied, as he removed the kite shield mounted on his back with his left hand and turned it toward the courtyard. "Ignorable Zone."

Haruyuki wondered when Cavalier had found the time to charge up his special attack gauge while bullets of silver light shot out from the shield and were sucked into the ground in front of the pond. A razor-thin dome of light stretched out from where they landed to neatly enclose a space a hundred meters across, including the courtyard and part of the palace.

Haruyuki felt nothing when the light touched his avatar, and Crococetus on the ground also did not react to it. But he could no longer see anything outside the dome, nor could he hear the wind that had only a second before been whistling through his ears.

"This light membrane blocks all detection abilities of both Burst Linkers and Enemies," Cavalier said. "There's no need to worry about intrusions when fighting beneath it…"

"Whaaat?" Cypress Reaper cried. "I've never seen this technique befooooore!"

Rose Milady nodded. "Me neither. Playing things close to the chest, as always, hmm?"

"I could say…the same about you," Cavalier replied.

"And this'll cut the Incarnate technique scent that tickles Enemy noses?" Milady pushed the point home.

"I believe I said…*all* detection abilities…," Cavalier retorted as he lowered the shield and turned to Haruyuki. "Zone's effect time is half an hour…You have that long to defeat the Enemy or you fail the trial."

Haruyuki nodded firmly. "Got it."

"If you keep your head and fight, you can beat it," Orchid Oracle told him.

Haruyuki bowed neatly before using the railing as a stepping stone to leap down into the courtyard.

6

The Enemies that lived in the Unlimited Neutral Field—also known as Beings—were so varied and numerous that it was impossible to memorize all of them. But if that list were limited to Beast-class Enemies, which inhabited the twenty-three wards of Tokyo, then there could be said to have been roughly a hundred different types. Haruyuki had done his best to memorize their names and appearances, along with attack strategies, but he'd never seen this Enemy, Crococetus.

He'd heard of rare Enemies, though, not just among the Beast class but also in the Wild and Lesser classes, which only appeared in a specific location, so Crococetus was likely one of those. Since the Minato City Local History Museum was smack in the middle of Oscillatory Universe territory, he had to assume that no outsiders had been able to approach it, which meant that the Enemy had been omitted from shared databases.

Thus, rather than immediately approaching the pond after he dropped to the ground, Haruyuki started with observing the creature. Cavalier had set a time limit of thirty minutes, but failing to subjugate the Enemy because he'd run out of time was vastly preferable to dying instantly in a reckless charge.

Crococetus was swimming leisurely through the silver water. The pool was only about twice as wide as the length of the creature, so it seemed a tiny bit cramped. But perhaps the massive body was more flexible than it looked; it didn't appear to have any trouble when it came to turning around.

Hiding behind a thick metal tree trunk, Haruyuki watched it patiently. The six spectators on the roof might have been annoyed by this, but he wanted to get a really good look at his opponent before he started in on it.

Two minutes later, Crococetus once again broke the water surface and stood. It supported its body with its hind legs and tail, while its front legs dangled down before it, and it moved its head slowly from side to side. The head looked like a whale and a dragon added together and then divided by two.

Haruyuki opened his eye lenses as wide as possible and inspected every nook and cranny of the Enemy body.

The bluish-gray skin looked pretty tough, and knife-sharp claws extended from the feet at the end of the front legs. Countless teeth lined the slightly open mouth, and the eyes were a dull yellow. Haruyuki couldn't see anything that could have been called a notable characteristic like horns or a crest. He could only see the upper body that was visible at the moment, but he imagined the lower half in the water was probably more or less the same. So this really wasn't a magical creature or a monster, just a pure animal type.

Many Enemies had a set weak point that could be destroyed to defeat them. For insect types, it was the nervous system; for mechanical types, the control module; for spirit types, it was the soul core. But for animal types like Crococetus, while the brain and heart were indeed places where it would be vulnerable, these weren't set weak points, so it would have been extremely ineffective to focus on damaging them.

"I guess I'll just have to chop at its gauge the usual way," Haruyuki murmured to himself and put his hand on his left hip.

Takumu had returned Lucid Blade to him after the meeting three days earlier. At the time, Takumu had been the same as always on the surface, but he had to have been at least a little shaken inside. Just when they were at last on the verge of fulfilling their vow to each other to fight for real, he'd been brought down two levels, far below the level seven of their promise.

I gotta talk with him, too. Haruyuki swallowed this uneasiness, took a deep breath, and shouted, "Equip Lucid Blade!"

White light appeared on his left hip and contracted to produce a slender longsword.

At the same time, Crococetus whirled around and looked at Haruyuki. Its yellow eyes flashed dully, and a three-level health gauge appeared above its head.

Haruyuki had thought about sneaking around from behind and getting in a surprise first blow. But even if he succeeded, he ran the serious risk of falling into the pond. And attempting to fight in the water when he was up against an Enemy that clearly lived in the water went beyond an excess of self-confidence and straight into pure foolishness.

"Over here, Whale-croc!" he shouted, as he leapt out from behind the metal trees and ran toward the main gate of the palace. There was plenty of space there, and if push came to shove, he could escape into the building.

Fortunately, Crococetus did not appear to have the intellect of a real-world whale. It accepted Haruyuki's challenge and pulled itself out of the pond before opening its massive mouth wide and roaring ferociously.

"Graaaaaaaaaooooooh!"

It scratched at the ground with a front leg like an excavator bucket, and then charged, making the ground shake. The behavior pattern might have been simple, but this was a Beast-class Enemy. If it body-slammed Haruyuki, he would be killed instantly, without a doubt.

Pushing back his fear, Haruyuki stayed where he was to lure the Enemy before sinking down at the very last possible second and jumping as hard as he could.

He just barely managed to leap over the battering-ram head, and flipped himself around to land on its back. He ran up the short neck, pulled Lucid Blade out of its sheath in a backhanded grip, and thrust it downward at the vertebrae popping up on the creature's back.

The skin he could feel through the soles of his feet was thick and hard, and if he tried to simply hack his way through it, it would no doubt have easily repelled his blade. Thus, he aimed for the tip of the spinous process jutting out at regular intervals, so that he could take advantage of the fundamental principle of Omega style Whole Blade: the extreme. This technique generated the maximum power at the minimum point, and if successful, could cut through a literal lump of steel.

Haruyuki slid the sharp tip of Lucid Blade into the bluish-gray skin before pushing down to plunge it in all the way up to the hilt.

"Graaaoooooooaah!" Howling with rage and pain, Crococetus threw its enormous bulk from side to side.

Haruyuki held the hilt of his sword tightly in both hands and tried for dear life to keep from being thrown from the creature's back.

This was the strategy for attacking Crococetus that he'd thought up on the fly. Given the range of motion of its head and limbs, it wouldn't be able to bite him or mow him down or stomp him into the ground if he was on its back.

The health gauge floating above the Enemy's head was still about ninety percent full in the first level, but the beast would continue to take damage as long as Haruyuki's sword was embedded in its spine. If he could just hang on until the third level of its gauge ran out, it would be his victory. If he was thrown, however, Crococetus would win.

"Hnngh!" Groaning, Haruyuki clung to his sword, shaken in all directions every time Crococetus flailed. As a metal color, Silver Crow was fairly lightweight, but all this swinging about was still putting an excessive burden on his sword. He'd enhanced it with the super-expensive fire damage nullification, so he could stab it into magma, and it would be totally fine. But it couldn't withstand this lateral bending for very long.

I've got nothing against you, but please die soon, he begged, as he looked up at Crococetus's health gauge once more. The first level had finally dropped below fifty percent. At this pace, it'd be about seven or eight minutes before all three levels were completely exhausted. He'd kill it within his allotted thirty minutes, but would his sword last that long?

Even if an Enhanced Armament was destroyed, it would return to its original state when the user left the Unlimited Neutral Field and dived again. But Haruyuki was opposed to the idea that this fact made it all right to handle these weapons roughly. He felt like he had to treat his sword right or it wouldn't be there for him in his moment of need.

He would have to let go of the sword when it seemed like it was reaching its limit, before it broke. Having made this decision, Haruyuki tried to predict Crococetus's movements and compensate for them to reduce the burden on his sword if possible.

The massive creature seemed to move entirely at random, but when he watched it closely, he found that there were only four basic moves: lean to the right, lean to the left, lift its rear, and throw back its head. If he watched for the signs of what was coming next and moved at top speed, he could to keep his balance before the Enemy flung him around.

He eliminated Crococetus's slowly decreasing health gauge from his field of view, and focused on nothing but the creature's movement.

Which is why he didn't immediately notice the dome of light above the museum bending and creaking, like something was pressing on it from above. A myriad of cracks raced along its surface, and the dome shattered soundlessly.

A tremendous roar transformed into a shock wave and slammed into Haruyuki.

"…?!" Reflexively, he looked up at the sky.

Darkness. A massive shadow was blocking the sun shining faintly beyond the clouds. Not a bird, not a plane. The silhouette was entirely smooth, no bumps or protrusions. Almost like an ancient idol...

The Super-class Enemy, the Deity of Demise, Tezcatlipoca.

"H...ow...?" Haruyuki said, his voice cracking, as he clung desperately to the back of the thrashing Crococetus.

Platinum Cavalier's Ignorable Zone had, until just seconds before, covered the entire courtyard. As long as they were isolated by that light, Tezcatlipoca was supposed to have been unable to detect the fact that an Enemy was being attacked.

But the one hundred-meter giant was descending directly toward this place, crimson flames jetting from the soles of its feet. Depending on what Tezcatlipoca did next, it was very possible that Haruyuki would fall into an unlimited EK once more.

"Everyone, run!!!" he shouted, in a trance, toward the right side of the palace roof.

Immediately, he heard Glacier Behemoth's clear voice in response. "We shall lead Tezca away and then depart! Shake off Croc however you are able and exit through the portal on the third floor of the museum!"

"G-got it!" Haruyuki shouted, as Tezcatlipoca landed on the roof of the left side of the palace.

The building was crushed with an earsplitting shriek, unable to withstand the weight of the giant. The thick exterior walls ripped apart as though exploding from within, and an ocean of sparks rained down onto the ground. Although not as untouchable as in a Demon City stage, large buildings in a Purgatory stage were supposedly so strong, they were basically impossible to destroy. This was how far outside the realm of the ordinary Tezcatlipoca was.

The giant had in mere seconds transformed the left wing of the palace into a mountain of rubble and at last stopped moving when its feet touched the ground. A heartbeat later, Haruyuki felt a shaking like an earthquake. From this close up, he could only see Tezcatlipoca's legs rising up into the air and the stomach that lay above them. Compared with this monster, even Crococetus, at six meters long, was a mere insect.

Crococetus kept thrashing around as though it hadn't registered the arrival of this reddish-black giant. This made sense, since Haruyuki still had Lucid Blade plunged into its back, but the moment he pulled the sword out, he would be thrown into the air. It would be great if he was sent flying toward the main entrance of the palace, but it would be very bad if he was thrown into the pond or toward the feet of Tezcatlipoca.

However, Glacier Behemoth and the others were in even more danger, given that they were trying to lure Tezcatlipoca away from here. If it hit them with the gravity attack of its right hand, Toxcatl, or the annihilation technique of its left, Miccailhuitontli, they wouldn't be able to escape certain death. And he had to wonder how Behemoth was planning on luring Tezcatlipoca away anyway.

The answer to this question was simple and bold.

"Congeal Ray!"

"Soul Squeeze!"

Behemoth and Reaper spoke at the same time, and two different-colored beams of light shot down from the right wing of the roof to strike the giant in the head. The ensuing explosion was like several hundred panes of glass shattering all at once.

Grrraaaaaaarrr. He heard a low, heavy rumble from far above. The unfortunately familiar voice of the titan.

The massive bulk slowly changed direction. For a mere blow— well, two blows—to draw the attention of the Super-class Enemy away from Haruyuki, they must have had exceptional power.

Clinging to Crococetus's back, he managed to turn his gaze upward and saw Behemoth and the others racing away on the east side of the palace, in the direction of Takanawa.

Tezcatlipoca began to give chase. Its movements appeared slow, but not only was its stride nearly fifty meters long, its tree trunk legs easily crushed any and all obstacles.

Please get away safely! Haruyuki called in a silent prayer toward the Burst Linkers as they quickly disappeared from sight.

If the majority of the Seven Dwarves were caught in an unlimited EK, the White Legion would be severely weakened. Considering everything that had happened, maybe he should have actually been hoping for that. But Rose Milady and Orchid Oracle were part of that group, and he found it hard now to wish for the other four to lose all their points.

Haruyuki chased this thought from his brain. Right now, he had to focus on doing as Behemoth instructed and shake off Crococetus, so that he could leave the Unlimited Neutral Field.

Tezcatlipoca receded from view, kicking up clouds of dust with a rumbling roar. The left wing of the palace was in a disastrous state, but the central part of the main building with the portal on the third floor was unharmed.

The moment Crococetus's thrashing eased up, he would yank his sword out of its back and use his wings if necessary to fly into the palace. Having decided on a plan, Haruyuki waited for the perfect moment to escape.

And then a silver line mowed across Crococetus's front leg as it jumped up. The leg, thicker and tougher than that of an elephant, was severed soundlessly mid-shin. The cross-section was too perfect, smooth, and clean, and Haruyuki opened his eyes wide, unable to process what had happened.

Crococetus screeched and fell forward, prostrate. This was his chance to get away. He pulled Lucid Blade out of the Enemy's back and jumped down to the ground. With the loss of its right front limb, the beast's health gauge had dropped to the second level, so he felt a pang of regret at leaving it alive. But he also had no idea why it had been so seriously injured, and he really needed to prioritize leaving right now.

Still gripping his sword in one hand, Haruyuki dashed toward the entrance to the palace up ahead to the left. But he stopped again abruptly after taking a mere five steps forward. A human silhouette was hovering in the dust in front of him. He swiftly raised the sword in his right hand and was about to demand whoever it was identify themselves when a breeze cleared away the last of the haze.

The sunlight shining down from the cloudy sky made the clear silver armor shine faintly. Standing there alone, shield on his back, longsword with a cross grip readied in his right hand, was Bashful, Platinum Cavalier.

Haruyuki had assumed he'd gone with the other members of the group to draw off Tezcatlipoca, but it appeared that he alone had stayed behind. It was Cavalier who had severed Crococetus's leg and created the opportunity for him to escape.

"Thanks a lot," Haruyuki said as he started toward Cavalier.

Glint.

The knight's right hand flashed.

The reason Haruyuki was able to take evasive action despite the fact that he was completely unprepared was perhaps because of the unconscious distrust of Platinum Cavalier lodged deep in his heart.

But it wasn't enough. The moment he saw the flash, he threw his upper body as far to the right as he possibly could, but the angled silver line that shot toward him still touched his left shoulder and left the sensation of a sharp chill before slipping away to the rear.

"...!"

A momentary silence. And then the armor on Silver Crow's shoulder slid off and tumbled to the ground.

He'd been cut in the same spot by Centaurea Sentry when she was instructing him in sword techniques. But unlike that time, when only his armor had been sliced off, this attack also took the naked body of his avatar. The cold sensation turned to incandescent heat, and a crimson-red damage effect erupted from the severed cross-section.

"Hngh!" Haruyuki readied Lucid Blade in his right hand. His left arm was still attached, but a two-centimeter chunk had been carved out of what would have been his upper arm bone, which rather severely impeded the movement of that arm. His health gauge had dropped nearly ten percent, but he was more surprised than anything else.

He wasn't surprised that Cavalier had attacked. His surprise was at the *speed* of the attack.

He'd come this far in the Accelerated World relying on his speed to get through the many duels he'd faced, and yet Cavalier's movement to raise and swing his sword had been essentially invisible. There were over five meters between the two of them, so the attack had likely been something that shot a slicing attack across a distance, much like the Coba-Manga sisters' Rangeless Scission. And given that Cavalier hadn't called out the technique name, Haruyuki was forced to assume that it had not been a special attack but a normal attack. And yet it was far too fast for that.

He hadn't been able to respond to Centaurea Sentry's slicing into him, either, but that was because his detection abilities had been inhibited by the Gou of the Omega style Whole Blade. Cavalier, however, had not disappeared from his field of view for even a fraction of a second. He could only assume that it was simply a tremendously fast slicing attack, but if that were the case, then it would be difficult—or impossible—to continue to dodge it.

Cavalier looked coolly at Haruyuki, frozen in place, through the slits in his visor. "I'm impressed you dodged that...I was actually aiming for your neck."

Haruyuki swallowed the word "why." It was a pointless question. Cavalier intended to kill him here and now—or even to drive him to total point loss.

So instead, he gave voice to a question he thought Cavalier might answer. "You said that light barrier blocks all Enemy detection abilities, right? So then why did Tezcatlipoca come to attack?"

"Fairy and the others asked me the same question...," Cavalier replied. "That wasn't a lie, you know. Ignorable Zone does block the sight, hearing, smell, and all other perceptions of both Enemies and Burst Linkers...You also didn't notice Tezcatlipoca's approach until it smashed the Zone, yes?"

Haruyuki stared hard at the knight. "So then how come?"

"Because Tezcatlipoca doesn't detect Enemies being attacked with its senses…That giant is connected directly with the system of this world. And it is indeed impossible to block something like that…"

From the way Cavalier was speaking, it sounded like he had known from the start that if Haruyuki attacked Crococetus, Tezcatlipoca would come to attack. But if that were true, then…

He tightened his grip on the hilt of his beloved sword and said, in a low voice, "If I don't burst out, Milady or Oracle will pull my Neurolinker off my neck. No matter how strong you are, there's no way you can keep killing me until I'm out of points."

"There are plenty of cheats and loopholes in the Accelerated World," Cavalier replied, and Haruyuki could hear no emotion in his voice. "You've learned that from your time here…"

"I'll tell you right now," Haruyuki snapped. "I'm not agreeing to a sudden-death match."

"Such a thing…I don't want to do that, either." Cavalier shrugged as he slowly raised his longsword.

Haruyuki immediately dropped into a fighting stance, but the knight was not moving to attack him.

Something shifted in the entrance of the palace that opened to the rear of Cavalier. A faintly white shadow appeared, as if oozing into reality out of nothingness. The silhouette was tall and slender, like a tapered pole. Its ivory armor had a texture reminiscent of unglazed porcelain. And the face mask was marked with an unsettling pattern instead of eyes or a mouth.

"Ivory Tower," Haruyuki murmured, and the fourth of the Seven Dwarves, the Burst Linker with the nickname Doc, bowed slightly.

"It's been a while. Or perhaps not so long as that, I suppose." As usual, his voice had little inflection and communicated even less emotion than Cavalier's. "The joint meeting, wasn't it, Silver Crow?"

There was no way that Ivory Tower's presence there was mere

coincidence. Cavalier had him lying in wait here. Right from the start, his intention in having Haruyuki execute the final task had been to set a trap for Silver Crow.

Ivory Tower was one and the same person as the vice president of the Acceleration Research Society, Restrainer, Black Vise. If he managed to grab hold of Haruyuki, he would be able to do all manner of things to him before Tsubomi or Megumi could get his Neurolinker off in the real world.

He had to do whatever it took to get out of this place. But Platinum Cavalier had his sword readied in front of him, and Crococetus behind him was recovering from the loss of his leg rather quickly. Silver Crow's only path of escape was the sky, but Cavalier would have naturally taken that into consideration in setting this trap. The knight's super-high-speed slicing attack would be impossible to evade in the air, and if his wings were severed, his back would well and truly be up against the wall.

The lone check in the plus column was the fact that Ivory Tower likely wouldn't join the battle. Black Vise was a powerful foe who used a variety of restraint techniques, but he had zero combat abilities when in his Tower form. In the Territories, he'd actually transformed into Vise in order to defend against Blood Leopard's special attack Bloodshed Cannon, making a grave mistake that Chocolat Puppeter caught on video.

Naturally, there was the possibility that he might transform now, but as long as he was Tower, he would likely stick to watching from the sidelines. Haruyuki's only option was to check Cavalier's movement somehow for even an instant and break away into the sky.

However.

He was rooted in place by the very strong feeling that if he left even the tiniest of openings, the knight would cut him down.

Was Cavalier keeping his distance rather than charging him because he wasn't completely sure he could sever Lucid Blade? But if that was the case, he could simply keep using this slicing move over and over until he broke through Haruyuki's defenses, given that it was a normal attack and not a special attack that used up his gauge. Was he not doing so out of some gentlemanly principle?

Either way, Haruyuki couldn't stay on the defensive forever. In less than three seconds, Crococetus would be up to full speed and charging Haruyuki again. The moment he let his guard down to deal with the Enemy, he was certain Cavalier would have his head.

He had two choices for possible action. One was to remove himself from Cavalier's view with Gou and attack. And the other was to also use Gou to disappear and then flee.

After working his brain at top speed for two seconds, Haruyuki decided on the best course of action for the situation.

"Graaarrrrrrarararrrr!" Crococetus's rage-filled roar erupted from behind him as the beast charged forward on three legs.

The ground rumbled. He felt the information pressure of the Beast-class creature prickling against the back of his naked avatar. If it head-butted or bit him, Cavalier wouldn't even have to draw his sword to take him down; he'd die instantly.

Not yet. Not yet...Keep drawing it in.

The instant Crococetus was within a meter from his back, Haruyuki activated Gou and dropped down.

Cavalier's hand twitched. But he didn't launch his slicing attack.

Gou, the secret Omega-style technique, caused a momentary glitch in the predictive ability of the Brain Burst system and erased him from the perceptions of others in the area. Since he was interfering with the system itself, Burst Linkers couldn't defend against this technique, no matter how excellent their vision might have been. In fact, the more finely honed a Burst Linker's senses were, the greater the shock when they lost sight of their opponent. Platinum Cavalier would have been viewing Haruyuki with an extremely precise sighting ability, which was exactly why he was unable to move when Haruyuki vanished.

Naturally, this trick wouldn't work a second time. Gou only

lasted for a fraction of a second, and he couldn't use it repeatedly because it required a deep and careful focus. Once Cavalier got him in his sights again in a one-on-one fight, he would be taken down.

But Cavalier wasn't the only one who lost sight of him.

Crococetus shot past where he was pressed firmly against the ground. Enemies were also part of the system, which meant they also lost their target when Gou was activated. Naturally, when the creature was disoriented and attempting to regain its target, it would turn to the person closest to it.

As soon as Crococetus's chest, belly, and then tail passed above his head, Haruyuki spread the wings on his back.

He pushed off the ground and vibrated the metal fins at full power. Even Cavalier would have to devote his full attention to dealing with the Enemy when targeted by a Beast class. Haruyuki had to get out of attack range while the Enemy's body was still shielding him.

"Yaaaaah!" Howling, he used up all of the special attack gauge he'd charged in the fight against Crococetus and shot up to the highest altitude.

"Laser Lance," came a quiet voice from far behind him.

Huh?

By the time this thought hit him, a pure-white light was already piercing his back. His right wing was ripped off at the base, and he fell into a tailspin. As he spiraled toward the earth, a single word played over and over in his head.

Why? Why? Why?

Just as he chanted this question for the fifth time, he crashed into the ground at the southern edge of the pond. He was unable to take even a protective posture due to his immense shock, and his health gauge dropped even further, cut down by half.

Lying dazed on his side, he looked down at his right side. A hole about two centimeters across had been gouged out of his metal armor, and a stream of red light was pouring out of it.

"Grrrraaaaaaaooon!"

He heard a throaty roar to his left and turned his head that way to find Crococetus flipped over onto its back. With every movement of its flailing limbs, an ocean of damage effect gushed from its mouth and right eye.

It was clear what had happened. As the Enemy charged with its mouth open, Platinum Cavalier shot through it using a long-distance Incarnate technique to strike Haruyuki as he flew up into the sky.

High-ranking Enemies were fairly resistant to Incarnate techniques. And Incarnate should have been even less effective on a close-range combat type like Crococetus. And yet this particular technique had pierced the Enemy's critical points in a single blow. But that wasn't what concerned Haruyuki.

"That technique," he rasped, as he pulled himself up into a sitting position.

Cavalier turned his gaze upon him, even though they were nearly twenty meters apart. He casually raised the longsword in his right hand. The platinum blade had Haruyuki in its sights. Once again, the technique name was called out:

"Laser Lance."

Shwnk!

A silver light jetted from the tip of the longsword and shot through both Haruyuki's left shoulder and wing at the same time. His already injured arm was severed at the shoulder and clattered to the ground. Pieces of metal fins scattered and dropped on top of it.

Laser Lance. This was the first-stage Incarnate technique Haruyuki had learned after much intense training, a range enhancement of his Laser Sword. The light of hope that he had found deep in his heart once he'd finally faced himself, after turning his eyes away for so long.

So how could Platinum Cavalier be using it?

Klak. Klak.

The knight approached, his boot-shaped armor sounding against the ground. The sword in his hand flashed, and a silver line ran across the neck of the overturned Crococetus; the Enemy instantly stopped moving.

The enormous head slid down off the neck and tumbled along the ground. The three levels of its gauge dropped to zero, and the disconnected head and body both shrank inward before exploding into pale flames and a universe of tiny particles.

Since Haruyuki had done some damage to Crococetus on his own, a not-insignificant sum of points was added to his total, but he didn't even notice this. He continued to stare up at the approaching Cavalier.

Klak. Klak. Klak.

The knight stopped about two meters away from him and murmured, "You likely…think it strange, hmm? I can…imitate just about any Incarnate technique I like."

"Imitate?" Haruyuki parroted, and Cavalier shrugged.

"That said, however…high-level techniques are beyond my reach. But I can copy simple techniques like your 'light line' series in a few days…"

"But," Haruyuki started to protest.

Incarnate techniques were the embodiment of the darkness—or light—hidden away in the depths of an individual Burst Linker's heart. They were supposed to be unique, inimitable abilities. Because no matter how simple the technique appeared to be, the mental scars that powered it were too varied and numerous to count. There was no way to reproduce them. For instance, even though they were both first-stage range expansion techniques, Haruyuki's Laser Sword and Niko's Radiant Heat were completely different, from appearance to effect.

A single possibility popped into his head, and Haruyuki clung to it.

"Do you have an ability like Dusk Taker's Demonic Commandeer?" he asked, desperately. "Is it like the Incarnate version of that?"

"Heh..." Cavalier let out a faint, uncharacteristic chuckle. "I myself had that question a long time ago and posed it to the King once...Is this power of mine an Incarnate technique to copy Incarnate? But the King's response was no...This is simply me."

He cut himself off and pressed the tip of his longsword to Haruyuki's brow.

"Let us leave it at that...I won't be...seeing you *as a Burst Linker* again, anyway." He sounded extremely nonchalant, in horrific contrast to the words he spoke. He pulled the tip of his sword upward a mere two centimeters.

A heartbeat later, a super-fast Incarnate slicing attack would come flying at Haruyuki and his head would be cut off. He had nothing left with which to change that future. He could use Gou, but it would have been pointless at such close range.

No.

Don't give up. Kick and flail and struggle. There was a good chance he could do *something* at least, even if it only extended his life for a fraction of a second.

In his mind, focused and pushed beyond all limits, Haruyuki tried to grab at the thread of this possibility. There was no way he'd have enough time to call the name of a special attack, and he wouldn't be fast enough to defend or attack with the sword in his right hand. Both of his wings had been destroyed, so evasion with a slide-dash was impossible. He had only one option left to him: silent, instantaneous activation of an Incarnate technique.

Unlike special attacks, which could not be activated without shouting the technique name, the calling of Incarnate technique names was nothing more than a trigger to focus the imagination. Ever since Niko had taught him how to use the Incarnate system, he'd always called the technique name either out loud or in his mind when using Incarnate techniques. But after all this time, he thought he should be able to do it silently now.

He had to believe. In the power of the image. And in the light inside of him. Even if he was cut off from the people he loved, the bonds they'd built wouldn't disappear. The light he'd gotten from Takumu, from Chiyuri, from Fuko, Utai, Akira, and Niko—and most of all, from Kuroyukihime—shone brightly, powerfully in his heart and would never vanish.

Amplify that light and release it.

Light Shell.

A pure-white light surged from the center of his cracked and broken chest armor where he was kneeling on the ground, formed a spherical shield, and expanded.

At exactly the same time, Platinum Cavalier's hand grew blurry, and the cross-shaped longsword flashed.

Silver sparks flew before Haruyuki's eyes.

His second-stage Incarnate technique, Light Shell, was one he'd produced to resist Tezcatlipoca's gravity attack. While it had proved to be a powerful defense against energy attacks, its effectiveness against physical attacks was an unknown variable. While Light Shell would maybe not be able to completely guard against the super fast, long-distance slicing attack that had cut through Silver Crow's metal armor like butter, he hoped he could at least knock it slightly off course.

The attack touched the barrier of light, but was unable to pierce it and bounced backward. And then Haruyuki saw it:

An ultra-slender, ultra-thin blade three meters long, twisting in midair like a ribbon made of pure silver.

The ribbon instantaneously contracted at Cavalier's feet and turned back into the original longsword.

Inside of the fading Light Shell, Haruyuki felt certain he'd seen through to the mechanism of the long-distance attack. The blade itself of Platinum Cavalier's cross-shaped longsword stretched out like a film, longer or shorter as required for the speed of the slicing attack. Because Cavalier's attack was so impossibly fast, the blade thinned out and lengthened to the atomic level, so that it easily severed Crococetus's head and Haruyuki's shoulder. That was the true nature of the silver line.

But when it was repelled and unable to cut its target, the thin film of the blade twisted in the air and revealed its true nature. Cavalier hadn't attempted to cut down Haruyuki with Lucid Blade earlier in an attempt to keep this from happening.

An attack so fast it was invisible to the naked eye and the proficiency required to handle the film-thin blade were god-level, but as a sword technique, it was as heretical as Omega style, or even more so.

"You have discovered...the mechanism, then, hmm?" Cavalier said, his voice tinged with a cold echo. "And you'd shown me that defense technique before, too...I assumed it didn't work with physical attacks, my mistake. But...now I have all the more reason not to allow you to escape..."

Rather than replying, Haruyuki slowly stood. He was a little unsteady on his feet, but he managed to get his sword up and looked at the knight's visor intently.

"I have no intention of running." It took all his strength to get these words out. In fact, he was certain Cavalier would slice his head off the moment he turned his back, so even if he wanted to run, he couldn't.

Fight and defeat the first of the Seven Dwarves. This was the only path that led to his survival.

Cavalier's health gauge was full, and Haruyuki's was at twenty percent. His left arm and his wings had all been destroyed, and there was a large hole in his chest. He was battered and bruised, but he could still move, and he still had his sword.

He would repel the long-distance slicing attack with Light Shell again, and in the opening that created, he would cut into a critical point with Omega style's Extreme. Having decided on a plan, Haruyuki adjusted his grip on Lucid Blade.

He wouldn't make it in time if he activated his Incarnate technique after he saw the light of the attack. He needed to keep his eyes on the whole of Cavalier and not only on his right hand, and perceive the start of the attack with all his senses.

At some point, he'd begun to see Platinum Cavalier not only as a duel avatar in the form of a knight, but also as a mass of shining, clear silver. It was almost the form he'd seen from the Highest Level, but he himself was unaware of this change in his perceptions as he intently waited for his moment.

Cavalier had defeated Crococetus, and now time was on Haruyuki's side. The five Burst Linkers who had drawn away Tezcatlipoca might come back here instead of leaving through the portal. He was confident that there was zero possibility that they were all complicit in Cavalier's plot—and doubly sure of that when it came to Tsubomi and Megumi.

The Two Burst Linkers remained still as statues as time alone moved forward silently.

And then, finally, a clear silver light inside of Cavalier shimmered the faintest hint to the right.

Light Shell.

The Incarnate barrier and the invisible slicing attack made contact with an earsplitting shriek. Repelled, the film blade danced into the air once again.

Haruyuki slid forward as he canceled the barrier and brought Lucid Blade down with the bare minimum of movement.

With impressive instincts, Cavalier twisted away from Haruyuki's onslaught. The end of the blade caught not his head but his left shoulder. Still, Haruyuki had him.

Extreme.

He felt a tremor of feedback as the knight's shoulder armor was severed vertically. The left arm slid off without a sound and dropped to the ground.

I did it!

But his exultation vanished a moment later, because he then perceived something impossible, something that should not have existed.

Missing his left arm, like a mirror image of Haruyuki, Platinum Cavalier should have had the smooth cross-section of an amputation on his left shoulder. But inside the thin armor, there was nothing but a gaping darkness.

"No avatar body?!" Haruyuki cried out, stunned.

Beneath the visor covering the knight's face, previously unseen eyes abruptly came to life, shining a blackish red. These were not regular eye lenses; the outline shimmered like flames.

"So you saw..." Cavalier's voice had an empty echo as he pulled his left leg back, bent forward, and hid the opening of his left shoulder with his right hand.

Unconsciously, Haruyuki took one step and then another backward.

"That body...is not a duel avatar?" he somehow managed to say. "A drone...? Or...an Enemy?"

But Cavalier made no move to answer. Instead, he removed his right hand from his shoulder. He brought it and the sword he held slowly above his head. Beams of a bluish-black overlay erupted from the platinum blade toward the heavens and began to tangle together like a swarm of snakes in an Incarnate technique unfamiliar to Haruyuki.

He intuitively knew he wouldn't be able to defend against that with Light Shell. Plus, his powers of concentration were nearly exhausted because he'd silently activated twice in a row an Incarnate technique he'd only just learned. Even so, he readied his beloved sword directly in front of him, firm in his resolve to keep fighting until the very last.

Then Cavalier abruptly leapt backward as a beam of pale light pierced the spot where he had been standing.

The overlay enveloping the knight's sword dispersed as another beam of light shot from the sky, only to be quickly followed by another and then another. Cavalier kept jumping backward to dodge the bolt from above until he was chased all the way to the palace entrance. Even the quiet observer Ivory Tower retreated a few steps into the building.

Here, finally, Haruyuki looked up.

A human silhouette was hanging there quietly against the backdrop of the cloudy yellow-green sky. But it wasn't a duel avatar. He stared at the long hair and skirt fluttering in the wind, the beautiful wings spreading out in the air.

"Metatron," Haruyuki whispered, his throat threatening to close over with emotion.

Legend-class Being, one of the Four Saints, the Archangel Metatron. Haruyuki hadn't heard from her once since they'd transferred together from Nega Nebulus to Oscillatory Universe. And now, for some reason, she was here.

Perhaps sensing his surprise, Metatron raised a hand as if telling him to wait, and then turned that hand toward the palace. Points of pale light popped up on the tips of her slender fingers and transformed into beams of light that shot toward the earth with a loud screech.

The lasers carved out complicated spline curves in the air and hit the ground in front of the palace entrance. The surge of energy contracted to a single point, became a ball of light, swelled, and exploded.

"Ngh!" Haruyuki squinted as he threw up an arm to protect himself against the Blast Wave. The walls and ceiling of the main building that had escaped being trampled under Tezcatlipoca's feet were unable to completely absorb the influx of energy and began to melt, red-hot.

He tried to find Platinum Cavalier and Ivory Tower in the midst of the roaring flames, but he couldn't spot them anywhere. Maybe they had gotten caught up in the explosion and died, or maybe they had managed to escape. If it was the former, death markers would have appeared, but he wouldn't be able to check for those until the fire died down. If they had survived, they wouldn't try to attack him, not with Metatron here. He nevertheless kept up his guard as he looked to the sky once more.

Having transformed the first floor of the local history museum into a sea of flames, the Archangel finally lowered her hand, folded the wings on her back, and dropped in a free fall to the courtyard. When she was on the verge of a collision, she spread her wings once again to brake abruptly and come to a gentle landing.

"Metatron, thank*mph!*" Haruyuki couldn't finish his sentence.

Because Metatron had thrown her arms out and embraced him with all her might.

"Honestly. You are always, always...," she said, her voice filled with fury, displeasure, worry, and a million other emotions. She squeezed him tightly for another five seconds before finally releasing him.

"Pwah!" Able to breathe again at last, Haruyuki checked to make sure the intense pressure of her embrace hadn't made his health gauge drop even further, before he looked at the face of the Archangel again.

It was a visage so beautiful it threatened to suck his soul in, so lovely it was almost impossible to believe that it was a 3D object. He suddenly wanted to reach out and touch it, but if he did that, she would push his gauge all the way down to a single dot for sure. So he restrained himself and returned Lucid Blade to its scabbard.

"Thanks, Metatron. If you hadn't come along, I'd probably be worse than dead right about now," he said, and let his gaze roam from her head to her feet and back again. "Um. Are you all healed up now?"

Metatron nodded regally, as if to say this was obvious. "Long ago. This time, there was no damage to my core."

"Yeah? That's great then." He let out a sigh of relief, but found himself at a loss for what to say next. He couldn't read from the look on Metatron's face how she was taking the tragedy of the Tezcatlipoca attack mission three days earlier, the departure from Nega Nebulus, and the transfer to Oscillatory Universe.

He wished that this could have been their chance to talk about all of this and more, but unfortunately, he didn't have the luxury of time at the moment. He didn't know what Platinum Cavalier/ Tomochika Kyobu would do after returning to the real world, and he was worried about how Rose Milady and the others had fared after luring Tezcatlipoca off toward Takanawa. And what had actually happened to Cavalier and Tower anyway?

He turned a questioning gaze toward the palace, and Metatron said, "You were fighting the horse rider from Oscillatory

Universe and the shadow diver from the Acceleration Research Society, yes? I attempted to strike them down with Tehillim, but before they perished, they fled into the shadows."

This was the first time he was hearing the name "Tehillim," but he was pretty sure it was what she called the lasers she shot from her hand. He was curious about when she'd learned a technique like that, but there were more urgent matters of conversation at the moment.

"The one you call the 'shadow diver,' Black Vise—he has a ton of secret passages set up in the permanent shadows around here," he told her. "I think they're pretty far away by now."

"I will kill them instantly with Trisagion during our next encounter," she declared, with no change in her tone or expression, and then furrowed her brow slightly. "However...The shadow diver is a separate concern, but why was the horse rider trying to kill you when he is also a member of the same Legion?"

Haruyuki shrugged. "I don't know the answer to that, either. Given that he called Ivory Tower—Black Vise—here, too, I think he wasn't planning to kill me, but to capture me and do something to me."

"I truly should have made the both of them charcoal, hmm?" Metatron replied. "But what concerns me is the question of whether or not White Cosmos approved of their actions."

"Oh..." Haruyuki's eyes grew wide as he considered this idea for the first time.

He couldn't say that it was outside the realm of possibility. The White King was an incomparably merciless tactician, and she was the mastermind behind any number of tragedies and catastrophes since the dawn of the Accelerated World. He could never forget that she had deceived her own little sister, Kuroyukihime, and engineered a surprise attack that led to the first Red King losing all his points. She may very well have accepted him into the Legion in order to set just such a trap as this.

He was at a loss for words, and Metatron also appeared to be deep in thought. Eventually, however, she shook her head slightly.

"No, Cosmos is likely not connected."

"Huh?" He frowned. "Wh-why do you think that?"

"Because while I was healing my injuries at Fufuan, I was analyzing Tezcatlipoca at Cosmos's request," the Archangel informed him haughtily.

"A-analyzing?!" he parroted.

"Yes. I was able to detect your crisis because Tezcatlipoca's movement pattern changed while I was observing it. If not for Cosmos's instruction, I would not have viewed these coordinates."

"R-right." Haruyuki nodded to himself. Metatron's reasoning made sense. If the White King had permitted or even ordered Cavalier's actions, it was hard to imagine that she would have instructed Metatron to analyze Tezcatlipoca, allowing her to potentially interfere with that plan.

In which case, Platinum Cavalier had drafted a plan that was not only *not* ordered by the White King, but might actually have gone against her will, and dragged the rest of the Seven Dwarves into it. Why would Cavalier go to such lengths to eliminate Haruyuki? He had just barely survived this time, thanks to Metatron. But if she hadn't come along, Cavalier would have no doubt struck the killing blow with that Incarnate technique and its bluish-black overlay, despite the fact that in terms of both level and actual ability, Cavalier far surpassed Haruyuki and could easily best him without Incarnate.

He raised his face with a gasp. "What happened to Tezcatlipoca?! Milady and them lured it away, but…"

"At the point when I stopped observing, it had shifted from the Tah-kah-nah-wah direction to Shi-bah-ooh-ra," Metatron told him. "I have no way of knowing from this position whether or not Rose Milady and the others are safe."

"You don't?" He sighed. "I guess you wouldn't. I hope they managed to get away okay."

Tsubomi and the others weren't using an automatic disconnect safety, either, so if they'd fallen into an unlimited EK, Haruyuki needed to pull their Neurolinkers off in the real world. He wanted to check whether they were alive or not before he entered the portal, but he was barely still standing himself. He wondered whether he should burst out for now, but if the other five were still not awake and he ended up alone with Tomochika Kyobu...

"Well then, shall we go?" Metatron said, and she pulled Haruyuki close to her once again.

"Huh?! G-go? Go where?!" he asked in a panic.

Skreeeeee!!

The sound of acceleration—well, hyper-acceleration—roared in his ears.

7

"Uhhh…um, hey, Metatron!" Haruyuki moaned, the second his senses stabilized. "If you're gonna shift, it'd help if you said so beforehand!"

"This isn't your first or second time coming here. Accustom yourself to it." The exasperated Archangel was depicted in minuscule, colorless points of light, as was Haruyuki.

The half-destroyed Minato City Local History Museum building, the ground cracked in the fierce fighting, and the yellowish-green sky were all gone; only a deep darkness stretched out endlessly around them. But when he turned his gaze downward, he found an ocean of stars looking very much like the Milky Way. This was the Highest Level, an even higher dimension of space than the Unlimited Neutral Field, aka the Mean Level.

Only their minds had moved to this plane; their avatars remained behind in the courtyard of the museum. But since time was even more accelerated here than on the Mean Level, there was no danger to their defenseless bodies. On the Highest Level, time and similarly distance had no meaning. You could see everything you wanted to see, and go anywhere you wanted to go. Except for Area Zero Zero, aka the Castle, that was.

"Right. From here…," Haruyuki murmured, finally realizing

what Metatron was up to, and he looked down at the galaxy spreading out at his feet.

The myriad of white stars indicated the locations of the social cameras that existed in the real world. In this portrait of central Tokyo produced by those cameras, he could also see here and there stars of various colors. These were either Enemies or Burst Linkers on the Mean Level, but there were currently close to zero parties hunting. Which meant that if he could find a group of five Burst Linkers in one place, there was a very good chance that it was Rose Milady and the Oscillatory team. He could have also sought out Platinum Cavalier and Black Vise on the run, but he wouldn't have been able to do anything about them from here even if he did find them.

Using the gaping empty space in the center of the ocean of light—the Castle—as a signpost, he shifted his gaze toward the south. The remarkably tall tower of light was Toranomon Hills, south of that were Shiba Park and the old Tokyo Tower, and even farther down was Shibaura—

"Ah!"

A shiver of cold raced through him, despite the fact that he had supposedly lost corporeal form. On the west side of the reclaimed land containing Shibaura-futo, a concentrated darkness swirled and twisted like a black hole in the place where several waterways came together. The dark star appeared to be on the verge of swallowing up everything around it. This was most certainly the Deity of Demise, Tezcatlipoca.

The sight of it threatened to suck in not only his gaze but even his consciousness, and Haruyuki squeezed his eyes shut.

Abruptly, a hazy heat enveloped his right hand. He looked over and saw Metatron standing next to him, holding his hand. There was supposedly no "collision detection" on the Highest Level, and yet the certain sensation of touch reached his mind.

"Th-thanks," he said in a small voice.

The Archangel turned her face away. "Observing *that* on your own carries danger for an inexperienced tiny warrior such as yourself. At any rate, I found them," she announced curtly, and pointed to the right of Tezcatlipoca with her free hand.

He squinted in that direction and saw five stars floating above the sea about five hundred meters from Shibaura-futo. Judging from the colors, that had to have been the Oscillatory group. He didn't exactly understand how they could be proceeding across the surface of the water, since even in the Purgatory stage, the ocean was the ocean. But it appeared that they had mostly succeeded in the difficult mission of leading Tezcatlipoca away and staying alive at the same time. They were advancing in the direction of Toyosu Market, one of the most famous landmarks in Tokyo, so once they made it there, they would be able to leave through the portal.

Haruyuki let out a sigh of relief and, still holding Metatron's hand, gazed at the inky black hole once again.

The center of the Chiyoda Ward and the Castle it housed was also shrouded in darkness, but the nature of it was entirely different. If the darkness of the Castle was a void where information was obstructed, then the darkness of Tezcatlipoca was a singularity of overwhelmingly concentrated energy. Even seen from the Highest Level, which was nothing more than a thought space, he would swear he felt the destructive intent of the malevolent Being radiating outward and becoming vibrations that shook his nonexistent body.

"The White King called Tezcatlipoca the god of the end. A devastator existing only to close the world," he murmured automatically. When he continued, he consciously tried to put his complicated, tangled thoughts into words.

"Before, Graph was talking about how Brain Burst had two developers, right? Developer A, who created the Castle and sealed the last Arc, the Fluctuating Light, deep inside of it; and developer B, who created the rest of the world to attack the Castle and free TFL. The White King said the thing actually running Brain Burst is a control AI set here by developer B, and it was that AI that produced Tezcatlipoca."

"AI." Metatron's voice was quiet. "That word refers to an intelligence created by people, yes?"

Haruyuki stopped breathing for a second. When he thought about it, he, Kuroyukihime, and his fellow Burst Linkers had likely never used the word "AI" in front of Metatron. Because they'd been reluctant to shove in front of her the idea that she had been created, when she had exactly the same intelligence and emotion as a human being.

"S-sorry," he apologized reflexively. Metatron shook her head gently.

"Apologies are unnecessary," she stated simply. "It is a fact that I am indeed such a presence. It's simply that the definition of the word 'person' is somewhat ambiguous, and so it unsettles me."

"Person?" He unconsciously tilted his head to one side. He was about to say that it meant a human being, but he was sure that wouldn't be the answer she needed. He had the thought that he would ask Kuroyukihime about it later, and then held his breath for a moment, waited until the pain in his heart was gone, and said, "I think of you as a person just like me, Metatron."

"Oh-ho! Do you then?" The Archangel sounded amused somehow and raised her hand again to point at the swirling black hole. "But my existence resembles far and away more closely that monster's than that of you inhabitants of the Lowest Level. Because we are both Beings in the end. Do you think that Tezcatlipoca is a person?"

"Huh? Um..." When he was stuck for words, Metatron gave his hand a slight squeeze.

"That was a mean-spirited question," she said. "For approximately seven years of your time, I have observed and analyzed that Being, but I've been unable to perceive any consciousness or anything resembling intellect. Tezcatlipoca walks an irregular path within a fixed radius centered on the Castle, and when it detects little warriors, it moves toward them and attacks. It takes absolutely no other action, and it does not respond to contact from me. I sense more intelligence from what you call the Lesser-class Beings."

"Yeah." Haruyuki nodded, remembering the Lesser-class Enemy

Coolu that was the friend of Chocolat Puppeter and the other Petit Paquet girls. Now that he was thinking about it, he hadn't talked with them or Rui Odagiri, either. He swallowed this thought and said, "But I heard Tezcatlipoca detects Burst Linkers from way farther away when they attack a Being than when they're not doing anything, and then it comes charging right in. That's actually what happened earlier. Doesn't that mean it's maybe trying to protect the Beings of this world?"

"No." The Archangel flatly rejected Haruyuki's hypothesis.

"Wh-why not?"

"Because when Tezcatlipoca attacks little warriors, it does not shrink from involving in the fight any Beings nearby. Did you forget that it attacked me without any hesitation whatsoever in the mission to rescue you?"

"Oh. No, no, I didn't forget." He shook his head vigorously from side to side and hurried to add, "Um, I didn't actually say this before, but thanks a lot for that. Your Meteor Slash was super amazing."

"Meteor Slash?" She frowned. "What is that?"

"Oh! Um, that thing where you bring your sword down while you're in free fall; it was like a meteor, so…" He trailed off weakly.

"Hmm. Then I shall give that technique that name." Perhaps it was just his imagination, but Metatron didn't seem displeased as she said this, before letting out a faint sigh. "But your thanks is not warranted. I failed in your rescue in the end."

"Uh-uh, that's not true. You saved me." Haruyuki swiveled around, reached out his other hand, and clasped Metatron's free hand. "You said you'd transfer to Oscillatory Universe with me. And I was thinking there when you mentioned how the White King had you analyzing Tezcatlipoca, maybe the reason she accepted my request and saved Takumu and them was because she actually wanted you."

"I had not considered that." Metatron blinked, bewildered for a moment, but soon she shook her head. "No, that's unlikely. Because at that time, White Cosmos could have easily—"

Haruyuki didn't get to hear the rest of her thought because a sharp voice came flying at them suddenly from the right.

"Hark, Metatron! How long shall thou make us wait?!"

"Heeah?!" Haruyuki let go of Metatron's hand and turned his body ninety degrees once more.

Standing a mere two meters away—although distance did not exist on the Highest Level, so this was just Haruyuki's personal perception of the situation—was a woman clad in dress reminiscent of ancient times, her straight hair tied up in loops on either side of her head. A crown with rays like the sun sat upon her head, and the fan in her right hand hid her mouth.

She was not a hostile presence, but she was also someone he absolutely needed to take care around. This was a Being of the same highest rank as Metatron, master of the Tokyo Station Underground Labyrinth, aka Ama-no-iwato, one of the Four Saints, Amaterasu.

When Haruyuki froze in place, Metatron took a step forward. "Keep you waiting? I have no recollection of promising contact with you here."

"What?" The Saint frowned slightly. "We sensed thy shift, so We assumed that thou wished to discuss the incident that occurred since last We met. But then thou didst speaketh so intimately with the boy that We thoughtfully stepped forward."

"In that case, you were merely waiting of your own accord! And we were not speaking intimately!" Metatron argued, squeezing her hands into fists, and then took a few seconds to force herself to relax as she cleared her throat. "No, none of that matters. Amaterasu, what is this incident of which you speak?"

"A moment, please. First." Amaterasu snapped her fan shut and turned the end of it toward Haruyuki. "Silver Crow. Have thou not forgotten something?" she asked, her low voice elegant and graceful.

Haruyuki blinked several times before crying out. "Ah! I—I

didn't forget. You're talking about the thing where I bring cake to Ama-no-iwato, right?"

Tsubomi Koshika's voice came back to life in his ears. *You'd best fulfill that soon. If you skip out on your promise and put her in a bad mood, you'll be in real trouble. Seriously.*

Fearing that he'd maybe already put her in a bad mood, Haruyuki gesticulated wildly as he made his case. "Um. Uhhh. The truth is, I was planning to come visit you right after the Inti mission was over, but then Tezcatlipoca came out from inside of Inti, and a bunch of stuff happened after that, so."

"Thou need not fret. We have also grasped the situation." Amaterasu stepped in close and tapped his forehead with her fan as if to tell him to relax. Just like with Metatron's forehead flick, he felt the slight snap of it, as if they had physical bodies. "We shall wait for a time. At some point, thou wilt most certainly offer Us a *nagabitsu* worth of cake. Naturally, they will all be different flavors."

"R-right. Absolutely." He had never seen a *nagabitsu* before, but he figured it was probably a container the size of a picnic basket. "So then what's this incident you wanted to talk about?"

"*That*, obviously." The leisurely extended fan indicated the inky black hole swirling in the distance below. Amaterasu brought her fan back to hide her mouth once more and snapped it open. "We cannot sleep from the noise such an enormous brute makes wandering the land morning and night. We feel that it is long past due to handle it somehow."

"You say that as though it were simple," Metatron interjected, sounding exasperated, as she put both hands on her hips and let out a deliberate sigh. "That giant has power that far surpasses that of the beasts that guard the Castle. Should you approach it lightly, you would be blown away with a single one of its breaths."

"Well understood," Amaterasu agreed readily. "We have no desire to approach it directly, but We also cannot leave it be. We have more than scant reason to assume that should any little warriors enter our Ama-no-iwato or thine Contrary Cathedral,

Tezcatlipoca would plunge through the earth itself to attack them."

"Ah!" Haruyuki inhaled sharply, not having considered this possibility before.

Now that she mentioned it, there was no reason why Tezcatlipoca wouldn't react to Burst Linkers inside of a dungeon. In the Mean Level of the Unlimited Neutral Field, the ground was as a general rule indestructible, no matter what the stage attribute, but that sort of everyday logic wouldn't apply to the god of the end.

"True," he said, nodding to himself. "It's possible the Legions that can't earn points anymore by hunting Enemies above ground might think the dungeons are still safe. But even supposing Tezcatlipoca destroyed your dungeons, wouldn't they go back to normal when the Change came?"

This was an obvious question for Haruyuki, but Metatron raised a hand and Amaterasu her fan, and they hit him with a forehead flick and fan chop at the same time.

"Ow!!" he yelped.

"You bring this upon yourself for speaking such foolishness," Metatron sniffed. "Do you think we are such cowards as to happily accept the destruction of our castles simply because they will be rebuilt at some point?"

"Nuh-uh." Haruyuki shook his head back and forth at top speed and then turned toward Amaterasu. "So then do you have a plan of some kind?"

"That is what We came to discuss," she replied. "We will tell thee now, however; We are not the only one who finds the colossus extremely tedious."

"Huh? What do you—?" Haruyuki started to ask when he was interrupted by a bell ringing in the infinite darkness.

Ting! Ting!

He couldn't identify the source, because it sounded like it was echoing, despite the fact that there were no walls or any surfaces to echo off of. He looked both left and right, and then quickly looked back.

He saw someone walking toward them slowly on invisible ground and instinctively braced himself, thinking it was another Burst Linker. But the figure drawn in minuscule points of light looked to be not a duel avatar, but rather a woman of the same origins as Metatron and Amaterasu.

Her outfit resembled a kimono, with the same broad collar overlapping across the chest and lengthy sleeves, but the square apron stretching out from the belt sash differed from a Japanese-style *furisode* kimono. Thin pleats made neat lines on the skirt that reached her ankles, and she was wearing a crown somewhat more subdued than Amaterasu's sun adornment. The source of the sound that came with her every step was the small bells that dangled on either side of the crown.

Is this maybe another of the top-ranking Beings? It can't actually be one of the other Four Saints? Haruyuki wondered and started to retreat backward with a sliding step, but Metatron pushed him back into place.

"There is no need to shrink back, servant," she told him. "Compared with Amaterasu, she has a rather gentle nature."

"You say '*rather*,' which is totally not reassuring at all," he protested quietly, as he stubbornly tried to retreat again.

"You are Silver Crow?" the third Being said, as she stopped in front of him, bells ringing.

Her voice was a clear soprano, different from both Metatron's crisp mezzo-soprano and Amaterasu's refined alto. Her eyes were of course closed, but the small face, with its faintly childish air, was so cute that he unconsciously stared.

Maybe she really isn't scary. Clutching this ray of hope, Haruyuki stood up straight and introduced himself. "Y-yes. I'm Silver Crow. And, um…You must be…?"

"Bari," she said crisply.

"B-Bari…?"

"Lady Bari."

"Lady...Bari," he repeated.

"Or Your Highness," she added. "Or Royal Abandoned Princess."

"A-abandoned...?"

See? I knew she wasn't going to be as straightforward as all that, he said to himself.

"That's enough for introductions," Amaterasu said, annoyed. "Bari, how does that look to thy Buddha eyes?"

"It is no Being," Bari asserted immediately.

"What say thee?" Amaterasu demanded. At the same time, Metatron stared at the princess dubiously and said, "What do you mean?"

Haruyuki also blinked in surprise.

The "that" Amaterasu spoke of was of course Tezcatlipoca. So what did "It is no Being" mean in relation to the Enemy? "Being" was the same thing as "Enemy," and there wasn't a creature that was more suited to the title of Enemy than Tezcatlipoca, in terms of both the game and as a hostile presence.

Haruyuki glanced down at the sea of light below him and the giant dark star swirling in one corner of it. "Um, Bari—I mean, Lady Bari. Does that mean that Tezcatlipoca doesn't have a light cube?"

"So close," replied the Abandoned Princess as she flipped her skirt to one side lightly and sat down in midair, where there was nothing.

Metatron to his left and Amaterasu to his right followed suit, so Haruyuki started to sit, too. But then he had the sudden feeling that he would end up flat on his backside, and so he earnestly stayed on his feet.

Sitting directly in front of him, Bari said, a faintly exasperated look on her face, "Looking at Beings as a whole, those who have light cubes are in the small minority. The egg Inti did not have one, so it is no surprise at all that Tezcatlipoca, born of that egg, would also not have one."

She spoke with just the hint of a lisp, and he got the nagging feeling he'd heard this somewhere before. And then he realized where: It was likely simple coincidence, but her smooth, slightly sweet speech reminded him of Snow Fairy.

He thought for a second about mentioning her name, but then reconsidered, given that now was not the time to go on tangents, and gave voice to a different question. "Um. How did you confirm you all had light cubes? It's impossible to actually see the light cubes, right?"

"We haven't confirmed. It's simply a guess," Bari replied evenly, and she shrugged adorably. "There is one large difference between the lower-ranked Beings that roam the field following a given algorithm, and Beings with castles like Metatron, Amaterasu, and myself. And that is whether or not we can use language to communicate. A loooong time ago, we discussed all kinds of theories as to why we could speak and proposed the hypothesis that it was because we had been given the same circuits for thinking as the little warriors. That hypothesis has yet to be proved, but it has also not been disproved."

"M-makes sense." Haruyuki nodded in agreement, before another question popped into his head. "Where is your castle anyway, Lady Bari?"

"The place that you call the National Stadium," she told him.

"Huh." He saw in his mind's eye the stadium that looked like a massive spaceship, which had been rebuilt for the Olympics a couple decades earlier. "So there's a dungeon there, too. I'll have to come and—," he started to say casually.

Amaterasu glared at him. Remembering his promise to bring a *nagabitsu* full of cakes to Ama-no-iwato, he hurriedly returned to the subject at hand.

"Uh, wait. We were talking about Tezcatlipoca. Um, if having a light cube isn't the condition for existing as a Being, then…Lady Bari, why is Tezcatlipoca not a Being? It walks around and has a health gauge."

"You surrender already?" A faint smile rose on her face, but Bari replied simply, without any pretension. "I found within it something that a Being would not have."

"Wh-what?" he asked, baffled.

"A circuit connecting the Mean Level and the Lowest Level," she said. "What you little warriors call a portal."

"What?" Haruyuki's jaw dropped beneath his goggles at this entirely unexpected response.

Perhaps Metatron and Amaterasu were also surprised; they maintained their silence without moving a muscle. Forced to bear the brunt of this conversation, Haruyuki took a moment to collect his thoughts before asking Bari, "A portal inside of Tezcatlipoca? But you'd get killed just getting close to it. No one can use a portal like that. Why on earth would the giant have a portal inside of it?"

"I cannot know that." Bari's response was extremely correct. If there really was a portal inside of Tezcatlipoca, the only ones who would know the reason for that were the giant's creator, the Brain Burst manager AI, or—to go a level higher—Developer B. Haruyuki might have been able to find more information about the portal and its creator if he defeated Tezcatlipoca and went through this portal. But the reason this was an issue at all was because Haruyuki hadn't been able to defeat the giant.

"I-I'm sorry," he said. "So you mean that Tezcatlipoca's true nature is not a Being but a portal?"

"If Inti's true nature is to be the egg for Tezcatlipoca," Bari replied, "then it's reasonable to assume that Tezcatlipoca's true nature is also inside of its own body."

"True," he agreed.

Metatron nodded her approval. "I cannot believe that your Buddha eyes would see wrongly, Bari. If there is a portal inside of Tezcatlipoca, then we should deem that to be directly connected with the destroyer's reason for existing."

"We suppose so." Amaterasu also nodded, and leaned far back against her invisible seat. "But what is critical is how we can link this information to an attack strategy against it. Portals are without exception indestructible. Hearing that such a thing is inside of it, we've come to feel that any possibility of defeating the colossus is actually receding."

"If that is the case, it is not my fault," Bari said, seeming the slightest bit put out, and she stood slowly from her air chair. "I'll keep watching it. If I find anything else, I shall inform you."

"Yes. Please do that," Metatron said.

Bari nodded, and then turned her closed eyes toward Haruyuki. "And Silver Crow."

"Y-yes!" he half yelped.

"When you come to my castle, bring cake," she demanded.

"R-right…" He bobbed his head up and down, and next to him, Metatron sighed.

"Your obligations only increase, servant."

"We must tell thee, however, that our cake comes first," Amaterasu made a point of saying, and Haruyuki agreed once more before adding inwardly, *Once we take care of Tezcatlipoca.*

After leaving the Highest Level, Haruyuki said good-bye to Metatron, who returned to Fufuan, and then moved to the third floor of the main wing of the Minato City Local History Museum.

In the center of the hall, which had so narrowly escaped destruction, an elliptical blue light shimmered like a mirage, just as Glacier Behemoth had said.

Thanks to Metatron, he now knew that Behemoth and the others were safe, making their way across the Shibaura Sea. Running along the water's surface, it would take them less than three minutes to cover the kilometer to Toyosu Market. If he burst out right at that moment, the delay between their leaving the Accelerated World and his own departure would be around 0.2 seconds.

Even so, he slowly counted to one hundred in front of the portal before making up his mind and jumping into the swirling blue light.

8

Haruyuki couldn't open his eyes right away, even after the sounds, smells, and gravity of the real world returned. But he felt like nothing had been done to his real body while he was accelerating. He took a deep breath before slowly lifting his eyelids.

Across from him, Rioh Koshimizu and Airi Sagisu were already waking up, and there were signs of movement from where Tsubomi and the others sat to the right. They appeared to have all burst out without incident after leading Tezcatlipoca away. The real issue, however, was...

Haruyuki ever-so-timidly shifted his gaze toward Tomochika Kyobu—Platinum Cavalier—and found that he was still leaning back in his chair, head hanging. He likely hadn't yet returned from the Unlimited Neutral Field. But nearly three hours had passed in inside time.

And then Tomochika's long eyelashes fluttered and shuddered upward just a hint. The exposed gray eyes shone with a faint, smoky light, but Haruyuki couldn't read any emotion in them. But he knew that Tomochika was actually human with human feeling. When he'd remarked on Haruyuki seeing the void in the place where his left arm had been, his voice had contained very definite emotion.

Tomochika might have been the first of the Seven Dwarves,

the student council president at Shirakabanomori Academy, and beautiful enough to have been a model, but Haruyuki was still going to have to speak up against him.

He opened his mouth to ask why Tomochika would conspire with Ivory Tower and go so far as to lie to Nanako and the others in order to lay a trap for him. "Uh. Um. Kyobu?"

But that was as far as he managed to get.

Tomochika abruptly leapt up out of his chair. The mesh chair was thrust backward to slam into the wall with a crash.

"Wh-what's the matter, Kyobu?" Rioh called out in surprise.

But Tomochika ignored him completely, cut across the room on quick feet, and disappeared behind the partition without so much as a glance at Haruyuki. The door flew open and swung shut, and then the room was quiet once again.

"Whaaat?" Airi's lazy drawl broke the silence. "What's wrong with Chikariiiin?"

"Right when we started to lead Tezcatlipoca away, he said something about how this was all his fault because his whatever zone didn't work, so he went back to the museum," Megumi said, and turned to Haruyuki beside her. "Did something happen, Arita?"

"Um," he stammered.

A whole lot more than "something" had happened, but he hesitated to tell the story. Explaining things now, when Tomochika himself was not present, felt sort of like snitching. But the other Burst Linker had renounced his chance to tell his side of the story and left the room of his own free will.

So Haruyuki set aside his reluctance and relayed in detail everything that had happened in the courtyard of the local history museum, excluding his conversations on the Highest Level. He told them how Platinum Cavalier had returned and cut off Crococetus's front leg and his arm with an invisible, super-fast slicing attack. How he had used the secrets of Omega style to somehow create an opening and then tried to escape with his flight ability, but had been shot down with a long-distance attack that copied his own Incarnate technique, Laser Lance. How he'd just barely managed to repel the killing blow with his Incarnate technique Laser Shell and taken off Cavalier's left arm in a counterstrike. How the Archangel Metatron had appeared and forced Cavalier to retreat with her laser attack. And how Ivory Tower had watched the whole thing from start to finish.

Five minutes later, once he'd finished telling them the whole story, Haruyuki wet his throat with the iced tea remaining in his glass.

Airi stood up without a word, went to the kitchen to get the jug, and refilled his glass. She topped up her own as well and drank it all down in one go before groaning at length, still standing up. "Aaaaaah, Chikarin, you never grow uuuuup. The stuff he did is obviously out, but sulking and running away is even more oooouuut." She sat back down, slowly shaking her head from side to side.

"Honestly," Nanako said from the end of the table, in the same exasperated tone. "I *thought* something was up when Bashful said he was going back to Crow. It was so unlike him. We should've made Sneezy go, too."

"But if Rioh had gone with him, we couldn't have crossed the ocean. In fact, if we'd been down even one Linker, we wouldn't have been able to make a clean getaway from Tezcatlipoca," Tsubomi pointed out, coldly. Most likely, they had made a path by freezing the ocean surface with Glacier Behemoth's abilities. And it seemed that Milady, Oracle, Fairy, and Reaper had also made use of their own abilities to cut open a path of retreat.

I'm glad they all made it okay, Haruyuki thought, and clenched his hands into fists underneath the table. One or all of the three Burst Linkers besides Megumi and Tsubomi might have known what Tomochika was up to. In which case, the most likely candidate was actually Rioh Koshimizu, who was on the same student council as he was.

It wasn't as though he could have read Haruyuki's mind, but this very Rioh suddenly stood up, pressed his hands to the table, and bowed his shaved head deeply. "Arita. I must beg your pardon. On behalf of Kyobu, please accept my heartfelt apology."

"O-oh, I mean…" Haruyuki pushed his hands out in front of him awkwardly, forgetting the fact that he had been doubting Rioh only a half-second earlier. "You don't have to apologize, Koshimizu. I mean, there was no actual harm done, so…"

"No, no. A mere apology is in fact not nearly enough. I have known Kyobu the longest of us all, so the fact that I did not glean his plan is an unforgivable error," Rioh stated, and bowed so low that his forehead was very nearly touching the table.

At a loss for what he should do, Haruyuki looked at Megumi and Airi, but they showed no signs of tossing him a lifeline. "Um. So then, I'd like it if you could tell me one thing?"

Rioh finally raised his head and looked at Haruyuki curiously.

He met the other boy's steady eyes behind his glasses and asked the all-important question. "Why do you think Cavalier would do something like that?"

"Well, that is—you see…," Rioh stammered.

Nanako answered the question instead. "For Bashful—for Tomochika—the King is everything."

"Everything?" Haruyuki parroted, unable to immediately grasp the meaning of this.

He could understand if she meant it in the sense that he sacrificed everything to his Legion Master as a Burst Linker. But the White King herself had approved Haruyuki's transfer to Oscillatory Universe. Cavalier's actions that day very clearly went against the will of his King.

Nanako continued, quiet and yet scathing. "The only driver for Tomochika's behavior is how he can serve the King, how useful he can be to her. So I'm sure he believes he has to eliminate you for her sake."

Not knowing how to respond to this, Haruyuki looked at the seat where Tomochika had been sitting, and then glanced at the seat that had been empty the entire time, at the farthest end of the table.

He abruptly remembered that there had been no avatar body inside of Cavalier's armor when he cut into it. For some reason, he had hesitated to tell the group this. What if it wasn't the figure of a gallant knight, but rather the empty armor itself that was the symbol of Tomochika Kyobu's mental scars? If that was the case, then did that mean that he was a metal color with the purest manifestation of the Mental-Scar Shell theory espoused by Argon Array?

Despite the fact that they were talking about the person who had set a trap and tried to kill him, Haruyuki felt a curious resistance to accepting Nanako's theory wholesale, and he earnestly searched for the words he needed.

"But," he said, slowly, "Cavalier is the student council president at Shirakabanomori Academy, right? That's a pretty tough job. Wouldn't he have run for election because he wanted to make his school better?"

"Tomochika became council president of the Shirakaba junior high division because the King told him to." Nanako cut his theory in half with a single stroke and pushed back her flowing blond hair as she blinked sapphire eyes dubiously. "Crow, why are you trying to take Tomochika's side here? He lied to you, betrayed you, and almost killed you."

"No, I mean, I'm not taking his side or anything like that." Haruyuki averted his eyes from Nanako's sharp, icy gaze. He couldn't really understand his own feelings himself.

Rioh turned the corners of his mouth up in a pained smile. "Thank you, Arita."

"S-sorry?" Haruyuki blinked a few times in surprise. "What for?"

"A number of things," Rioh said, and leaned across the table, his large right hand extended.

Haruyuki gaped for a moment and then hurriedly stood up. He nervously extended his own hand to clasp Rioh's, which was surprisingly warm. He suddenly felt ashamed of having suspected the larger boy of conspiring with Platinum Cavalier. Naturally, he couldn't eliminate the possibility entirely, but at the very least, Rioh's concern about Tomochika felt like the real thing.

After shaking hands for a full three seconds, Rioh finally released his hand and urged Haruyuki to sit, before sitting down himself and getting a serious look on his face.

"Arita," he said solemnly, "this incident today was due to my own and the Seven Dwarves' carelessness. According to our Legion rules, you have the right to request a boon that will balance the uneven scales."

"Sc-scales?" Haruyuki automatically furrowed his brow, but then realized what Rioh wasn't saying. They probably had a rule that said if someone incurred some disadvantage because of someone else in the Legion, there had to be compensation paid between the persons involved. Or something like that.

Still, he couldn't immediately decide how great the damage here was. Cavalier had indeed wronged him. The scales would probably be balanced if he directly dueled with Rioh as a proxy for Tomochika, cut off one of his arms, broke his horns, and pierced his chest. But not only would that not make Haruyuki feel better, he would have been very unhappy about doing it.

"Um, you did apologize and everything, so—?" he started, and Nanako cut him off.

"Don't hold back," she urged him. "Burst Points, Enhanced Armament, whatever you want. Although it will have to be within the scope of what I'm authorized to give."

"Um. It's great of you to say that, but..." Even as he was saying these words out loud, his mind started racing wildly. *Maybe like fifty points? Wait. Would they get mad if I said a hundred?*

And then he had a flash of inspiration and sat up straighter as he made up his mind.

"Um. Juholt?" he said.

"Nanako's fine."

"Uh. Okay, then Nanako. Can I cede that right to someone else?"

"Well, sure." Nanako shrugged.

He turned his gaze to the two people sitting to his left and declared, "Then I cede that right to Koshika and Wakamiya."

"Huh?" Tsubomi looked extremely suspicious.

Koshika, please ask to leave Oscillatory Universe! He earnestly sent this thought at her.

Perhaps his telepathic message was received; Tsubomi blinked as if she'd understood something, and then made eye contact with Megumi. In the taxi, he'd wondered why Fairy and the others had called Megumi here, even though they knew she was the one who betrayed Oscillatory Universe in the Territories and changed the field back. Perhaps there was unfinished business yet today.

Megumi brought her mouth to Tsubomi's ear and whispered something. The analogue secret chat was over soon enough, and Megumi cleared her throat before speaking, her voice serious. "Nanako, our request is…"

9

Five PM.

Haruyuki was standing alongside Tsubomi Koshika and Megumi Wakamiya on the sidewalk, about ten meters away from the main gates of Eternal Girls' Academy. The sun was still very much high in the sky, and the temperature didn't feel like it had dropped at all. There was also the fact that they'd only just come out of the air-conditioned student council office, so that even as he stood still, sweat was beading on his forehead.

After wiping this away with his handkerchief, Haruyuki spoke the words he'd been holding inside all this time. "Um. Wakamiya, that was your big chance. So why would you ask for something like that?!"

"It's just, it's hot out," Megumi replied nonchalantly, and next to her, Tsubomi offered a hint of a shrug.

"I really appreciate the thought, Arita," she said. "But getting them to let me and Orkki leave the Legion is too big of an ask. First of all, the only one who can make that decision is Cosmos. And Fairy herself said it had to be within her own scope of authority, y'know?"

"Okay, yeah, that's true, but…" Haruyuki was forced to agree, and then he asked the question that had been bothering him this whole time. "Why was the White King not there anyway? I know

I'm new to all of this here, but that was a pretty important meeting, wasn't it? I mean, if Cavalier hadn't done what he did, we'd be fighting in the Territories right about now."

"Mmm. Yeah." Tsubomi nodded her agreement.

Early that afternoon, before they dived into the Unlimited Neutral Field, Tomochika Kyobu had said he had two reasons for asking them to the meeting that day. One was the test of Haruyuki's abilities. And the other reason, which Haruyuki did not get to hear directly from Cavalier himself, was that he was putting Haruyuki and Megumi on a team to attack Minato Area No. 3 in the Territories, set to start at four. In other words, if Nega Nebulus had dispatched a defense team, Haruyuki might have been at that very minute fighting his beloved comrades.

But Tomochika himself had ruined the test and the Territories. He hadn't come back after he'd marched out of the room, and Rioh's mood had also cratered after the incident in the Unlimited Neutral Field. So Nanako decided that there was no way they could charge into the Territories when they were in such disarray, and the mission to take back Minato Area No. 3 was postponed until the following week. But if Cosmos had taken part in the meeting, Tomochika wouldn't have dared to try to kill Haruyuki, and there was a good chance that the Territories would have gone off as planned.

"True, to us, that seems like it should be higher up on her list of priorities," Tsubomi said quietly, as she adjusted the brim of her white capelin hat. "But Cosmos is one of those people who just sort of throws on different outfits on a whim. She's always popping up at the tiny, meaningless meetings and totally skipping out on the ones that are all hands on deck, super serious. I'm sure she doesn't have any real reason for missing today."

"Oh. So she's just like that?" Haruyuki asked, as he recalled what the White King had said to him at Heimwert Castle.

That's why I made her a Burst Linker on a whim myself.

If even the act of making her own sister into her child was nothing more than mere fancy, then he guessed that things like attending a meeting barely warranted her notice and she was probably very quick to forget them. In other words, she might have readily assented to Tsubomi and Megumi leaving the Legion, but it was equally likely that she would have used Judgment Blow to destroy both of them on the spot.

So then rather than stepping up in a front attack and directly asking for permission, maybe the best strategy for Megumi and Tsubomi was to simply leave the Legion with no announcement and somehow keep running until the end of the month of the White King's Judgment Blow authority? Transferring to a solidly powerful midsize Legion and counting on them for a deterrent effect was also one way of handling it, but having actually faced the Seven Dwarves, Haruyuki was starting to think that this sort of superficially clever move wouldn't work with them.

To be honest, they were a friendlier group than he'd imagined. Setting Platinum Cavalier aside, anyway. Even the Snow Fairy had not a bit of thorniness in her demeanor. In fact, just the opposite—she had treated them to cheesecake.

But that was exactly why they were so frightening. They had to have been aware of the possibility that Haruyuki had joined Oscillatory Universe under the pretense of obeying with a secret plan to turn on them, and yet they hadn't questioned him or searched him. Because they were confident that whatever he threw at them, they could handle it.

"Um." He sidled up to Megumi and asked, "So about up there?"

"Huh?" She turned to look at him.

"By the time you all made it to Tokyo Bay, you'd drawn Tezcatlipoca off nearly a kilometer, right? But that thing moves in straight lines and has a stride of fifty meters. Plus, it kicks buildings and stuff all over the place. So how'd you manage to get that kind of lead on it?"

"Ohh...Hey. Wait a second." Twirling the parasol, Megumi looked at Haruyuki dubiously. "You were supposed to have been at the museum, Arita. How could you know the distance between us and Tezcatlipoca? Did you see us from the air?"

"Oh. Uh. Um," he stammered. "Something like that."

There was no need to hide what had happened on the Highest Level from Megumi and Tsubomi, but once he started to tell the story, they'd be there for a while. He decided he'd have another chance to tell them all about that, and Megumi looked more or less satisfied with this explanation for now.

"Well, the MVP was Nanako, you know?" she reported. "The four of us lured Tezcatlipoca out to the waterways, and Nanako, who'd gone around ahead of us, froze it and all the water around it with Brinicle."

"O-oh, that makes sense then. That water's over ten meters deep and all. Even the giant's not going to be able to break free so easy as that if both of its legs are frozen in place." Haruyuki was very much impressed, and he also felt like he could see a ray of light into the Tezcatlipoca attack strategy he'd despaired over.

If its movement could be checked in the Shibaura waterways, then maybe it could be lured to a place in Tokyo Bay where the water was nearly a hundred meters deep. Frozen from the neck down together with the surrounding water, the Enemy wouldn't be able to move either hand, effectively putting its Toxcatl and Miccailhuitontli attacks out of commission. Then they might be able to carry out a concentrated attack on its head.

"Hey, Crow?" Tsubomi called to him from the other side of Megumi, and Haruyuki yanked his head back up.

"Y-yeah?"

"Don't go thinking you can do anything about that thing," she warned. "Even with the direct hit from Brinicle, Tezcatlipoca's health gauge barely dropped at all. And while we were running away, it nearly wiped us all out with the Blast Wave once and the gravity wave twice."

"Y-yeah." His shoulders slumped dejectedly, and then he heard the sound of an expensive motor from the left side of the road. He turned and saw a large black car approaching with its signal light on.

Megumi and Tsubomi had used his hard-won right to ask

Nanako to get a driverless taxi for them. But the car that stopped before them was not an SUV like the one they'd come in, but rather a wide and low sports car.

"H-huh?" Peering inside the door that opened automatically, Haruyuki blinked rapidly before looking back at Megumi. "Wakamiya, this is a two-seater, though?"

"It is." She nodded agreeably.

"'It is'?" he questioned. "But there are three of us."

"Whatever. Just get in, Arita." Megumi gave his back a push. "Me and Rosie are going shopping in Azabu."

"O-oh." The momentum of her push forced Haruyuki to climb into the navy seat of the sports car. When the door closed, he hurriedly opened the window and called, "Um, thank you for today! Please take care on your way home!"

"You, too. See you."

"Later, Crow."

Megumi and Tsubomi waved at him, side by side, and Haruyuki bowed at them. When he put on his seatbelt, the taxi quietly pulled into traffic.

He waited until he could no longer see the girls before closing the window. The noise of the outside world was essentially completely cut off, and a synthetic voice announced, "*Thank you for using Smart Cab Tokyo automatic taxi service…*"

Haruyuki let the announcement wash over him as he leaned back into the genuine leather seat, which felt like it might actually swallow him whole, and exhaled at length. He'd been a bundle of nerves ever since he'd stepped through the EG gates, and he'd also been very nearly killed in the Accelerated World, but at least his first face-to-face meeting with the Oscillatory Universe executive hadn't ended in total failure. Or so he wanted to believe.

Naturally, he had some regrets. He hadn't been able to do anything to fix Tsubomi's and Megumi's precarious situation, he was still in conflict with Tomochika Kyobu, and he hadn't been able to get any information about Wolfram Cerberus.

Cerberus was most likely a student at Shirakabanomori Academy with Tomochika and Rioh. Haruyuki very much wanted to get out of the taxi right that second and charge into Shirakaba, but he knew there would be basically no one there in the middle of summer break, and he didn't have permission to go onto the campus. He had to, at the very least, pin down Cerberus's real name first, or he wouldn't get anywhere trying to collect information.

Pushing down his panic, Haruyuki turned his gaze out the window and caught sight of the gently curving lines of Shirakabanomori Academy on the left side of the road.

I've come this far. I will *come and see you. Just hang on a bit longer,* he called out in his mind to Cerberus, who probably attended that school, and he sat back again.

On the front windshield, the predicted route was displayed, and when he glanced up at it, he let out a short cry. "Huh?"

His destination was the Arita house in Suginami's Koenji, but the route shown was a bit off. The fastest way would have been to turn right at the next intersection and head down Meiji-dori, but the route drawn out on the windshield went straight, turned left, and passed by the north side of Ebisu Garden Place.

Maybe traffic was bad on Meiji-dori. But in that case, there would have been a display to that effect, some message about how the car was taking a detour because of traffic. As he wondered about this, the car was already turning left at the intersection in front of the Ebisu post office and pulling onto Shinbashi-dori. Garden Place was dead ahead.

Well, even if it was the long way around, it was only a difference of two or three minutes, Haruyuki told himself as he forced himself to relax.

After two hundred meters, the taxi turned right and started down Kusunoki-dori. The imposing figure of Garden Place came into view on the other side of the trees lining the street.

This was Meguro Area No. 1—Great Wall territory. He had cut his global connection after getting into the taxi, so there was no risk of being challenged, but he was still a little antsy. Maybe because he was still very much a baby in the Accelerated World, or maybe because even experienced veterans were nervous in the Territories of other Legions.

As he thought about this, he stared absently at the stylish brick shopping center, and the taxi suddenly started to decelerate. The left turn signal came on, causing Haruyuki to yelp, "Uh-wha?!"

The route shown on the windshield led all the way to Suginami, so this couldn't have been the end of the ride. Nevertheless, the car slid toward the shoulder of the road and stopped neatly in the loading/unloading zone partitioned off with LED markers.

"*A scheduled passenger will be entering the vehicle,*" the synthetic voice announced. "*Please move to the right-hand seat.*"

"Huh?!" Panicking, he raised both hands to his virtual desktop. But it was Megumi who had set the taxi's destination and other details, so canceling that would require some rather tricky maneuvering. He told himself that if necessary, he could throw open the door on the driver's side and escape that way, and then scooted over to the other seat.

He heard the sound of the door unlocking, and then the passenger-side door opened. Slipping into the car with the heat of summer and the clamor of the world outside was a girl with long black hair, in a navy pin-striped dress, carrying a folded-up black parasol.

As she sat down, she pushed down the handle of her parasol. "Sorry, Megumi, for having you come get me—" Obsidian eyes grew wide as saucers, and after a full three seconds of being utterly speechless, the girl—Umesato student council vice president, Nega Nebulus leader, World End/Black Lotus, aka Kuroyukihime—cried out, her voice upset in a way he'd never heard before, "H-H-Haruyuki?! What are you doing here?!"

Before he could say anything in response, the taxi said, "*We are departing. Please fasten your seatbelt.*"

Still staring at each other stunned, they half-automatically fastened their seatbelts. The doors were locked, the turn signal blinked, and the car began to move.

When the car had finished accelerating, Haruyuki finally

managed to open his mouth. "Uh. Um. Wakamiya told me to take this taxi home to Koenji. Why are you...?"

"Megumi told me to wait here and she'd send a taxi for me," Kuroyukihime said slowly.

At last, Haruyuki understood what was actually going on. Megumi Wakamiya—and Tsubomi Koshika probably in cahoots with her—had discovered at some point that Kuroyukihime was near Ebisu and sent the taxi to pick her up along the way.

Megumi and Tsubomi had told him again and again to talk to Kuroyukihime, but he couldn't believe that they would come up with a strategy like this. *Wait. Why's she even in this area to begin with...?*

Haruyuki belatedly realized that Kuroyukihime wasn't in Ebisu to shop or enjoy a summer Saturday afternoon. She had come to defend Minato Area No. 3, the territory Nega Nebulus had taken from Oscillatory Universe the week before. Ebisu Garden Place wasn't in Minato ward, but she had no doubt left Minato once the Territories were over.

"Um, were you on the defense team yourself?" he asked, without any real preamble.

A slight smile crossed Kuroyukihime's face as she leaned back in her seat. "Hold on." She slid her bag off her shoulder, pulled a small thermos out of it, took the cap off, and put the thermos to her mouth. But then she scowled. Apparently it was empty.

"Uh. Here!" Haruyuki hurriedly said. He was about to hand her the thermos he pulled out of his own cross-body bag when he hesitated for an instant. "Oh. I already drank out of it, though."

"No matter. Thanks." Kuroyukihime accepted the bottle and took three sips, her slender throat moving up and down. "Fwah. That brings me back to life. I appreciate it."

"Well, it's pretty hot again today, so," Haruyuki replied, and then realized he was also thirsty. But he thought drinking from the bottle when she had just returned it to him would be a whole thing, so he refrained. He'd enjoyed two glasses of iced tea at EG, so this thirst was probably psychological.

"It really is so hot these days," she murmured, and turned her gaze toward the windshield.

The taxi went south past the SDF Meguro garrison and crossed the Meguro River. They'd be on Yamate-dori Street from the next intersection, but it was late Saturday afternoon, so it would probably be full of people on their way home from a day out. Just as he had this thought, the taxi spoke again.

"At this time, level-six synchronized driving is in effect on highway three-one-seven, Yamate-dori. There will be no stopping at traffic lights."

Per the announcement, all of the traffic signals were blinking purple to indicate that only synced vehicles were allowed to proceed, and the car ahead of the taxi plunged into the lane of cars flowing past at sixty kilometers an hour on Yamate-dori without braking. The reason there were no accidents was because a single traffic control system (TCS) was operating all of the vehicles, including motorcycles.

A notice popped up on the windshield, to the effect that control of the taxi had been ceded to the TCS. The system made minute adjustments to the sports car's speed, and the vehicle slalomed smoothly from left to right between the smallest gaps in the flowing lanes of traffic.

He'd experienced synced driving any number of times since he was little, but for some reason, he froze up now. But of course, there was no danger in the taxi cutting in front of the other vehicles as it smoothly shifted to the right and merged with traffic on the outside lanes.

"Hmm. I never get used to this, no matter how many times I do it," Kuroyukihime said, and Haruyuki bobbed his head up and down.

"I heard there's never been an accident because of the system," he said. "But I always feel like a really big something's gonna happen one of these days."

"I feel that all the more so when I hear that the Accelerated World is controlled by an AI," Kuroyukihime said, tongue in cheek, and then changed her tone as she continued. "As to your earlier question. I demanded to be a part of the defense team. Naturally, Utai and Fuko tried to stop me, but I threw a serious temper tantrum, and so they let me."

Even if that last part was a joke, it was a fact that Utai and the others would have tried to stop her. *He* would have totally tried to stop her if he'd been there. Kuroyukihime insisted that since there was no transfer of Burst Points in the Territories, the level-nine sudden-death rule did not apply. But given that the veracity of this information was unconfirmed, no one in the Legion was willing to expose their Master to the risk of total point loss in the course of defending their territory.

Haruyuki frowned, confused. "But, Kuroyukihime, I'm pretty sure you can participate in the defense of any area as long as you're in a territory with a connected border, right? You didn't actually have to come all the way to Minato; you could've defended Area Three from Suginami, couldn't you?"

"True," she assented readily. "But that's no longer possible. Nega Nebulus abandoned Shibuya Area One and Two after Great Wall ceded them to us."

"What?!" he cried, but he had known that this might happen. He sat back down in his seat. "Oh, yeah? Well, I guess it would be too hard to defend all the way to Shibuya with Suginami Area Three in there, too. So what happened to Shibuya One and Two, then?"

"I haven't confirmed it yet," she replied. "But we informed them in advance, so I assume that GW reoccupied the areas. Those were originally their territory, after all."

"But before that, it was the first Nega Nebulus's territory, right?" he insisted. "And they didn't cede that territory for free. You paid points for it."

"*I* didn't pay those points. Graph did," Kuroyukihime stated with a cool look, and she casually crossed her legs. The large, two-seater sports car had plenty of leg room, and even the long-legged Kuroyukihime had more than enough space around her knees for this movement.

The taxi smoothly proceeded north on Yamate-dori. At a large intersection, another car cut across in front of them at incredible speed, so Haruyuki couldn't help nearly jumping out of his skin. But their car didn't slow down in the slightest, despite the heavy traffic, thanks to the synchronized drive. It had only been implemented on a few main roads like Yamate-dori. But what kind of system, exactly, could force thousands of vehicles to drive with such precision and impeccable control?

Haruyuki blinked hard and yanked back his thoughts wandering off on some traffic tangent. "Um. So who else was registered for the defense of Minato Three?" he asked casually, before panicking that he'd messed up. This was probably confidential Nega Nebulus information.

But Kuroyukihime seemed to be entirely unconcerned as she replied, counting off on her fingers. "Let's see. Fuko, Utai, Akira, Choco, Satomi, Yume, Rui, Rin, Seri, Utan, Olive…That's it. Chiyuri, Takumu, Niko, and Pard insisted on joining us, but I left them to defend Suginami and Nerima."

"What?" He raised an eyebrow. "Rin came, too?"

"Oi! *She's* who you focus on?" Kuroyukihime glared at him, and Haruyuki squeaked and shrank into himself.

"N-no, it's…Rin—I mean, Ash, Utan, and Olive were only supposed to be temporarily with the Legion until the fight with the Acceleration Research Society was finished. So I just figured they'd gone back to GW," he concluded weakly.

"The finish of that fight's still a long way off," she said, and she was exactly right. They'd exposed Black Vise's true identity, Ivory Tower, and also that the Acceleration Research Society was actually the dark underside of the White Legion. But they still hadn't stopped that group's scheming. Ivory Tower's appearance at the local history museum was proof of that.

"Of course. I'm sorry." He bowed neatly before picturing again in the back of his mind the battle formation of the defense team. Instantly, a cold sweat ran down his back. "So then…That's basically the biggest guns, right? What if—?" He cut himself off there.

If Oscillatory Universe had carried out the attack, Haruyuki would have been a part of a massive fight with the Four Elements and the Seven Dwarves clashing, but that wasn't the reason why he couldn't finish his sentence. He couldn't finish it because he had very nearly said, *What if we had attacked?*

It was a fact that he had transferred to Oscillatory Universe, and he was prepared to do what he had to as a Legion member. But he had no intention of surrendering his heart. That's what he had thought, anyway, but had his heart been so easily swayed, by nothing more than a few hours in the real and some cake? *Am I so fickle a person as that?*

Haruyuki shrank inward, and a gentle hand reached out from his left to pat his shaking shoulders.

"Come now. Take a deep breath. Have a drink."

"Right." He earnestly focused on getting air down his trembling throat before opening the thermos he'd been holding all this time. He gulped down the still barely chilled liquid, and then let out a long breath. "Um. I'm sorry about that. Out of the blue."

"No worries," she replied kindly. "You don't have to tell me why it happened."

Haruyuki's eyes grew hot.

Even though I haven't contacted you in three days. Even though I'm making you worry by dueling recklessly every day. Even though you have the right to be angry, to tell me off...in fact, you have the right to "judge" me. So how is it that you can be so kind?

He closed the lid of the now-empty thermos, wiped at his eyes with one hand, and said, "I...Snow Fairy sent me a message and...I went to Eternal Girls' Academy with Wakamiya and Koshika."

"Mmm." Kuroyukihime nodded evenly. "Megumi didn't tell me that, but I thought as much."

"The White King wasn't there," he continued. "But Fairy, Glacier Behemoth, Cypress Reaper, and...Platinum Cavalier were. We had tea and cheesecake in the student council office. And then I was almost killed by Cavalier, but everyone was just like me, like…I mean, they're all super strong in the Accelerated World, but they're actually regular kids, and I…I…"

His eyes grew hot once more, and he was unable to hold back this time; tears slid down his cheeks.

All this time, he'd believed that the culprit behind all of the calamity and tragedy that had happened in the Accelerated World was the White King. He'd made up his mind that she, the Acceleration Research Society, and Oscillatory Universe were pure evil, and they had to be eliminated from the Accelerated World.

But after meeting Nanako, Rioh, Airi, and even Tomochika in the real for the first time, it was impossible for him to feel as though they were opponents to be despised. They were all the same as he was. They had their mental scars, so difficult to bear, and they'd become Burst Linkers, found their place in the Accelerated World, and were doing everything they could to protect it. If he was going to trust them and pledge his loyalty from the heart, then…even the supposedly absolutely evil White King, too, was perhaps…

"Well, I suppose so," Kuroyukihime said, her voice calm. "Even if our positions and principles differ, at the end of the day, we're all Burst Linkers. Which is why I'm not worried about you. I know you'll be able to perform magnificently, even if you have transferred to the White Legion, Haruyuki. As long as you stay true to yourself—"

"*We will shortly be turning left onto Highway Number Five, Oume Highway,*" the taxi said abruptly, and drowned Kuroyukihime out, "*at which point the level-six synchronized driving will be released.*"

And just as it had announced, the taxi pulled into the left lane and turned at the Nakano-Sakaue intersection. After it drove another dozen meters or so, control reverted from the TCS back to the car's AI. There was the faintest hint of a change in their speed, but then the car accelerated powerfully and entered cruise mode.

"We're almost at Suginami," Kuroyukihime said.

"Yeah." Haruyuki nodded. "Oh! Please drop me off once we're on the other side of Kannana."

"That's nearly a kilometer from your house," she protested. "Don't stand on ceremony. This is Megumi's treat, at any rate."

"Um. It's actually Fairy's treat," he said, and Kuroyukihime blinked a few times in surprise before chuckling.

"Ha-ha! Is it then? All the more reason not to stand on ceremony. Perhaps we should simply keep going all the way out to Mount Takao."

"That'd be fun, actually."

While they chatted about nothing, the taxi continued its smooth progress. Only five more minutes until it reached his condo.

But I want to talk more. There's still so much I want her to hear.

The irresistible urge made his mouth move. "Um. Kuroyukihime!"

"Mmm." She glanced at him. "What is it?"

"Uh. I know you're probably busy, but if you have time, would you like to come over for just a little bit?"

10

After getting out of the taxi in front of his condo building, Haruyuki and Kuroyukihime bought drinks at the shopping center inside before taking the elevator to the twenty-third floor. Although it had only been eight hours since he'd left the house to take care of Hoo, it felt like he hadn't been home in days.

Well, I didn't expect it to be a day with all of this happening when I left this morning, he thought as he unlocked the door. He placed his hand on the door handle, and then gasped.

"Mmm. What is it?" Kuroyukihime furrowed her brow.

"Oh, it's nothing serious at all," he said quickly. "It's just, I announced I'm basically on the matching list every day around ten in the morning and three in the afternoon, and I realized I skipped out on the morning today."

Instantly, the look on Kuroyukihime's face changed from dubious to worried. "Is that it? Utai told me that you've been dueling dozens of times a day. And I won't say that dueling is itself bad, but—"

"Uh. Um. It's a bit awkward to talk here…" Haruyuki managed to cut in and gave Kuroyukihime a push toward the door. "Come inside at least!"

He had turned on the air conditioning via the condo's local net while they were shopping, so the heat in the living room had been completely swept away. His mother had still been in bed when he left the house, but she'd left for work now and likely wouldn't be home until late again. Even with Haruyuki on summer vacation, they were still always just missing each other. But lately, he hadn't really felt the same abandonment he had before. And the fact that she always came home late meant that he could invite his friends over.

"Whenever I come to your house, it's always impeccable. Your mother likes things neat?" Kuroyukihime asked him as she set her shoulder bag down.

Haruyuki looked around the living room. "Yeah, Mom definitely does like things neat, but I do clean, too."

"Oh-ho!" She raised an eyebrow. "Impressive. And your own room as well?"

"Um. M-more or less." He panicked suddenly as he realized his T-shirt was still where he'd tossed it on the bed, but it wasn't like she would see it. He hurriedly went into the kitchen and washed his hands before putting some ice into two glasses. He portioned out the lime-flavored carbonated water they'd bought and popped a titanium straw into each glass.

When he returned to the living room, Kuroyukihime had moved to the window facing the balcony and was gazing out at the darkening sky.

"Here you go, Kuroyukihime," he said, holding the tray with the glasses out to her.

"Oh. Thank you." She took a glass with one hand and put her mouth on the straw.

For a moment, he was entranced by her face in profile. He hadn't turned on the lights in the apartment, so the golden glow of the western sun pouring through the window made her silken ebony hair and her piano-black Neurolinker shine faintly. Despite the fact that it was nearly the end of July, there was no hint of a tan on the arms that peeked out from the short sleeves of her dress.

What was I so anxious about these last three days? Haruyuki asked himself, still holding the tray in both hands. He should have called her sooner, called her the very evening of the Tezcatlipoca mission. He should have had faith in his beloved master and parent, Kuroyukihime, and talked to her about everything on his mind.

No, but it's not too late even now. Megumi and Tsubomi created this chance for me, and I have to really use it and tell her everything. With this thought, Haruyuki was about to open his mouth.

"That reminds me. I have a message for you," Kuroyukihime said as she pulled her mouth away from the straw, like she'd just remembered something.

"What? Fr-from who?" he stammered.

"Graph and Lead," she replied. "Let's see, first Graph's. 'Sorry I was no use in the Tezcatlipoca fight. I'll train more with Lead and be back.'"

"Tr-train?!"

"Mmm." She nodded. "Lead left the message 'I will return when I'm stronger. Please keep fighting, Crow.'"

For a moment, he stood and gaped at her, but then asked the first question that occurred to him. "Where is this training?"

"At Mount Fuji in the Unlimited Neutral Field, apparently," she said. "Graph's always been a wanderer. It might have been a mistake to free him from the Castle."

"M-Mount Fuji?" Without thinking, he looked out the window at the western sky. On clear winter days, Mount Fuji was visible from his condo on the twenty-third floor, but maybe because the air was hazier in the summer, he could only see as far as the mountains of Okutama. "Is Mount Fuji in the Unlimited Neutral Field some kind of special place? I guess Metatron went to Mount Fuji, too, to heal from her injuries. And Master Sentry said there's an infinite pool of sake there."

"There's no mistake that it's a special place," Kuroyukihime assented readily, and indicated the window with the glass in her right hand. "There are dungeons and fixed Enemies in the Unlimited Neutral Field at nearly all of the famous landmarks in Tokyo, yes? Mount Fuji is the most famous landmark in all of Japan. It would be strange if there *wasn't* something there."

"I guess that's true." He nodded slowly. Even the Minato City Local History Museum, the name of which he had only learned that very day, had the Beast-class Enemy Crococetus living there. It made sense that Mount Fuji would have Legend-class or even higher-class Enemies living there.

He felt like he wanted to go check it out and at the same time like he wanted to stay away from it at all costs. He lifted his own glass and sucked hard on the straw. The shock of the carbonation and the fragrance of lime shot through his head, washing away part of the complex layers of thought bogging him down.

He didn't know what was going to happen to him—to Silver Crow—from here on out. The Minato Area No. 3 Territories had only been postponed, so next week, he might actually have to fight the Nega Nebulus defense team as a member of the attacking team. And there was also the possibility that Platinum Cavalier would set another trap for him. That said, however, he couldn't exactly go pulling his Neurolinker off his neck and locking himself away somewhere. In the end, there was only one thing he could do, one thing he had to do: get stronger. Strong enough to resolve all of these problems and reach the objective he had his sights set on with Kuroyukihime—the end of Brain Burst.

"Um. Kuroyukihime?" With his gaze still turned toward the evening sky, Haruyuki tried once more to tell Kuroyukihime the things he hadn't been able to say before. "I'm sorry for transferring to Oscillatory Universe without consulting you...and for not calling you at all after that. But I—"

"Don't say it!"

He jumped at the sudden shout, and a little carbonated water spilled from his glass. He turned eyes wide in surprise to his side and found Kuroyukihime hanging her head low. The long hair that spilled over her shoulders hid basically all of her face, and he couldn't see her expression.

As he stood there, rooted to the spot, he heard a hoarse voice. "I'm sorry for yelling."

He realized that her hands on the glass were trembling. He returned his own glass to the tray, took two steps to one side, and gently took her glass from those trembling hands. After setting both glasses down on the dining table, he hurriedly turned back to her.

He placed a hand on her back to lead her to the sofa, where he guided her to sit down, before sitting next to her himself. But he had no idea what to do next. Even if he wanted to apologize, he didn't know what he'd said before that had caused her to react like that.

"If you...," she murmured abruptly, so he listened attentively. "If you apologize to me about the transfer, I feel like it will all become reality. In the car, I said you would perform magnificently even after this transfer to the White Legion. That wasn't a lie, but the idea of it actually happening is very...very frightening to me. This is the first time since I became a Burst Linker that I've feared losing something this much."

"You don't—! Please don't talk like that!" he said earnestly, leaning forward. "You're not losing anything, Kuroyukihime! I have been and will always be your child. And I know the time might come that I have to fight Nega Nebulus, but the bond that connects us isn't going to be cut by something like that. I mean... *you* were the one who taught me that once you accelerate, there is only the duel!"

Even after Haruyuki broke off, Kuroyukihime's mouth remained closed. Eventually, he heard a voice that threatened to fade into silence.

"I suppose. I am your parent, you my child. As long as we are Burst Linkers, that will never change. But...that very relationship produces an invisible wall between us."

"Huh? A...wall?" He frowned. "Where would that...?"

"Here," Kuroyukihime said, and finally lifted her face. She brushed away the tears clinging to her long lashes with a fingertip and brought that hand to his face. But she stopped ten centimeters in front of his lips, and a faint smile crossed her own.

He finally understood what she wasn't saying. The wall was a mental boundary, the awareness of being parent and child—in other words, "family" was putting a type of limiter on Haruyuki's heart.

Six days earlier, on Sunday, he'd taken a bath with Kuroyukihime at her house. Naturally, they had both been stark naked, but he'd only thought that her nude body was beautiful and hadn't felt any kind of physical desire. This was partly because he'd been so nervous that he thought he might die, and because she had confessed some rather shocking things to him. She'd explained that she was a "machine child" born from an artificial womb, and part of an experiment to overwrite a body's original soul with one with an unknown history.

But there was one more reason. He hadn't been aware of it until now, but he had inside of him a solemn awareness that he was Kuroyukihime's child, and this awareness was creating an invisible wall between them.

Nine months earlier, Kuroyukihime had used the Physical Burst command in order to save him when he was about to be hit by a car. When they were alone in the frozen blue world then, she had told him to his face that she liked him, but he hadn't taken that declaration seriously.

Why was he so fixated on the parent-child relationship?

The truth was, he knew why. It was because he had no confidence in himself. Whenever something bad happened, he ran away; he'd hurt his beloved childhood friends any number of times because of his inability to stand up to bullying. He hated, hated, hated, hated this self so much he could hardly stand it. So he'd allowed himself to lean into the comfortable parent-child relationship regulated by the Brain Burst system.

But.

Now. This was the time for him to smash the hard, thick shell he had locked himself up in. He mustered all the courage he'd built up bit by bit in both the Accelerated World and the real world, and raised his hands.

The words Kuroyukihime had spoken to him nine months earlier, when he'd only just become a Burst Linker, came back to life in his mind: *Do these two virtual meters feel that far to you?*

At the time, those two meters had been infinity. They still felt that way. But it was a distance that he himself was creating.

Haruyuki reached out trembling hands and wrapped them around the cool hand of the long-suffering Kuroyukihime. He pulled it toward him and touched the teardrops on her fingertips to his lips.

"Kuroyukihime," he said, with all the emotion in his heart. "Kuroyukihime. I like you. Not as a Burst Linker, but as me, Haruyuki Arita. I like you, Sayuki Kuroba."

The black, crystalline eyes before him flew open in surprise. Tears welled up in them once again, and absorbed the red afterglow coming through the window, shining like tiny stars. Two of those stars slid downward, leaving a glittering trail behind. Her lustrous lips trembled slightly and then formed a delicate yet definite smile.

Kuroyukihime lifted the hand she had pushed down onto the sofa, laid it on top of Haruyuki's hands, and murmured in a voice like a silk thread being strummed:

"I do, too. I like you, too."

Using their clasped hands as a support, the two slowly brought their faces closer. Kuroyukihime's hair slid forward, and a sweet scent wafted through the air. Ebony eyes containing small galaxies closed without a sound. A heartbeat later, Haruyuki closed his eyes, too. As if pulled together by some invisible force, lips touched lips.

Warm. Soft. Smooth. It wasn't only these physical sensations; a vast amount of information was communicated to him as if every nerve in his body were responding. He could feel the sadness and pain and loneliness Kuroyukihime had been carrying around all this time…and the love that she was feeling in that moment.

He wanted to communicate the same—no, even deeper—emotions to her. With this fervent desire in his heart, Haruyuki leaned forward a little too far. The balance between their two bodies, supported only by their four hands, wavered, and they fell onto the sofa with Kuroyukihime below and Haruyuki on top.

But they didn't move to pull their lips apart. In fact, they each pulled the other closer to them with their now-free hands, and tried to connect more powerfully, more deeply. The boundary separating them grew hazy and then broke apart; their bodies and minds melted into one.

More. He wanted to feel more. He squeezed the arms wrapped around Kuroyukihime's slender frame as tightly as he could.

At some point, their mouths had opened, and now tongue tangled with tongue. An impossibly sweet sensation pierced his body, turned into sparks, and lit up his entire nervous system. A rainbow light bloomed in the darkness behind his eyelids. It became a shimmering circle that spread out and covered everything.

Skreeeeee!!

Haruyuki's consciousness shattered into countless pieces.

"Ah! Wh-what?!"

By the time he heard Kuroyukihime's cry, Haruyuki was already leaping up. He snapped his eyes open and looked around.

Dark. A gloom so deep he couldn't see the ceiling or the walls. Had night actually fallen without him realizing it?! If that were the case, though, the lights of the streets of Koenji would have been shining through the windows.

"Hey…Hey, Haruyuki."

He heard a voice from immediately behind and whirled around.

Standing there was Kuroyukihime. But her long hair, her slender limbs, and her entirely naked body were formed of particles

of white light. He quickly looked down to find that his own body was the same. And in the distance far below, a vast galaxy sparkled quietly.

"Huh?" He frowned. "This is...the Highest Level?"

"It does appear to be." Kuroyukihime shrugged. "But why did we shift so abruptly?"

"Um." He checked his surroundings once more. But there was no one else in the infinite darkness. Which meant they hadn't been forced to shift by Metatron or some other Being. Which meant...

"I think I brought you here, Kuroyukihime," he said slowly.

"Huh?" She stared at him, uncomprehending. "But, Haruyuki, we're not accelerated or directing."

"W-we're not," he agreed. "But the way this feels...I can't think of any other explanation."

She was speechless for a few moments before she finally shook her head slowly. "Of all the things...So then will I be sent to this place every time I kiss you?"

"K-kiss..."

That's right. I kissed Kuroyukihime.

After reconfirming this fact, he froze, not able to process how he should react. Instantly, Kuroyukihime reached out and poked him in the shoulder.

"Hey! You're the one who started it, so what are you getting all awkward for now? You're going to make *me* embarrassed, too."

"Huh?" He blinked rapidly. "D-did I start it?"

"You did," she told him firmly. "No ifs, ands, or buts."

He turned his face away in shyness, and she looked down at the sea of stars below them as she continued in a softer tone. "Well. I do like it here, so I've no complaints about the fact of you bringing me, in and of itself. But last time, we were both duel avatars, and now we're our real selves. Not to mention we're both stark naked. How does that work?"

"Dunno. This is the first time I've shifted like this, too," he replied, belatedly trying to hide himself.

But a voice in his brain denied this. *No.* When he came to the

Highest Level for the first time with Metatron, the shell of his duel avatar had peeled away, and he'd been transformed into his real self. That might have been a clue to understanding their current situation, but he got the feeling that it would be dangerous in numerous senses to bring up Metatron's name now.

"A-anyway, should we be getting back?" he suggested, unconsciously lowering his voice.

But Kuroyukihime took a step forward and said, "Regardless of the fact that it was an unintentional shift, we were able to come here without using any Burst Points, so why don't we enjoy it a little longer? We would never get this sort of opportunity to leisurely take in Tokyo from this altitude in the real world."

"Okay," Haruyuki agreed, and looked down.

Because he'd been visiting the Highest Level on a regular basis lately, he had gotten used to being here. But normally, this was a place of miracles, a space that was impossible to reach, no matter how many stars you wished upon…

Suddenly, he felt like he'd stumbled onto the answer to a question that had been stuck in a corner of his brain.

The words that Snow Fairy had said—*on top of that, Crow's a level-three accessor.* That had to have meant a person who could reach the Highest Level. Most likely, level one was someone who was led there by a Being; level two, someone who could shift long-distance in resonance with a Being; and level three, someone who could shift on their own.

He'd only been able to move here on his own three times, excluding right now, when he'd shifted spontaneously. The first time, he'd shifted after hacking at a virtual steel sphere thousands of times in the Unlimited Neutral Field. The second time, he'd had the help of Utai's late brother, Mirror Masker. And the third time, he'd shifted in the extreme situation of the awakened Tezcatlipoca trampling his comrades before his eyes. So it was natural for Fairy to note the "on top of that" part.

He had no guarantee that there would be a fourth time, and like Kuroyukihime said, he hated to waste this opportunity.

After thinking everything over, he squinted at the sea of stars and immediately found what he was looking for: the swirling inky vortex that threatened to swallow everything up.

However.

"H-huh?" he wondered.

"Mmm." Kuroyukihime turned to him. "What is it?"

"Oh. You can see Tezcatlipoca's marker over there, right?"

"Of course. I was looking at it myself. In the Ueno Park area, hmm?"

Haruyuki slid his extended hand just a little to the left. "Can you see the small markers fixed around a kilometer away from it?"

"Mmm." She leaned forward. "Ohh, I see them. Are those Burst Linkers?"

"The color's a little different from the white markers of the social cameras, so they're either Enemies or Burst Linkers. But Enemies basically never form groups, so they're probably Burst Linkers. But what are they doing so close to Tezcatlipoca?" he muttered, half to himself.

Tezcatlipoca's basic detection range was about a kilometer. Meaning that if they went just a little closer, they would be targeted by the god of the end. And unless they were Seven Dwarves–level skilled, they would be slaughtered.

"You don't know who they are or where they're from, either?" Kuroyukihime asked, and Haruyuki shook his head.

"I can tell who it is from the color or the kind of feel of the marker if it's a Burst Linker I know well, but..."

"Not Oscillatory members?"

He shook his head. "It's not the Seven Dwarves, at any rate."

"Hmm." Kuroyukihime placed a finger on her chin. "Rabble coming to have a look at something scary? Or—"

"That's the Exercitus scouting party."

The voice came from above, and Haruyuki jerked his face up.

A silhouette enveloped in phosphorescence danced soundlessly down from the starless heavens. The figure, with slender arms slightly open and long hair swinging gently, seemed to be a real girl. For a second, he thought it was a Being, but she didn't seem to have any clothes or accessories, just like Haruyuki and Kuroyukihime.

"Impossible…," said Kuroyukihime, her voice hoarse, while basically at the same time, Haruyuki also swallowed hard.

"Huh? Is that maybe…?"

The aloof aura, as if to make all of creation bow down before her. This ambience, this sense of presence…

"The White King?" A second after he gave voice to this name, the elegant tips of her toes touched the invisible ground.

Hair fanned out behind her like wings slid smoothly together to hang flat down her back. The slender body leaned forward slightly.

Haruyuki gaped at the face this movement revealed. An extraordinary beauty that still shone in this colorless world. If he hadn't had the faint sense of déjà vu, he might have decided she was a Being after all. Her visage somehow resembled Kuroyukihime's, but instead of the severity of a finely whetted blade without a single blemish, hers displayed an absolute purity like a flawless diamond.

His brain went numb, and he was unable to think at all.

Next to him, Kuroyukihime spoke in a calm, yet extremely strained voice. "Been a while, Cosmos—I mean, Enju."

"It really has," the White King replied, with a smile full of love. "You look good, Sayuki. I'm glad."

As he listened to the girls, Haruyuki managed to at last get his brain back up to half speed. He was about to ask about the name "Enju," but as if anticipating this, the White King turned her gaze toward him and smiled again.

"Now that I'm thinking about it, I haven't told you my real name. Enju Kuroba. Nice to meet you, Haruyuki Arita."

"I-it's nice to meet you." He reflexively bowed before earnestly setting his brain to work. He didn't care at the moment how the

White King knew his name when they'd never met in the real world. The issue at hand was why she had appeared before them now.

Snow Fairy had manifested on the Highest Level in a similar fashion and had tried to sever the link between Haruyuki and Metatron. She'd also tried to suffocate him. And if Fairy could do it, then the White King most certainly could. There was no one else in the Arita house, and they hadn't set up a timed safety, so if she hit both him and Kuroyukihime with that suffocation attack at the same time, they would suffer for what was basically an eternity in the stopped world.

Should he burst out right that second with Kuroyukihime? But if he did that, he wouldn't find out the meaning of this "Exercitus."

As if seeing right through him, the White King—Enju Kuroba—announced in a sweet, kind voice, "Don't be so afraid. The two of you are my precious child and grandchild. I'm not going to hurt you for no reason."

She turned around so that her back was to them, clasped her hands behind her, took a couple steps forward, and looked down at the black hole swirling in one corner of the white galaxy.

"Um, Cosmos?" Haruyuki mustered his will and called out to her when he could no longer stand being put on hold. "That Exercitus you mentioned..."

"It means 'army' in Latin." It was Kuroyukihime who answered him.

The White King nodded without looking back and added, "To be a little more specific, it's the idea of the high-ranking 'legio' in the ancient Roman army. 'Cohors' come together and form a legio; legio come together and form an exercitus. Taking all that into consideration, the choice of name is quite bold, hmm?"

"So then does that mean they made, like, a joint Legion army in the Accelerated World?" he asked.

"It does. It was officially launched this afternoon, apparently, so it's no wonder that you're not aware of it." The White

King stopped for a moment, before adding, as though she'd just remembered, "Aah, it might be a joint Legion army, but the Kings' Legions aren't involved. The central group are powerful midsize Legions: Night Owls, Ovest, and Cold Brew. Many of the small Legions and solo Linkers are also a part of it."

"Many?" Kuroyukihime asked, and the White King tilted her head slightly to one side.

"I don't have a perfect grasp on the situation myself," she said. "But it seems that there are more than five hundred members."

"Five hundred?!" Haruyuki cried, shocked. There were said to be about a thousand Burst Linkers residing in Tokyo. Five hundred meant half of that number. This was clearly more than all members of the seven Great Legions combined. "Wh-why would such a large group suddenly...?"

"It's not as though it was sudden," the White King told him. "The movement to create an alliance to resist the Kings' Legions has been ongoing for quite some time. But whenever it starts to gain momentum, the Armor of Catastrophe runs wild or ISS kits get passed around, and the new problem takes the wind right out of those sails."

"You're the one pulling those strings behind the scene, Cosmos," Kuroyukihime pointed out icily.

That was only natural. Not only had the White King created the reason for the crisis of Haruyuki becoming the sixth Chrome Disaster, and for Takumu and Rin being parasitized with the ISS kits, she had also incited Kuroyukihime into a surprise attack on the first Red King, Red Rider, and caused his total point loss in order to control him with her ability to revive the dead.

But the White King apparently did not consider her own actions to be crimes in the slightest. "I am." She nodded evenly. "And once again, a crisis in the form of Tezcatlipoca has appeared. If it were still under the control of the Luminary, the children in those midsize Legions might very well have feared being targeted by it and thus put any plans for an alliance on hold. But while Tezcatlipoca is still extremely powerful freed from that control, its movement patterns are simple, so this has actually accelerated movements to form an alliance."

After taking a few seconds to digest this, Haruyuki asked quietly, "That's...sounds like you don't want the Burst Linkers to come together as one?"

He was prepared for this question to turn her mood sour, but the White King let out a happy chuckle.

"Ha-ha! If we're speaking the unvarnished truth, then yes, that's exactly right. Grandé is the one bringing them together, so I'm working hard to keep them from doing that."

Grandé was the head of Great Wall, and the Green King. And indeed, by indirectly distributing the Burst Points he earned hunting Enemies to lower-ranking Legions, he was defending against the intensification of fighting in the Accelerated World and any increase in the number of players forced to retire.

Haruyuki could never do the same himself, but without these efforts on the part of the Green King, there would be far fewer Burst Linkers than there currently were. It was even possible that Brain Burst itself would have long ago met its end. And even the White King couldn't want that. So then why...?

Once his thoughts had reached this point, he heard the echo of something the White King had once said to him. Unconsciously, he turned that echo into words. "Accel Assault 2038 was filled with excessive fighting, and Cosmos Corrupt 2040 with excessive harmony. That's why they fell."

"Exactly."

"So then everything you've done has been so that no excessive harmony happens in Brain Burst 2039? Is that it?!" Haruyuki half shouted.

The White King shrugged shoulders, slender like a doll's. "I won't deny it, but that is definitely not the whole of it. When I spoke to you of this at your school before, Sayuki, you did get so angry at me. You said I shouldn't try to legitimize what I've done with flowery words."

The White King giggled, and Haruyuki shifted his gaze from

her back to Kuroyukihime beside him. But the Black King's face was unexpectedly calm.

She parted her lips, and in quiet notes declared, "Cosmos—Enju. There's no point in you revealing your objective here. Whatever you say, there's no proof that it's true. But I will say just one thing."

A lurid light shone in the eyes that stared at her older sister's back. "I *will* eliminate you and the Acceleration Research Society from this world. Even if the end result of that is the destruction of Brain Burst due to this excessive harmony or what have you."

Despite the fact that this was coming from her sister/child, the White King did not so much as twitch. She looked back abruptly, hair that was the slightest bit longer than Kuroyukihime's swinging, a saintly smile on her innocently beautiful visage. "Can you, though? If the day comes when you and I face off against each other, it might be that Haruyuki will be standing not by your side, but by mine."

Haruyuki gasped sharply. He wanted to deny it. He wanted to shout that there was no way.

But the current Haruyuki was a member of Oscillatory Universe; he had dedicated his sword to the White King. If she ordered him to, he would have to fight Kuroyukihime and protect the White King. It wasn't because he was afraid of the Judgment Blow. If he didn't want to stain his own sword with deceit, he had no choice but to do as she asked.

He stood there, head hanging, but Kuroyukihime took his hand and squeezed it tight. "Even then, Enju. Even if that happens."

The White King turned a gaze on Kuroyukihime that was almost fond somehow. "You really have grown strong, Sayuki. I've said this before, but I look forward to the time when you stand in my way."

She took a light step backward.

"Well then, I should be on my way. Oh! One more thing. It's lovely that you two are getting so close, but please, everything in moderation. You must act appropriately for students."

"Wh—? Th-that is none of your business!" Kuroyukihime snapped, losing her temper.

The White King laughed merrily, and then her body sank down with a graceful gesture. She kicked off the invisible ground and—

"Ah! R-right! Please wait!" Haruyuki cried out to stop her, and the White King simply did a little hop before returning to their plane.

"Whaaat? If it's about Exercitus, I've told you all I know."

"No, it's not that." He shook his head. "It's about Tezcatlipoca. You instructed Metatron to observe it, right, Enju? Have you received her report yet?"

"No, not yet." The White King shrugged again. "Hmm? Are you saying that child went past me, the Master, and reported to you?"

Referring to a Being of the highest rank who had lived for over eight thousand years as "that child"...Haruyuki shivered in fear. "N-no, it's not like that. I just happened to see her, and..."

The one who gave us reason to meet was your very own Cavalier, you know!

With effort, he swallowed this complaint and continued, "Um. Metatron is getting help observing Tezcatlipoca from these Beings Amaterasu and Lady Bari—I mean, the Abandoned Princess Bari. She said it was weird."

"Bari," the White King said, lowering her lashes for a moment before quickly raising her face again. "And what did she say is weird, then?"

"She said Tezcatlipoca's not a Being," he told her.

""What?"" the White King and Kuroyukihime said at the same time.

"What is that supposed to mean, Haruyuki?" Kuroyukihime demanded. "A Being is an Enemy, yes? I don't think there's anything more fitting to be called Enemy than *that*."

"Yeah," he agreed. "I thought so, too. But Lady Bari said there's a portal inside of Tezcatlipoca, and that that's its true nature."

"A portal?" Kuroyukihime furrowed her brow dubiously.

"And what does that mean?" came a quiet voice, causing Haruyuki to turn to the left.

The White King had one hand on her elbow and the other up against her mouth, while her head hung deeply. "There was no portal in the Tezcatlipoca *before*. Although I didn't exactly confirm this. Nothing like that appeared in the moment the world closed, either."

Unable to understand what she was talking about, Haruyuki gaped.

But actually, he felt like the White King had said something similar before. He was pretty sure it was when Tezcatlipoca had been freed from the control of the Luminary and was running wild. The White King had said that of all the Burst Linkers, she alone might be able to stop it once again. And the reason for that was because she'd been eaten by it long ago.

Did that mean that she had once been eaten and killed by "the Tezcatlipoca before"? In that case, this wasn't the first time that Tezcatlipoca had appeared in the Accelerated World? But if something this big had happened before, the veteran Linkers would have definitely known about it. One question after another popped up to overwhelm him, and he was rendered speechless.

And then the White King abruptly lifted her face and looked directly at him. "Silver Crow, I command you as your King," she said, her tone and entire aura suddenly completely different from before. "Contact the other highest-ranking Beings as soon as possible and link with them if you can."

Haruyuki stared, stunned, as he managed to squeak, "O-okay. But I don't know where any of the other Beings are. I mean, other than the three I've already met."

"And those three are the Archangel Metatron, Ohirume Amaterasu, and Abandoned Princess Bari, yes?" the White King asked.

"Th-that's right."

"Then the remaining four are..." She paused for a moment before continuing, "Goddess of the Dawn Ushas, Queen Mother of the West Xiwangmu, Storm King Rudra, and Night Goddess Nyx. Ushas is in the Shinjuku Government Building Underground Labyrinth, Xiwangmu is in the Tokyo Dome Underground Labyrinth, Rudra is in the Tokyo Big Site Underground Labyrinth, and Nyx lives in the Yoyogi Park Underground Labyrinth. But Yoyogi's sealed presently, so it's fine if you leave that one for later."

"Okay," he started to say, but then quickly shook his head. "No, but the government office, Dome—you're talking about the four great dungeons! I'm supposed to charge in there by myself?! I will definitely die, though?!" he argued desperately, as he brought his arms together in front of him to form a giant X.

The White King waved a hand to the side lightly. "I'll talk to Fairy. Select whichever members of Oscillatory you need, including the Dwarves, and put together an attack team. When you need to contact me, go through Fairy. Please and thank you," she said at twice the speed of anything else she'd said thus far, and prepared to jump once more.

This time, Kuroyukihime called out to her. "Enju, stop! Haruyuki may very well be your subordinate now, but if you're going to order him to take on such a large mission, how about you at least explain the objective to him!"

"I would explain if I could," she said. "Right now, I can only say it's a gut feeling. Sayuki, if you're worried about Haruyuki, you're free to help him. All right then!"

The White King sprang hard off the ground and shot up into the air at incredible speed. In the blink of an eye, she disappeared into the infinite darkness.

Haruyuki stared upward even more baffled, but Kuroyukihime's voice brought him back to himself with a gasp.

"Honestly, what was that...?"

"For real. You said it..."

They looked at each other and sighed heavily at the same time. They'd managed to get out of the encounter without any suffocation attacks at least, but in exchange, he'd been ordered to undertake an extremely tough mission.

Attack three underground labyrinths, including two great dungeons, break through the first form of the final bosses—Beings of the highest rank—and make them take on their true forms. Build a friendly relationship with these thoroughly crusty creatures and form a link with them. No matter how much help he got from Snow Fairy and the others, he couldn't even imagine how many days this would take, with all the prep work included.

"So how soon is 'as soon as possible,' then?" he muttered, and Kuroyukihime sighed again.

"Enju—well, Cosmos—said 'as soon as possible,' so that means now if not yesterday," she replied. "But she said to put together a team. If you're tackling the great dungeons, you want at least three parties of ten people. And it normally takes an evening to make sure you have the right balance of people in your parties and put together a schedule. This is where you get to show off your leadership and planning abilities."

"I—I don't have any, though." Haruyuki shook his head vigorously, and Kuroyukihime patted his shoulder.

"Well, you can lean on Fairy and Glacier Behemoth if you need to," she said, with a sly smile. "Work them to the bone as revenge for all the trouble they've given you."

"R-right," he said, less confidently.

"Now then, we should also be getting back." She paused briefly. "And how do we go about doing that, do you suppose?"

"Um," he said. "You basically have, like, an image and then you sort of just *snap*," Haruyuki started to say, and then decided it was hopeless to try and explain in words. He reached out a hand, and when Kuroyukihime clasped it in hers, he called in his head, *Burst Out.*

11

When he returned to the Lowest Level—aka the real world—
Haruyuki was unable to immediately understand the position-
ing of his body, and he froze in place. Eyes still closed, he tried
to process the vast quantity of information pouring into his nervous system: a sweet scent, warmth, suppleness, and a softness
touching his lips.

At last, he remembered that he and Kuroyukihime had kissed,
or rather that they were currently kissing at that moment.

He very nearly threw himself backward, but then he realized
at the last second that doing that from this position would put
his full weight onto Kuroyukihime. He turned his focus to con-
trolling his clumsy real-world body and ever so slowly pushed
himself upward.

When he had created a distance of about thirty centimeters
between himself and Kuroyukihime, he finally opened his eyes
to find that she was already staring at him. After a moment of
silence, her cherry-pink lips broke into a faint smile.

"Hmm. Even I didn't expect to be sent to the Highest Level in
my real body during my first kiss."

"Uh. Um. I'm, um, sorry," he stammered.

"You've nothing to apologize for. Thanks to this little detour,
I'll likely never forget this moment," she said, and slid backward

a bit. She grabbed on to the hand he held out and sat up. She spun herself ninety degrees, dropped her legs over the edge of the sofa, and tidied her slightly mussed hair and rumpled dress.

Haruyuki was absently entranced by this movement, and then came back to himself hurriedly. "Um. I'll get drinks! Is tea all right?"

In the kitchen, he filled new glasses with ice, poured some chilled green tea, and returned to the living room, where Kuroyukihime was leaning back into the sofa, twisting from side to side, deep in thought.

So as not to disturb her, he set the tray down gently on the low table, then placed the glasses on ceramic coasters and slid one in front of Kuroyukihime.

She noticed this a few seconds later. "Thank you." She picked up the glass and took a sip before saying, "A portal inside of Tezcatlipoca. Where could it possibly lead?"

"Right?" He sat down next to her and put his own thinking on the matter into words. "If we're looking at it from a game theory kind of view, then it'd be something like the portal becomes usable when Tezcatlipoca is defeated. But I don't know if there's any place you'd want to go so badly that it's worth the risk of challenging an Enemy even stronger than the Four Gods."

"Hmm!" Kuroyukihime said, in a little cry of realization. "So if we're thinking along those lines, then wouldn't the portal exit into the Castle? Defeat Tezcatlipoca and you get a free pass inside without having to deal with the Gods?"

"O-oh, I guess maybe." He nodded. "If it exits into the Castle, then the risk and the benefit maybe just barely balance out."

They looked at each other and then sighed in unison.

"Well, given our current situation, it's all the stuff of dreams," she said. "I don't have the first hint of an idea on how to defeat that giant."

"Me, neither," he replied. "But the thing that kind of bugs me is that thing Enju—I mean, the White King—mentioned before, the E-Excer…"

"Exercitus," she offered.

"That's the one. This Exercitus, does the fact they sent a scouting party to follow Tezcatlipoca mean they're maybe planning to attack it?"

"I'd like to say that's absurd, but I honestly don't know. If they really do have five hundred members, we can assume that at least half are level four or higher and thus able to enter the Unlimited Neutral Field. I wouldn't be surprised if they were working on an attack strategy, at the very least." Kuroyukihime brought her iced tea to her lips once more.

Haruyuki also felt thirsty and gulped cool liquid from his own glass. He crunched down on the ice that tumbled into his mouth and then sighed.

"Overall, I think it's a good thing," she said, out of the blue, and Haruyuki turned to look at her.

"Huh?" He frowned. "What is?"

"Exercitus," she replied simply. "For a long time, the Accelerated World has stagnated under the control of the six Great Legions. When I revived Nega Nebulus last fall, it was with the intention of overthrowing that status quo. But not only did I not take the heads of the Kings of Pure Color, I merely changed the system of six Great Legions to that of seven Great Legions."

"That wasn't your fault, though," he protested. "There was so much that was totally beyond your control. The whole Chrome Disaster thing was in January, and then the fight against the Acceleration Research Society's been going on since April, so."

"Well, hmm. At any rate, if the small and midsize Legions have formed an alliance to upend the stagnation created by the seven Great Legions, then the Accelerated World might begin to move in big ways again. And then a flood that not even Enju can control will come rushing in and sweep us away. I have to say, I'm a little looking forward to it." She murmured the last part as if she were more talking to herself, raised her glass to eye level, and made the ice rattle in a gesture that seemed to celebrate those who would challenge her.

Haruyuki watched this with a pain in his heart. Even if the Legions under the Exercitus umbrella did attack the Suginami area, he wouldn't be able to stand and face them alongside Kuroyukihime, Chiyuri, Takumu, and everyone else. In fact, next Saturday, he would definitely be added to the attack team in the attempt to take back Minato Area No. 3 from Nega Nebulus. If only Exercitus would attack Minato and upset these plans for a showdown between Oscillatory Universe and Nega Nebulus... Haruyuki shook his head firmly to shake off such thoughts.

"What's the matter?" Kuroyukihime asked gently, and he shook his head once more.

"Oh. It's nothing. Anyway, um, Enju's kind of an unusual name, huh?" Even he was aware that this was a rather obvious subject change, but Kuroyukihime only nodded with a smile.

"Yes, and it feels all the more so, given how common my own name is."

"I-it's not, though!" he cried. "I love your name!"

"Heh-heh, thank you. I like it now, too, you know. And it has a character in common with your name." She smiled brightly, and a faint light flickered in her eyes as she continued. "The truth is, there's a story behind both of our names. I told you before that my mother was born into the Kamura Company family, yes?"

"Uh-huh."

"The Kamura family has long had a curious custom," she said. "Girls born into the main family are given a name derived from a tree species, while girls born into the branch families are named after herbaceous plants. My mother left the Kamura main family, but since she married into a branch family, the Kurobas, she should have given her girl children names derived from plants. My name, Sayuki, is from a species, *Hemerocallis*, called 'early snow.'"

"*Hemerocallis*," Haruyuki murmured, and Kuroyukihime moved her fingers in the air to send a file to his virtual desktop. He opened it to find a flower with petals as white as snow, and stared at it for a while before tentatively saying, "It's incredibly beautiful, a lovely flower. Um. It really suits you."

"Hee-hee, thanks." She moved her fingers in the air again. "And this is the plant my sister's name comes from."

He opened this new image file and saw another snowy white flower. But it was blooming from the branch of a magnificent, large tree. He furrowed his brow in confusion. "Huh? This isn't a plant. It's a tree."

"Mm-hmm." She nodded slightly. "It's a pagoda tree. In kanji, it's 'enju,' written with the tree radical next to the character for demon. It's quite the impressive tree. It can reach up to twenty meters."

"B-but why is your sister named after a tree?" He didn't get it.

"Why indeed? When I learned of the Kamura family custom, I also thought it strange that I had a plant's name while my sister had a tree's. But for some reason, this was one question I couldn't pose to either my sister or my mother," she said, with a faraway look in her eyes.

Haruyuki wanted to comfort her somehow, but he didn't know what to say. Instead, he reached out a hand, and after hesitating for a few seconds, he touched it to her back. When he did, she leaned over and rested her head on his shoulder.

After a little while, she said calmly, "You've gotten stronger, Haruyuki."

"Huh?" He blinked rapidly in surprise. "I—I don't think so at all, though."

"Have more faith in yourself," she told him. "You managed to become my boyfriend, didn't you?"

No, no! I mean, I couldn't actually be—! he very nearly shouted and just barely managed to hold the cry in. They'd told each other how they felt and even kissed, so seen through the lens of society, that meant they were dating—and that made them none other than boyfriend and girlfriend.

"Um. Thanks for having me," he somehow managed to say.

Kuroyukihime chuckled before clearing her throat and saying, "Ah, I'm sorry. Thanks for having *me*. But if you're going to date me, there's one mission that you absolutely must clear."

"Huh?!" he yelped. "I–in the Accelerated World?"

"No, in the real world." She sat up and turned her gaze on him directly, glaring slightly. "Listen, Haruyuki. From what I've seen, Rin, Niko, and Chiyuri consciously like you. And although they themselves may not be aware of it, Fuko, Utai, and Choco are extremely suspect. Aah, and Metatron, too. I'm not sure about Lead yet, though."

"Whaa?!" This time, he couldn't hold his baffled cry in. He set his glass of iced tea back down on the coaster before waving trembling hands in the air. "R-Rin did actually, um, tell me that she likes me. But Niko's the same as always, and Chiyuri won't even talk to me lately. Master Fuko, Shinomiya, and Choco totally don't have that vibe at all, Metatron's a Being, and Lead's actually a guy, so."

"Boy or AI, they nonetheless have the right to love you," she declared. "You have to square off with all of their feelings and tell each of them how you actually feel."

"Um. Okay." What she was saying was absolutely correct, and he could only agree with her. At the very least, he had to take the time to give Rin Kusakabe a proper answer, given that she had gone so far as to put her feelings into words for him.

"Understood," he said, finally. "I'll try calling Kusakabe tomorrow."

Kuroyukihime shifted her glass to her left hand and then patted his shoulder. "Good luck. Sorry to rush you, but the more you put things like this off, the harder they actually get."

"Right." He nodded again, and Kuroyukihime smiled as if to cheer him up.

"Now then," she said, getting to her feet. "I should be on my way. It wouldn't do for me to listen to you discussing this and that with Fairy."

"I...guess not." Shaking off his sadness, Haruyuki also stood up.

It had already been a long day, but he still had so much left to do. He had to put together a team as per the orders of the White

King, but he also wanted to call Niko and Utai to check in on how Hoo handled the move. Plus, he needed to talk to Reina about the student council election, and do at least some of his summer homework. And he was also very curious about the movements of Exercitus.

Thinking he'd accelerate to finish that day's homework, Haruyuki headed for the front door to see Kuroyukihime on her way.

12

Zelkova Verger, level-six Burst Linker and member of the small Legion Gallant Hawks, crossed his arms tightly in front of him to push down his impatience.

The rooftop of Toshima Ecomuse Town, the super skyscraper soaring above the Higashi Ikebukuro area in the Unlimited Neutral Field, was crowded with over a hundred Burst Linkers on standby like he was. Sunshine 60 three hundred meters to the northeast and the roofs of the other nearby skyscrapers were the same.

The fact that this many people had assembled in the span of a mere hour demonstrated the serious expectations they had for the brand-new, unified Legion army, Exercitus. When he'd first heard this name, which meant "army" in Latin, a part of him had thought they were putting on airs, but once he got here, that opposition melted away. Because the central members of Exercitus had set into motion an outrageous attack and were actually, unbelievably succeeding at it.

He looked out from his spectacular vantage point of one hundred eighty meters above the ground to take in the sight of Higashi Ikebukuro covered in pure blue water as far as the eye could see. The only things poking through the water's surface were skyscrapers like Sunshine 60 and any nearby condos that were over a hundred meters tall. Because as of the present moment, seven PM, July 27, the attribute of the Unlimited Neutral Field was an Ocean stage.

Naturally, more than three hundred Burst Linkers had not come together to take in the spectacle of a rare Ocean stage. They were all looking down with bated breath at the terrifyingly huge human-shaped Enemy held captive in the center of a circle of frosty ice about four hundred meters across. Frozen up to the chest was the Super-class Enemy that had run rampant in the Accelerated World for the last three days, the Deity of Demise, Tezcatlipoca.

Exercitus had formed with the objective of defeating Tezcatlipoca, rather than waiting for the seven Great Legions to do something about the terror it was inflicting on their world. But to actually get to this stage where they were about to go on the offensive, the central members had gone through hell.

First, there was the scouting party. A single misstep there meant certain death, and yet they'd carried on for a total of over a year of inside time. While the party gathered intel on the giant, other members of the group desperately investigated various methods of attack. An away team had even been dispatched to the city of Nagoya far outside the one hundred kilometers of Tezcatlipoca's reaction range to earn the points needed for the mission.

Initially, Zelkova had taken a skeptical view, wondering if the midsize Legions called to form Exercitus—Cold Brew, Ovest, Gouen, and Night Owls—simply wanted to usurp the place of the current seven Great Legions. But after seeing the tremendous effort they'd put into this mission, he was forced to recognize that they were the real deal.

They'd spent pretty much all of the points they'd saved up hunting Enemies in Nagoya to first buy up a large amount of the Rainmaker item in the shop. They'd then used these to increase the probability of a water-affiliated stage and drawn an Ocean stage in the Change immediately after that. They'd laid multiple traps and set up a variety of teams in this spot in Higashi

Ikebukuro before attacking a Lesser-class Enemy and luring Tez-catlipoca into their snare.

The giant shot over like it was jet propelled, and the moment it sank chest-deep into the eighty-meter-deep ocean, they exploded the countless ice bombs they'd sunk in the area in advance, while over twenty Burst Linkers with freezing abilities attacked in unison. Their combined efforts froze a vast quantity of water and succeeded in trapping the giant.

Locked away in the jail of thick ice, Tezcatlipoca sometimes moved its boulder of a head from side to side, but it showed no signs of being able to break free. Even as he watched from on high, a semicircle of ice users to the rear of the giant were showering it with beams of pale light, ice bullets, and snowstorms to strengthen the prison.

"Hope this goes well," a smaller Burst Linker murmured anxiously, as she looked down on the scene of the battle from beside him.

"It'll be fine," Zelkova Verger remarked confidently. "Now that we've come this far, victory's basically guaranteed."

"Yeah." The F-type who agreed vaguely was Taupe Cape. Although she was the parent who'd given him the Brain Burst program, she was a year behind him at the junior high they attended in the real world.

Normally, Zelkova tried to speak in a more polite way to add a bit of character to his avatar, but when he talked with Taupe Cape, he always reverted to his real way of speaking.

Taupe Cape's parent and previous Gallant Hawks leader had fallen prey to one misfortune after another and lost all their points last year in an unlimited EK. Taupe had a tendency to brood ever since, and Zelkova tried to do what he could to cheer her up somehow, but it wasn't going too well. That morning, he had dragged a reluctant Taupe on the journey to neighboring Suginami, so that she could watch him beat the Betrayer, Silver Crow, who had caused this whole Tezcatlipoca thing. But that had backfired pretty spectacularly.

Folks like Crow appeared from time to time in the Accelerated World. They got lucky and drew a rare color or ability, hopped straight into a Great Legion, and raced up the ranks without doing much of anything. The Great Legions had a points surplus, so they could easily set up young members at the enhancement shop or with Enhanced Armament, and they also excelled at providing information to new recruits. Zelkova had only just learned Conic Smiter recently, and he was sure the reason Silver Crow had been able to turn its weak points—the fact that he couldn't move while it was activated and the fact that he would be hit with the spikes if the target jumped directly above him—to his advantage was because he'd bought Zelkova's information in advance or learned about attack methods from his veteran comrades.

But today would change the situation in the Accelerated World.

The seven Great Legions were the ones that had gone out of their way to attack the Sun God Inti, despite the fact that the Enemy was pretty much harmless so long as you stayed away from it. And the result of that attack had been to break Tezcatlipoca out from inside of it.

The Kings of Pure Color had been strutting around like they owned the place, but if Exercitus could destroy Tezcatlipoca, then their authority would plummet to the bottom of a lake. Exercitus could demand a vast sum of points as compensation for all the damage the Kings had done to them, and not only that, they would even be able to insist that the Kings abandon their Territories. Naturally, there would be a stream of people leaving the seven Great Legions, and if Gallant Hawks could absorb some of those players, then it wasn't out of the realm of possibility for them to grow into a massive Legion that controlled the areas from Mitaka to Suginami, and all the way out to Nakano. And when that happened, their leader, Taupe Cape, would definitely be excited to play again, the way she used to be.

After hesitating for a second, Zelkova lightly tapped the shoulder of Taupe's grayish-purple cape-type armor. "Look. Phase two's gonna start any second. We're part of the long-distance attack team, so the danger's pretty minimal. But that also means the close-range team has the advantage in terms of dealing damage. We gotta really work to carve away Tezca's gauge and earn those points."

"Yeah." Her voice finally had some life back in it, and she jabbed Zelkova in his side with her small fist. "Hey, so Zel, don't get all carried away and get too close."

"I won't." Zelkova smiled wryly, just as the amplified voice of the mission lead began to echo in the valley between the rows of skyscrapers.

"Phase two starts in sixty seconds! Groups two, three, and four, get into position, and wait for the countdown!"

"Wohkay! Here we go!" Zelkova Verger nodded at Taupe Cape, and then leapt up onto one of the countless ropes set up to drop down from the roof. He adjusted the strength of his grip and slid to the frozen water surface a hundred meters below. When he shifted his gaze slightly to the east, he saw that the captive Tezcatlipoca was already covered in white frost right up to the back of its head.

According to what he'd heard while they were on standby, the central members had gotten the idea for this freezing strategy from the shameful sight of Oscillatory taking a stab at an Enemy in the Minato area, like they were playing a little game, and then being chased around by Tezcatlipoca. As they fled, they led Tezcatlipoca to the waterways near Shibaura, froze the ocean water, and stopped the giant. And the Exercitus scouting party had witnessed the whole thing.

If its movement could be slowed down by freezing just the area up to its ankles, then...They'd been quick to realize the possibilities, but even if any one person could come up with that idea, it was no simple task to actually execute it. Among the central Exercitus members, the Night Owls based out of Ikebukuro had played an even more central role, and it was fair to say that their power was already on par with that of the seven Great Legions.

The one thing that concerned Zelkova was the fact that the

midsize Legion Helix, based in the Itabashi area, was not taking part in this mission, nor in the Exercitus alliance itself. There was no great difference in terms of membership between them and Night Owls or Ovest, and he'd heard that their leader, Beryllium Coil, was a pretty skilled player, so he thought they would have readily joined in.

Zelkova Verger snorted lightly. They were probably just coasting on easy mode, having fun picking fights in the Territories with Nerima area's Prominence and continually losing. They would have only gotten in the way if they had taken part in the mission. If they chose the path of fading into obscurity with the Kings' Legions, well, they would do what they wanted.

His feet touched hard ice, and a fraction of a second later, Taupe Cape slid down the rope next to his. The other members of their Legion had been placed at Sunshine 60 because of the abilities they brought to the mix, but they should have also dropped down at the same time as he and Taupe.

"What d'you think? Should we look for the gang and try to meet up?" Zelkova asked softly, but Taupe shook her head slightly.

"Nuh-uh. They're close-range types, so even if we did find them, we'd have to split up again pretty quick. The two of us'll have to do what we can together here."

"Guess so," he agreed. "And if we dawdle, all the good spots'll be taken. Let's go!"

"Yeah."

They nodded at each other and started to run at the same time.

At the advance briefing, there had been talk of how the ice scaffold was thinner the farther out to the edge you went, so if they ran too hard, there was the risk that it might break. But the feedback he got from the soles of his feet told him that it was far firmer than he had imagined. The ice users that made up group one were probably doing whatever they could to strengthen the ice.

Tezcatlipoca was held captive in a place that was a school ground in the real world, wedged between two main streets. Of course, the roads and the buildings were all sunk beneath the water of the Ocean stage, and the only thing in the area now was the pure-white, enormous circle of a battleground.

A myriad of battle cries roared from the right, and when he glanced that way, he saw that the hundred and some warriors who had dropped down from Sunshine 60 were charging ahead as one. Zelkova and those around him yelled, too, just as loudly.

"Yaaaaaaaaah!!"

Up ahead, a group of ice users who had depleted their special attack gauges were waving at Zelkova and the others charging in, cheering in welcome.

"Go get him!"

"Take that thing out!"

"We got this!" Zelkova shouted back as he passed by them and ran even harder.

Less than thirty meters to Tezcatlipoca. The head and shoulders protruding from the ice were enormous, like small mountains.

"*Counting down…Twenty…Nineteen…Eighteen…*" The leader's voice rang out once more.

Zelkova and Taupe put on the brakes, cutting into the ice, and took up the best positions twenty meters directly behind the giant to wait for the signal to begin the attack.

The Enemy had immense and terrifying power, but its attack patterns were simple. Outside of physical attacks like kicking and hitting, it only had the gravity attack of its right hand, the fireball attack from its left, and the Blast Wave that radiated outward from its mouth.

Since both of its hands were completely locked away in the ice, all they had to watch out for was the Blast Wave. But the scouting party had been thorough in their work, and the effective range of that attack had been made clear. Although it reached up to a hundred meters in the direction the giant was facing, it could only extend thirty meters to either side and twenty meters to the rear. In other words, as long as Tezcatlipoca couldn't change the direction its head faced, Zelkova and Taupe were in the safe zone. The

Burst Linkers on either side also carved out a smooth quadratic curve that just barely kept them out of range of the Blast Wave.

"*Twelve...Eleven...Ten...*"

As he listened to the countdown, Zelkova crouched down and pressed his hand to the ice. Naturally, he'd charged his special attack gauge to full in advance. First, he'd get off ten direct hits with Conic Smiter and make the leaders watching over the battle from Ecomuse Town pay attention to him.

"*Nine...Eight...Seven...*"

"Zel," Taupe Cape murmured, abruptly.

Wondering what she could possibly want six seconds before the start of the attack, Zelkova looked to his side and followed her gaze down to the ice at his feet.

Dark, red...light. The depths below the thick ice were shining crimson like blood.

Boshhm! He heard a bizarre sound from immediately behind. And then again from either side.

Zelkova Verger looked up to see snowy-white steam jetting up from a massive hole in the ice.

The countdown was still going on, but there were cries of confusion all around him. The ice scaffold shuddered, and countless cracks ran up and down it.

The crimson shining rapidly rose to the surface from the depths. This was no ordinary light. It was superheated flames.

"Zel!" Taupe shrieked.

Zelkova peeled his hand off of the ice, stretched it out, and grabbed Taupe's hand in a trance as his field of view was filled with bright-red light.

13

"C'mon! Hurry up! Hurry! Hurry!" came an impatient voice as hands shoved and pushed at Haruyuki's back, forcing him to advance down the hallway at a trot.

"Okay!" he yelled "I get it! Stop pushing me!"

"Huuuuuurrryyyyyy uuuuuup!" Absolutely not having any of this was his childhood friend, Chiyuri Kurashima.

She'd contacted him for the first time in three days a little before eight PM. In the end, he'd finished his quota of homework without relying on acceleration, had a dive chat with Utai, Reina, Niko, and Kao to find out how Hoo was doing, and he was finally thinking about messaging Snow Fairy when the mail from Chiyuri had arrived.

All it said was "I'm bringing food." While he wrestled with the question of whether this sounded angry or not, the doorbell rang, so he opened the front door timidly. The moment he did, however, Chiyuri blew in like a storm, the only word coming out of her mouth being "hurry."

Forced to retreat to the living room, he dashed away from her, whirled around, and shouted, "Hurry, hurry, hurry! What is all this hurrying for?!"

"This!" Chiyuri pulled two XSB cables out of the pocket of her culottes.

"Huh?" He gaped at the cables. "W-we're directing?"

"No! Nooot thaaat!" she snapped impatiently. "Sit down and plug your Neurolinker into your home server, Haru! And do maybe…thirty seconds for the cutoff time."

He finally understood that she was planning for them to dive into the Unlimited Neutral Field together. But her objective was still unclear, and more importantly…

"Huh? What about food?" he asked, pointing at the reliably bulging tote bag in her left hand.

Her response was unequivocal. "After the dive! Come *on*! I'm telling you, we don't have time for this!"

"O-okay. Fine." Realizing that something big was going on, Haruyuki accepted the cable Chiyuri held out to him and sat down on the sofa. He plugged one end into his own Neurolinker and the other into the port to connect to the home server embedded on one side of the low table. He set the automatic disconnect timer for thirty seconds and glanced to his side.

He also had a whole bunch of things he needed to talk to her about: his transfer to the White Legion, the fact that he'd gotten her mail about it but hadn't responded, and the whole thing with him going out with Kuroyukihime. But right now, her mission came first.

"I'll count down," he said. "Two, one…"

And then they shouted together, ""Unlimited Burst!!""

His second visit to the Unlimited Neutral Field that day was to a Wasteland stage where a dry wind whistled. Since all the buildings had been changed into solid rock, he and Chiyuri appeared at the top of a massive stone that was roughly the same shape and height as his condo building in the real world.

"So? What was all the rush for?" he asked again.

"Um, so." Chiyuri—Watch Witch Lime Bell—tilted her vivid green pointed hat to one side. "I have this friend in Nishi Tokyo's Ovest."

"Huh?" He stared at her, stunned. "You do?!"

"You don't have to act so surprised."

And she was exactly right. It had already been three months since she had become a Burst Linker as Takumu's child. Given that much time, it was absolutely natural that she would have built relationships he knew nothing about.

"I guess, yeah." He nodded. "So what's their name?"

"This girl, Cotton Marten," she replied. "I got a mail from her today at six thirty, and, like, it was kinda weird and rambling. She said there was this secret mission in Ikebukuro in the Unlimited Neutral Field, and she didn't want to go, but she had to. So if I hadn't heard from her again by eight, I should come look for her."

"Mission?" He frowned. "What mission?"

Chiyuri blinked her cute, round eye lenses. "That's what I wondered, too, so I mailed her back right away, but I haven't heard from her since. And then I was trying to figure out what to do and eight o'clock came around, but I thought it was maybe dangerous to go by myself. Sorry for dragging you into this."

"No, you were right to come with me. This maybe had something to do with Exercitus."

"Excer...?" Now it was her turn to frown. "What?"

"I'll explain later," he said. "Anyway, we should charge our special attack gauges."

"Yeah."

After nodding firmly at each other, they began to smash the nearby rocks.

Haruyuki set his mind to work at the same time as his fists. When he ran into the White King on the Highest Level, she had mentioned Ovest as one of the Legions that formed the core of the newly launched Exercitus. And Exercitus had a scouting party keeping an eye on Tezcatlipoca. These facts plus the "secret mission" in Cotton Marten's mail gave rise to a single possibility in his mind.

What if on the very day Exercitus launched, they attempted to attack Tezcatlipoca? If their mission had succeeded, Cotton Marten would have contacted Chiyuri by now. So the fact that she hadn't meant…The mission start time was seven, and it was already eight now. An hour in the real world was a thousand hours in the Unlimited Neutral Field—forty-one days and sixteen hours.

He pushed back this uneasy feeling as he kicked and shattered his nth rock to fill his special attack gauge. He raced over to Chiyuri and called, "I'm all good! You?"

"Now." Chiyuri pulverized a massive rock with the Choir Chime Enhanced Armament of her left hand, whirled around, and jumped toward him. "I'm full up!"

"Hup!" He hurried to catch her and deployed the wings on his back. After a second of thought, he looked up at the pale-yellow sky and called the voice command, "Equip Metatron Wings."

A pure-white light shot down from the sky, collected on Silver Crow's back, and produced a new set of wings. A gift from the Archangel Metatron, these wings dramatically increased his flight speed and duration. Normally, he tried to use them as little as possible, but he felt they were warranted in this situation.

"Here we go," he warned.

"Let's do it!" Chiyuri chirped in response.

He kicked off the ground and lifted off.

From his condo, Ikebukuro was about six kilometers east by northeast. At the time of the fifth Chrome Disaster incident six months earlier, he had flown this very same course to Ikebukuro. Back then, the flight had taken more than ten minutes, maybe because he'd been carrying Kuroyukihime in his right arm, Niko in his left, and had Takumu hanging from his legs.

But now he vibrated his own wings and the Metatron wings at about half power. Even at that low level, his avatar accelerated like it had been launched from a gun, and in a mere minute or so, he had crossed Nakano and entered the ward of Toshima, home of the Ikebukuro area.

He passed Yamate-dori, which was re-created in the Wasteland stage as a massive ravine, and the overhead JR train bridge, transformed into a long razorback ridge, and then two incredibly tall rocks came into view up ahead. The one on the left was Sunshine

60, the one on the right was Ecomuse Town. And between them, a massive shadow writhed.

"Haru!" Chiyuri cried from his arms.

Graaaaaar!

An angry roar he'd heard before shook the air around them.

Despite the fact that he was still over a kilometer away, the shock waves traveled through the atmosphere to hit him hard. As he decelerated, he made a right turn and carefully approached on a course from the south, with Ecomuse Town wedged between them and the shadow.

"I'm taking us down!" he said, and cut the thrust to his wings to glide down onto the roof of Ecomuse Town. At the last second, he applied a hint of reverse thrust to cushion their landing. He set Chiyuri on her feet and made eye contact with her before bending over and pointing to the edge of the roof. Although the building had been transformed into a rock, there was a parapet standing on the edge. They hid themselves behind it, and then poked their heads out carefully to look down at the ground.

Even seen from the top of Ecomuse Town nearly two hundred meters up, the giant was still incredibly huge. Smooth, reddish-black physique. Abnormally long arms. Faceless face. The god of the end, Tezcatlipoca.

As Haruyuki and Chiyuri watched wordlessly, the giant raised one foot high and brought it down on the reddish-brown earth. *Thm, thmmm.* A shock like an earthquake radiated out from that epicenter, and Ecomuse Town shuddered.

And then Haruyuki saw them. A variety of colored lights blinking and disappearing.

"There," he said, and immediately, a faint sound—no, a voice—reached him. A shriek, filled with despair.

The lights were duel avatar death effects.

"Haru, those are…," Chiyuri said, her voice trembling.

At the same time, Haruyuki noticed countless lights shimmering weakly at the feet of Tezcatlipoca, sinking into the shadows of the skyscrapers. There had to have been over a hundred of them.

"They're all...death markers?" He shuddered in fear.

A hundred was a terrifying number. But the White King had said Exercitus membership was over five hundred Burst Linkers. In which case, he found it impossible to believe that only a hundred of them had convened for the Tezcatlipoca attack mission. It would have been more like all of the level four and higher members, around three hundred people on the high side.

Even mobilizing that kind of huge force, they hadn't been able to defeat the god of the end. They had probably been annihilated in an instant, and all three hundred had transformed into death markers. And then they had regenerated and died over and over again for a thousand hours. This was an unlimited EK on an overwhelming scale, like nothing seen in the Accelerated World before. It was quite possible that a hundred to two hundred Burst Linkers had already been pushed to total point loss.

"Why?!" Haruyuki cried, his voice cracking as he clenched his hands into tight fists.

If they'd been observing the Enemy all that time, then they should have known there was no way they could take on Tezcatlipoca. So then why?

Below, the giant began to move again. It reached its left hand out toward a place where a number of death markers were concentrated. Rings of pale light popped up above the massive palm. The instant their number went from seven to eight to nine, the circles changed color to a glittering crimson red.

At the same time, over twenty Burst Linkers regenerated as one, and an enormous fireball shot out from Tezcatlipoca's hand. The extermination attack, Miccailhuitontli.

Striking the ground in a direct hit, the fireball swirled and swelled upward, causing what was without a doubt the largest explosion Haruyuki had ever seen in the Accelerated World. The flames reached the belly of Ecomuse Town and shook the rocky mountain with a thunderous roar.

The regenerated Burst Linkers were all killed instantly, helpless in the midst of the flames. Two of them did not turn into death markers, but instead broke apart into countless ribbons that danced up into the sky. In that moment, they lost all of their Burst Points and were banished from the Accelerated World.

"No…No!" Chiyuri cried weakly. Haruyuki opened his clenched fist and gripped her hand tightly.

He wanted to help the hundred Linkers who still hadn't lost all of their points. But no matter how he racked his brain, there was no way. If he and Chiyuri came down from their rocky mountain perch and approached Tezcatlipoca, they would be caught up in some attack, die instantly, and join the crowd of death markers.

He thought about bursting out for a moment and getting together as many people as possible, but even assuming he took ten minutes to prepare, over one hundred and sixty hours would pass on this side. In that time, almost all of the remaining hundred Burst Linkers would lose their points, and there was a strong possibility of the rescue team falling to the same fate.

This really was the god of the end. Hundreds of Burst Linkers, with all the knowledge and courage they could muster, were still powerless against it. And Haruyuki was the one who had released it into this world.

I'm sorry.

I'm sorry.

I'm sorry.

He said the words over and over in his heart, tears filling his eye lenses, while ahead of him, the giant moved again.

It turned the face with nothing but a cavernous mouth toward the sky. And then it roared deeply, at length, like the sound of an earthquake itself.

Graaaaaaaaan…

But its voice wasn't colored with the same desire for slaughter as it had been before. In fact, it even sounded like a satisfied song.

Suddenly, countless cracks raced across Tezcatlipoca's body. Motionless, the giant lost its reddish-black coloring, turning into inky, lusterless black stone bit by bit. The stone crumbled and fell to the earth.

"Huh? Wh-what's going on?" Chiyuri murmured, and Haruyuki could only shake his head.

Was it really satisfied? Had its role ended with pushing a couple hundred Burst Linkers to total point loss and now it was dying?

He couldn't believe things could work out so conveniently, but Tezcatlipoca continued to fall apart. It had already lost its entire head, and once the destruction reached its shoulders, its arms were cut off and plunged downward. The right and left hands that had brought about so much devastation crashed into the ground and shattered. The destruction of the torso proceeded down from the neck to the chest. At the giant's feet, the several Burst Linkers who had regenerated during this time stared upward in amazement, not even trying to run from the rocks raining down.

Finally, the giant broke down from the chest to the stomach. A red light gushed from inside the infinite fissures running along the cracked surface. The true nature of this light was revealed little by little as chunks of rock fell away. It wasn't an Enemy or an item. The swirling red light was an elliptical object without physicality.

"A…portal?" Chiyuri whispered.

That was exactly what it looked like to Haruyuki's eyes, too. But the portals all over the Unlimited Neutral Field were without exception blue.

The destruction of Tezcatlipoca stopped once it reached the center of its stomach—the bottom edge of the portal.

This was followed by another unprecedented phenomenon.

Massive hexagons the same color as the mysterious portal popped up in the pale-yellow sky of the Wasteland stage. The word WARNING was engraved on each in unadorned letters. It took a mere five or six seconds to fill the entire sky from the northern to the southern horizons with the crimson hexagonal patterns.

There was no way that this was the end. The next thing that happened would be the climax of whatever was happening.

Certain of this, Haruyuki shifted his gaze away from the red sky and brought it back to the portal shining on top of the last half of Tezcatlipoca.

Shf. Something appeared from inside the swirling light.

A foot. And then an arm. Followed by a body.

Someone basically the same size as Haruyuki and Chiyuri was manifesting in this world from the other side of the portal.

Instantly, Haruyuki understood everything. The portal inside of Tezcatlipoca, the existence of which the Abandoned Princess Bari had predicted, wasn't an entrance to take Haruyuki and his fellow Burst Linkers to the Castle or some other place. It was the opposite: an exit to bring someone from some unknown place to the Accelerated World.

When the someone had stepped out of the portal entirely, another shadow immediately appeared. Three. Four. They kept coming. And they were very obviously not duel avatars. They didn't have the characteristic semitransparent armor, or face masks, or eye lenses.

The first person to come out of the portal looked to be a real person, more or less. He appeared to be a boy, but long hair fluttered behind him, and his frame, not so large but sturdy, was wrapped in a form-fitting red suit.

The second person had a totally different physique. And their entire body was covered in robot-like silver armor, while three lenses shone with pale light on the face area.

The third was a girl. Surprisingly slender body clad in a black dress, she had a witch's pointed hat on her head, and carried a long twisted staff in her right hand.

The fourth and fifth people again had a totally different appearance; there was no sense of unity. They were all over the place, like they had each come from a different world.

Wait. No. As they lined up to either side of the first person, Haruyuki got the impression that although there were no commonalities in terms of design, they were all based on a single concept. And that concept was…

Hero. So-called superheroes.

With the tenth person, the output from the portal stopped at last.

The heroes stood in a neat row on top of the crumpled Tezcatlipoca's stomach, below the sky ripped apart into hexagons.

A small-statured person taking up position on the right side, wearing a blue mask that hid their entire face, glanced at the Burst Linkers looking up soundlessly from the ground and said in a voice that carried well, "Y'hang on for eight whole years, and those are the looks on your faces. Is what I'd say, but I can't even see any of your damned faces."

"You're not exactly one to talk," the witch in the pointed hat retorted. Looking closely, Haruyuki saw that her feet were floating just a little above the ground.

Blue Mask glanced at her and shrugged theatrically. "That's just how it is. The masked man's the hero standard. Anyway. Listen up, gang!"

Blue Mask leaned far forward, seemingly unafraid of the fifty-meter height, and declared in a loud voice to the Exercitus survivors, "Trial Number Two service ends today! Any of you wanna disappear, you go right ahead. Anyone sticks around, and we'll give you your final notice. This game's official version, the name's *Dread Drive 2047!!*"

To be continued...

AFTERWORD

Thank you for reading *Accel World 26: Conqueror of the Sundered Heavens*. I feel like lately I start every afterword with an apology, but I must offer up a giga-apology this time for this volume being delayed the most out of any previous volume! I was planning to bring it to you a little sooner, but I was in poor health from August to September 2021. I couldn't quite get back into my writing rhythm after that, so the schedule ended up being delayed. As of the time of this writing in January 2022, I'm essentially back to full strength, so I will be working hard this year!

(I'll be touching on the details of this volume in the note below, so please be aware, if you haven't read it yet!)

In the afterword for the previous volume, I wrote that I was planning to end the White Legion arc in volume twenty-five and start in on the Seven Arcs storyline. But in terms of details, it does feel more like this volume is actually the White Legion arc? After all, the Seven Arcs and TFL appear in name only. But it was actually a lot of fun to write the Seven Dwarves in the real world. Unfortunately, White Cosmos, aka Enju Kuroba, does not make an appearance in the real, but if Haruyuki has another opportunity to visit the Eternal Girls' Academy junior high division student council office, then…I have a gut feeling about this.

If I could comment a little here, Cypress Reaper, aka Airi Sagisu, serves as vice president of the EG junior high student council, Rose Milady, aka Tsubomi Koshika, as the treasurer, and Snow Fairy, aka Nanako Juholt, as the secretary, which would make it seem that Cosmos is the president. But she is in high school, in grade ten, so the job of junior high student council president is assigned to another person. That person is scheduled to make an appearance in the next volume, so please look forward to that!

In this volume, not only is the real name of the White King made clear, but that of her younger sister, the Black King, aka Kuroyukihime, is also revealed: Sayuki Kuroba. That said, however, Haruyuki learned it in the last scene in volume one, and Fuko and Utai, who call her "Sacchi," also clearly already knew it. Kuroyukihime says that she likes her name, but the reason she goes so far as to use an SSS order to overwrite her name tag despite this is related to her mother's family, the Kamuras. I do hope I can go into a little more detail on this in a future volume.

Additionally, I suppose I must address the people who appear—or rather invade—the Accelerated World at the end of this volume. I believe that some among you will recall that in the previous volume, when Haruyuki tries to escape from Snow Fairy's suffocation attack, he perceives the existence of a new world that is very small, but very active. This fourth world, after AA2038, BB2039, and CC2040, is Dread Drive 2047. "Dread" means "to be feared" and "drive" is "to charge." As to whether the name of this game indicates the BB world of Haruyuki and his friends, or...Well, I hope you will be excited to find that out.

And now that I've written that, I've gone over the usual two-page spread for the afterword, so I'll go ahead and lay out the start dates of the three—now four—games, alongside the ages of Kuroyukihime and the others.

- Sept. 2031: Start of commercial Legion sales
- Dec. 2031: Birth of Enju Kuroba
- Sept. 2032: Birth of Sayuki Kuroba
- April 2033: Birth of Haruyuki Arita

■ April 2038: Distribution of Accel Assault 2038 program. The originators are one hundred children who started first grade that same month (born between Apr. 2031 and Mar. 2032).

■ April 2039: Distribution of Brain Burst 2039 program. The originators are one hundred children who started first grade that same month (born between Apr. 2032 and Mar. 2033).

■ April 2040: Distribution of Cosmos Corrupt 2040 program. The originators are one hundred children who started first grade that same month (born between Apr. 2033 and Mar. 2034).

■ 2047: Distribution of Dread Drive 2047 program. The originators are unknown.

That's basically how it looks. The time line around this becomes a bit important in future volumes, so I believe that if you could keep this in some small part of your mind, you'll be able to understand the story that much more smoothly. And I will work hard to bring you Volume 27 before your memory grows hazy!

Related to the discussion of time, I have one item that I must atone for.

At the time I was creating the plot for the OVA *Accel World: Infinite Burst* (*IB*), released in theaters in 2016, I put together a time schedule with the intention of merging it with the main story at some point, but with this volume, I at last catch up to the time in *IB*. To be more specific, it is July 21 when Risa Tsukiori, the heroine of *IB*, falls into a coma (this incident is mentioned in Volume 22, *Sun God of Absolute Flame*), and it is a week later, on July 27, that the dark cloud is generated in the Accelerated World. But I was unable to take care of the Tezcatlipoca threads by that time...I sincerely apologize to anyone who was anticipating Risa's appearance. The time line of the main story looks like it will be about a week (probably) off from that of *IB*. Well, with this and that, the OVA main story and the bonus stories ("Leap to

Infinity" and "Return to Eternity") have already diverged a fair bit from the main story, so I suppose it's a bit late to be on about this now. I do intend to have Risa and Nyx join in the climax of the story, so please wait a little longer!

And now I've come to the end of another two-page spread, so I'll write another two pages.

This year is the thirteenth year since Dengeki began to publish *Accel World* (the fifteenth if you start counting from the "Transcendent Accelerated Burst Linker" serialized online), and I've come to feel that my expectations for changes in social structures and scientific and technological advances largely missed the mark. (lol) Meanwhile, the age of majority will be lowered in April of this year (2022) from twenty to eighteen, and I'm forced to consider a number of things about this, the reason for the change supposedly to encourage the productive participation of young people in society.

To be blunt, I believe they merely wanted to increase the number of taxpayers. In Volume 6, released in 2010, there is a passage that reads, "Japan in the 2040s was on the brink of a total collapse of the nation's social security system due to the unbounded decline in the birth rate and the rapidly aging population. …Thus, it appeared the government intended to also increase the number of young people legally allowed to work by lowering the age at which a person could obtain certifications or qualifications, typified by the driver's license."

When I wrote this, I thought that it likely wouldn't actually happen, but it does appear that things are indeed heading in this direction. I am a person who has postponed engagement in the real world, doing nothing but watching anime, reading manga, and playing video games from my school days until now, and because of that, I was able to become the light novel author that I am. So it's unfortunate that we're shifting to a society that demands labor from young people even earlier, or rather there is something shameful about this to me as one adult. At the very least, I would like to keep doing whatever I can to bring you a story that you can enjoy just the same whether you're in school or out working in the world.

With all that said, we come into our customary recent update section. In the afterword I wrote in July 2020 for the previous volume, I noted, "I think that everyday life won't be going back to pre-COVID times for the time being or even ever if we blunder too badly," and the situation as I write this now in January 2022 is such that I can't see any exit whatsoever to this COVID pandemic. Naturally, I still haven't been able to return to my family restaurant workplace, so I'm doing what I can to write at home and in my office. I've gotten somewhat used to this environment as compared with the previous volume, and if I really make the effort, I can get into fifth gear now. But it is truly irksome that there is no drink bar, and I can't order a dessert as a treat to myself when I meet my quota! I'm sure you're all encountering all kinds of difficulties as well, and I would be very happy if this book could replenish your energy so that you can overcome them.

Once again, my deepest gratitude to HIMA and my editors Miki and Adachi, all of whom I inconvenienced so greatly with a series of postponements. Let us meet again in the next volume.

Reki Kawahara
A day in January 2022

HAVE YOU BEEN TURNED ON TO LIGHT NOVELS YET?

86—EIGHTY-SIX, VOL. 1–11

In truth, there is no such thing as a bloodless war. Beyond the fortified walls protecting the eighty-five Republic Sectors lies the "nonexistent" Eighty-Sixth Sector. The young men and women of this forsaken land are branded the Eighty-Six and, stripped of their humanity, pilot "unmanned" weapons into battle...

Manga adaptation available now!

WOLF & PARCHMENT, VOL. 1–6

The young man Col dreams of one day joining the holy clergy and departs on a journey from the bathhouse, Spice and Wolf. Winfiel Kingdom's prince has invited him to help correct the sins of the Church. But as his travels begin, Col discovers in his luggage a young girl with a wolf's ears and tail named Myuri, who stowed away for the ride!

Manga adaptation available now!

SOLO LEVELING, VOL. 1–8

E-rank hunter Jinwoo Sung has no money, no talent, and no prospects to speak of—and apparently, no luck, either! When he enters a hidden double dungeon one fateful day, he's abandoned by his party and left to die at the hands of some of the most horrific monsters he's ever encountered.

Comic adaptation available now!

ACCEL WORLD, Volume 26
REKI KAWAHARA

Translation by Jocelyne Allen
Cover art by HIMA

ACCEL WORLD Vol. 26
©Reki Kawahara 2022
Edited by Dengeki Bunko
First published in Japan in 2022 by KADOKAWA CORPORATION,
Tokyo.
English translation rights arranged with KADOKAWA CORPORA-
TION, Tokyo, through Tuttle-Mori Agency, Inc., Tokyo.

English translation © 2023 by Yen Press, LLC

Yen On
150 West 30th Street, 19th Floor
New York, NY 10001

Visit us at yenpress.com
facebook.com/yenpress
twitter.com/yenpress
yenpress.tumblr.com
instagram.com/yenpress

First Yen On Edition: August 2023
Edited by Thalia Sutton and Yen On Editorial: Payton Campbell
Designed by Yen Press Design: Andy Swist

Yen On is an imprint of Yen Press, LLC.
The Yen On name and logo are trademarks of Yen Press, LLC.

Library of Congress Cataloging-in-Publication Data
Names: Kawahara, Reki, author. | HIMA (Comic book artist) illustrator. |
    bee-pee, designer. | Allen, Jocelyne, 1974– translator.
Title: Accel World / Reki Kawahara ; illustrations, HIMA ; design, bee-pee ;
    translation by Jocelyne Allen.
Description: First Yen On edition. | New York, NY : Yen On, 2014–
Identifiers: LCCN 2014025099 | ISBN 9780316376730 (v. 1 : pbk.) |
    ISBN 9780316296366 (v. 2 : pbk.) | ISBN 9780316296373 (v. 3 : pbk.) |
    ISBN 9780316296380 (v. 4 : pbk.) | ISBN 9780316296397 (v. 5 : pbk.) |
    ISBN 9780316296403 (v. 6 : pbk.) | ISBN 9780316358194 (v. 7 : pbk.) |
    ISBN 9780316317610 (v. 8 : pbk.) | ISBN 9780316502702 (v. 9 : pbk.) |
    ISBN 9780316466059 (v. 10 : pbk.) | ISBN 9780316466066 (v. 11 : pbk.) |
    ISBN 9780316466073 (v. 12 : pbk.) | ISBN 9781975300067 (v. 13 : pbk.) |
    ISBN 9781975327231 (v. 14 : pbk.) | ISBN 9781975327255 (v. 15 : pbk.) |
    ISBN 9781975327279 (v. 16 : pbk.) | ISBN 9781975327293 (v. 17 : pbk.) |
    ISBN 9781975327316 (v. 18 : pbk.) | ISBN 9781975332181 (v. 19 : pbk.) |
    ISBN 9781975332716 (v. 20 : pbk.) | ISBN 9781975332730 (v. 21 : pbk.) |
    ISBN 9781975332778 (v. 22 : pbk.) | ISBN 9781975332754 (v. 23 : pbk.) |
    ISBN 9781975321338 (v. 24 : pbk.) | ISBN 9781975335083 (v. 25 : pbk.) |
    ISBN 9781975367848 (v. 26 : pbk.)
Subjects: CYAC: Science fiction. | Virtual reality—Fiction. | Fantasy.
Classification: LCC PZ7.K1755Kaw 2014 | DDC [Fic]—dc23
LC record available at https://lccn.loc.gov/2014025099

ISBNs: 978-1-9753-6784-8 (paperback)
       978-1-9753-6785-5 (ebook)

    10 9 8 7 6 5 4 3 2 1

LSC-C

Printed in the United States of America